CHILI

C000226290

Lucy English was born in Sri Lanka and grew up in London. She studied English and American Literature at the University of East Anglia and has an MA in Creative Writing. She works for a charity in Bristol, is a performance poet and the mother of three children. Her first novel, *Selfish People*, is also published by Fourth Estate.

CHILDREN OF LIGHT

Lucy English

FOURTH ESTATE • *London*

This paperback edition first published in 2000
First published in Great Britain in 1999 by
Fourth Estate Limited,
6 Salem Road,
London W2 4BU
www.4thestate.co.uk

Extracts from 'Magali' on pages 121, 123, 175–6, 244
are from *Memoirs of Mistral* by Jean Roussière.

1 3 5 7 9 10 8 6 4 2

A catalogue record for this book is available from
the British Library.

ISBN 1-84115-116-5

Typeset by MATS, Southend-on-Sea, Essex
Printed in Great Britain by Cox & Wyman Ltd, Reading

FOR MY PARENTS
BECAUSE THEY
INTRODUCED ME TO PROVENCE

INTRODUCTION

A bus stopped in a village in the south of France and a woman
with grey hair descended. She wore walking boots and tough,
practical clothes. She hauled a large rucksack on to her shoulders, but she was out of season. The village was shut like a
mussel on a rock. She didn't walk away but watched the nearly
empty minibus drive out of the village and back down the hill.
The village looked over a valley to another, almost identical
village, whose houses clung to the sides, which rose to a church
tower. All around were steep wooded hills of dark green pine.
A white tumble of clouds fell out of the whiter sky and hung in
the valley like a lost baby. A sudden squall of wind and a flash
of rain, the mother sky wailed with grief, then it fell too and the
whole valley became a swirling mist of wet cloud. It was March.

Wednesday
Dear Stephen,
I'm sorry we parted on such bad terms. I know it seems
crazy what I'm doing but I feel so much better now that
I'm here. It took me much longer than I expected. The
railway no longer runs to Draguignan and I had to bus
it. I was afraid I would arrive in the middle of nowhere
in the dark, but I managed to reach St Clair by early
afternoon. Oh, Stephen, Jeanette still runs the café. I
think she recognised me but I was tired and I didn't
want to talk. The village is different, it's nearly all
holiday homes, much smarter, there's no weeds
growing in the walls. I wonder how many real villagers
are left. I didn't see any.

You were wrong about the hut being derelict. You see, it's not England here. If you left a place in England for 20 years the brambles and the damp would take over, but here the summers are so dry they scorch plants to the ground. The pine trees are taller. The one near the hut is quite large, but that will give some shade in the summer. When I opened the door it was just as I left it, a cup on a hook, the pans hanging on the walls, the candle in the window alcove. Nobody has been here. There're so many huts in this valley, each olive plot has one, I suppose they don't attract attention. Can you imagine this? In England a forgotten house would get trashed, but there is nobody down here, absolutely nobody. It's such a strange feeling.

I'm writing to you in the morning. I'm still in my sleeping bag, sitting up at the table. The loft bed smelled so much of mice I slept on the floor. I couldn't sleep at first, I felt alone and stupid, I kept remembering what you said, 'Why on earth do you need to go back there?' It was also freezing. I will have to wait until May until it gets warmer. I'm writing this with my gloves on. I'm wearing two jumpers and my jeans. My first task when I finish this is to find some more wood. I got a little fire going last night but it didn't do much. Up in the woods behind the hut a big tree has come down. I managed to saw off some of the branches. I will have another go today. I remember it does eventually get cosy in here. The saw and the axe were in the tin trunk, a bit rusty but they do work. I'm making plans already. I want to put a *cannise* up, a sunshade. Now, that has rotted away and is in shreds round the back. I reckon that by the summer this place will look so smart. I can clear the scrub out the front and make a place to sit under the tree. Last night I could hear that tree like a whisper and that's what got me to sleep. It's all you can hear, the wind in the pine trees. In the early morning it rained and now it's so fresh outside, cold and bright. I want to go walking. It's the time of year for orchids, pink spotted ones, bee orchids, lizard orchids. I shall walk to the village later and post this and see if I can find any. The cherries are in blossom. It's so very beautiful. People miss this when they come in the summer, the grass is cracked and brown and there's no flowers. In a few weeks the fields will be flower filled. I remember they used to be dazzling. The water is just boiling on my camping stove, thank you for lending me that, it will be most handy until I get the stove going properly.

Please write to me care of Jeanette Blanc at Le Sanglier. She will be delighted to get my letters, I'm sure. Oh, Stephen, I feel so alive I cannot tell you. I'm still sad and I will be for a long time yet. I miss Felix so much and I miss you, but in England I felt so numb.

With all my love,
Mireille

She wriggled out of her sleeping bag and made a cup of coffee. There were two windows in the hut, but only one was unshuttered, consequently the inside was in half light. Through the tiny window a beam of sunlight shone so brightly it seemed solid, slicing across the stone floor and on to the table. Dust particles danced in it like joyous faeries. Mireille put the cup to her face to feel the warmth and smiled. She felt unwashed and crumpled, but it was a feeling she associated with being young, when her hair had been thick and dark, curling down her back, and soft. Her hair, though grey was still soft, cut straight round her ears. She looked at her jeans and knobbly walking socks. When she was young she used to wear a bright red gathered skirt with a yellow ribbon round the hem and an embroidered shirt, deep midnight blue. An amber necklace which held pieces of insects.

She went outside. In the sunlight the wet pine trees smelled strongly of resin. The clouds raced fast in the sky, white puffy clouds like washed flock blotting and unblotting the sun. Then, there they were, the mountains, like clouds themselves, white and indistinct in the far distance, but only for a moment before the real clouds blew into the valley and obscured them.

Later, she walked to the village, not up the overgrown track but down the terraces to a small road. On the other side on level ground was a large olive grove, well tended, its trees clipped and neat and the grass underneath cleared away in a circle around each trunk. Beyond the field was a farmhouse and beside it two pencil-like cypresses, dark bottle green. This was the last dwelling place, past here the road petered out into another track, which picked its way through dense woods to Rochas, the third village in the area. But Mireille didn't go that way. She followed the road to St Clair.

Near the village plenty of stone huts had been converted to holiday cabins, *cabanons*, some simple and rustic, others flagrantly pretentious, with coloured shutters, stripy awnings, brass lamps and even swimming pools. They were all empty. Of her own hut nothing could be seen except a glimpse of the rock it sat on. In her absence the tree cover had effectively removed it.

Six hairpin bends took the main road from the valley floor to the top of the hill and the small road joined it at the fourth. From here it was a steep, long haul. The locals drove round the roads as if pursued by the devil and every time a car came down she had to jump into the verge. She arrived panting and with aching legs.

The entrance to the village was a tree-lined road guarded by the statue for the heroes of the Resistance. A sturdy modernist woman with large flat feet. Her torch, held high, looked like a triple-whip ice cream cone. She had been placed at the far end of the *boules* yard, slightly too anatomically correct to be any nearer the church. Mireille rested on the wall of the *boules* yard to get back her breath. The village of Lieux was in a patch of sunlight, suddenly golden and shining. Behind it rose the high dark ridge, the end of the empty plateau of the Canjurs which spread all the way to the Gorge du Verdon. Lieux was the last village before this wilderness.

The plateau was owned mostly by the military. From far away she could hear the whump of shell fire. The dogs in the village started barking.

The café was busy. French people eat lunch whether it's March, January or June and that morning there had been a mini-market in the square. Two vegetable stalls, a cheese van and a butcher. At this time of year Jeanette's customers were traders. In the winter she served one dish and today it was *bourride*, a garlicky fish soup. Her mother helped wash up and serve and at the back of the café, as usual, the huge Macon drank beer and watched television.

Jeanette's mother, Auxille, was a tiny old woman with thin, dark hair. She wore a Provençal apron in much the same material as her daughter's flouncy dresses. She was as nosy as her daughter and twice as uninhibited about showing it. Mireille came out of the post office and went towards the shop. As she crossed the square they both rushed out to look. Their comments were quite audible.

'I'm sure she's a scientist, a botanist perhaps, she looks like one. She's not American, she speaks French too well. She could be Canadian.' In her hand was a glass of lager for one of the van drivers.

'She won't like Odette's prices,' said Auxille. 'The Villeneuves should have told her about the market. I got a fine piece of lamb.'

11

'But they get deliveries from Lieux.'

'Perhaps she's buying newspapers.'

'Where's my beer then?' called out the driver. 'And I want the soup.'

'*Tais toi!*' shouted Jeanette.

'Here she comes,' said Auxille and opened the door as Mireille was reading the board outside. 'It's a fine soup today, a good thick soup.'

Mireille sat in the café under the eyes of Auxille, who stood by her table like a perching raven. The van driver grumbled. 'Tourists, when they start arriving who cares about us?'

Jeanette banged his lager down next to him. 'She's a Canadian, you idiot, she can understand you. And let me tell you tourists are more *gentil*, and they tip better.'

'*Encore de bourride*,' called out Auxille. Auxille smiled sycophantically and Mireille smiled back. She knew this little game. She was not going to speak first.

'So . . .' said Auxille. 'You're the Canadian botanist.'

Mireille laughed out loud. 'I wondered what you would make of me,' she said in English. 'No, I'm not. I'm British.'

'Can this be right? The Villeneuves don't have British friends, surely.'

'I'm not at the château,' said Mireille, still laughing.

'The British people are the Gregsons and they don't come until May. Their place is empty. I know this. Madame Cabasson's niece looks after it.'

'I'm at La Ferrou,' said Mireille.

Auxille retied her apron. 'There's nothing at La Ferrou, an old hut and a spring . . .'

'It's my home,' said Mireille.

Auxille stared at her closely. She put her hands to her mouth. 'It cannot be! The Blessed Jesus and his Virgin Mother!'

Jeanette was bringing in the soup, an extra large portion with a whole basket of bread.

'Where's mine?' yelled the driver. 'Or do I have to wait until summer?'

'Shut your mouth, yours is coming. Maman, what's wrong, are you having a fit?'

'Jeanu, Jeanu, it's her, from La Ferrou, who sang the songs, and the little boy with the drum . . .'

'Mireille?' said Jeanette, and she looked too, and shrieked too, and they all hugged. Macon turned off the television.

'Look, hers is going cold and I haven't had mine yet,' said the van driver.

'You be quiet, Enrique,' said Auxille. 'This is a miracle and I know your mother.'

'She's in the graveyard, where you should be.'

'My family are in the oldest graveyard.'

'Go and join them. God, I hate old women!'

'Don't insult my family,' said Macon, loudly, and everybody looked at him. Even balding and with a paunch he was a head and shoulders higher than the driver. The man was quiet.

Auxille stood up '*Quel miracle! Quel drame!* What was it? One soup?'

'With extra bread like hers.'

After lunch Jeanette closed the café. She wiped the tables, washed up, swept the floor and folded up the table cloths, unaided because Auxille hadn't stopped talking once and Macon had gone into the cellar to find some celebratory wine.

The café was warm and moist and filled with a garlicky fish aroma now being attacked by bleach and cleaning fluids. Mireille rested her head against the window and listened as Auxille filled her in on the last twenty years' gossip. The topics were the same as ever. Fecundity, hunting dogs and who had married whom. Family connections were important in St Clair.

The top family were the Villeneuves, who owned the château. They were respected but not loved. In the war they had been

13

collaborators. They had very little to do with the village. The next family were the Cabassons, who owned the bakery. The current mayor was a Cabasson. They also owned several farms and ran the *cave*, the wine cellars, and the olive press. Auxille's husband had been a Cabasson. He was a hero of the Resistance. He had been shot trying to steal wine from the cellars of the château when it was occupied by the Germans.

There were four strands of the Blancs. The best Blancs had moved away years before and now lived near Nice. The next best Blancs were Auxille's family, who had owned the café for several generations. The third best Blancs were farmers at the château. The worst Blancs were Macon, his drunken father, his Italian mother, his no-good brothers. Other families were the Cavaliers, the Aragons, the Perrigues and the Gués. Auxille's mother had been a Perrigues, and her mother a Cavalier. Odette, who ran the shop, was also a Cavalier, her mother a Gués, and so it went on, the whole village woven together into a knotty carpet of rivalries and jealousies. Bottom of the heap and the subject of much rumour were the people who lived in the social housing behind the *mairie*. Half gypsies, the unemployed, half Moroccans, and Algerians. When anything was stolen or broken, they were blamed.

Macon brought in the wine and glasses and finally Jeanette sat down.

'So . . .' she said, 'when did you become a botanist?' She had a habit of believing her own fantasies.

Mireille did not want to tell her or anybody else in the village why she had come. She wanted to be left alone and now she was wondering if it had been a good idea to reveal who she was. 'I'm not,' she said, 'but I am interested in wild orchids. In fact, I'm making a small survey.'

'Doesn't Madame Cabasson's niece's husband-to-be know a scientist at the university?' asked Auxille. 'Perhaps I could introduce you.'

Miréille thought quickly. 'How kind of you, but it won't be necessary. It's only La Ferrou I'm interested in, it's just for . . . a nature magazine in England . . . it's not scientific . . . but I do need peace and quiet.'

'You'll get that at La Ferrou,' said Macon. 'That's all you'll get.'

'And you have no car. Can you stay for two weeks without a car?' asked Auxille.

'I'm going to be here until the summer.' Mireille wanted to go back immediately to the stillness of the hut. Three pairs of incredulous eyes were already picking holes in her story. 'The habits of wild orchids are very strange,' said Mireille.

'Of course,' said Auxille and they all nodded.

'And . . .' said Mireille, definitely thinking fast now, 'I need to rest . . . I need fresh air and stillness . . . the doctor said so.'

At the mention of a doctor Auxille and Jeanette moved close, like birds of prey. 'You have been ill? No? You look so well.'

'Mental . . .' said Mireille, groping around for an explanation that would satisfy them. 'Fatigue . . . brought on by stress . . . depression.'

They all stared at her. Mireille said nothing else. She hoped Jeanette's fertile imagination would fill in the gaps. It did. 'Your poor mother,' said Jeanette.

'My poor mother,' said Mireille and her sigh of relief could have sounded like an exclamation of sadness.

'How tragic to lose your mother. I thank the blessed Virgin that dear Maman is so well for her age.' Auxille was in her seventies but she looked about ninety.

'So tragic,' said Auxille.

'And how kind of her to remember us and send the money. I bought a pretty little carpet.'

'And Macon drank the rest,' said Auxille. Macon growled and drank his wine.

'And your son? He is well?' Jeanette changed the subject.

15

'My son is a successful young man,' said Mireille.

'How lucky you are to be blessed with a child,' said Auxille, glowering at Macon.

Macon ignored her. 'Do you still play the accordion, the one my father gave you?' He always remembered that his father had given it to Mireille.

'I didn't bring it with me. It was too heavy.' She hadn't played any music since November and this loss added to all her other losses. She desperately wanted to go back to the Ferrou.

'What was that song?' said Auxille. 'How did it go?' She began one of the old Provençal ballads. Mireille knew it and joined in. She had a splendid deep voice and eventually Auxille stopped her crackly accompaniment to listen. Mireille closed her eyes and sang to the end, a sad tale about lost love and forlorn, forgotten females. She finished. The others clapped. 'I have to go back now,' she said.

She was glad to be in the solitude of her hut. The light was beginning to fade now and clouds were coming down from the hills, tucking up the valleys and telling them to be quiet. But Mireille was restless. Everything she looked at reminded her of something she still had to do. Get a mattress for the loft bed. Cut more wood. Buy another lamp. In the ceramic sink the one tap dripped on to unwashed plates. There was no hot water at the Ferrou. What water there was came from a spring in the woods and it flowed into the tap, banging and complaining along the pipe. There was no toilet either. That was another job to be done. Dig a pit in the woods.

I am too old for this, thought Mireille, but she liked tiny spaces. Her houseboat in Bath had been tiny, but warm and tiny, and comfortable, with a bed taking up one end and padded seats by the table. In the hut there were no chairs, but a stone ledge along one wall. She was sleeping on this because the loft was littered with dead insects, mouse debris, and a

16

huge spider had built a tunnel-like web under a tile and crouched in there sulking, waiting to creep over her face in the night. A gust of wind rattled the door and blew ash down the chimney. She felt completely alone.

She put on her waterproofs and walked up into the woods. Behind the hut the land was more rocky and if it had ever been terraced, this had been long lost to the pine trees; but there was a path. It led to a gully thick with cherry and apple trees and a dense jungle of sarsparilla. In the summer this was the only green place when the rest of the land was scorched brown. The path followed the water up the hillside. She could hear it trickling over the rocks, the sides of the gully steeper here, the trees on each side taller and darker. It felt like the hill was crowding in. The path stopped in a clearing. There was a pool, a natural basin in the rock.

It was a dark, cold place and unbelievably still. She had forgotten how still it was here, sheltered from the wind. The pool was about ten foot across and when she looked into the water it seemed shallow, but it wasn't, she knew. It was deep enough to swim in, but swimming was the last thing she was thinking about. The water looked like liquid ice. Three worlds in one. A thin skin with leaves and pieces of twig floating on it. The rocky sides and the visible stony bottom of the pool. It looked so near, but it wasn't. It looked so still, but it wasn't. The water coming out of the spring was always flowing out of the pool and down the gully. And the third world. The sky on the water, her dark silhouette, the trees behind her perched up the hillside, and in front of her the massive, split, brooding rock that was La Ferrou. She looked up, out of the water, at the rock itself, creamy pale limestone, the cleft running down it as black as Satan's foot. The head of the pool, the source of the water. She had dreamt about this place. When the water lapped against her houseboat in the night, she was here. At The Heathers, when the fountain

17

outside her window dripped into her dreams, she was here. And over the last few months, when she couldn't cry but lay on Stephen's sofa under a travel rug. She was crying now because it was all water. The mist above the Roman baths and the clouds coming down the valley. This valley, and the valley in England by the river and the canal. That life was lost now, like her babies. The one who used to play here and throw stones in the water and her winter baby, who opened his eyes just once, and he had such dark eyes, like the bottom of the pool. He was lost and she was lost with him.

ROCHAS

CHAPTER ONE

A letter had arrived. Jeanette practically ran out of the café
when she saw Mireille. She had not been seen much over the
previous two weeks. Studying the orchids, Jeanette told
anybody who would listen. But there she was by the largest
plane tree, putting her shopping into her rucksack.

'A letter! A letter!' panted Jeanette, waving it in the air.
'From England. Your son? Your husband?' Mireille looked
up, her expression that of somebody who hadn't expected to
be spoken to. She was dirty. She had mud on her hands and
bits of twig in her hair. In fact she resembled Macon after a
day's work, which was so rare now that Jeanette had
forgotten how dirty a person can get.

'For me?' said Mireille.

'Four days ago it arrived, and we were waiting for you.
You were not at the Tuesday market and I said to Macon, do
we deliver it to her? But who can find La Ferrou these days, it
is so overgrown.' She handed over the letter reluctantly. It
had been the source of much conversation in the café. If it had
been in French she might well have been tempted to open it.
'From your son? A relative?' Mireille looked at it and put it
into her pocket.

'What about lunch? Today it's a good piece of chicken with
wild mushrooms.' At the café door Auxille was shaking out a
cloth and looking obviously in their direction. Odette and her
daughter were arranging newspapers outside the shop and
doing the same.

'I won't stop, thank you,' said Mireille. 'I've been making
my hut more habitable. It's taking up a lot of time.'

21

'On your own? You should have asked Macon. No wonder you look so tired.'

'Do I?' and Mireille smiled, a pale version of her usual dazzling one. 'It's finished now, but thank you.'

'On Saturday we go to the market in Draguignan. They have everything there. There would be room for you.'

'I do need a *cannise*,' said Mireille slowly, 'and some cooking pans, and some rope . . .'

'Then it's settled. Meet us by the café at eight. When we come back we shall have lunch.' She still didn't go but stood there smiling furiously in her navy and pink dress, like a sturdy, gaudy, hot-house plant. All this for the contents of a letter, thought Mireille.

She took the letter out of her pocket and opened it. The frisson of anticipation coming from Jeanette was almost audible. She read it. There was a pause between her reading and relating the contents to Jeanette. Jeanette took this pause to be the translation from English to French, not Mireille's attempt to alter it completely. 'He says he's very well. He wishes me a good holiday and he sends his love to everybody in St Clair. He's been windsurfing recently and he had dinner with his girlfriend's parents. That's about it.'

'Ah . . .' said Jeanette, hoping for more but already creating a suave sophisticated young man having a candlelit banquet in a castle. The girlfriend's parents were aristocrats, surely.

'I'll see you on Saturday,' said Mireille.

She was furious. Not with Jeanette. She crunched down through the woods like a wild boar. In her hut she threw the letter on to the table. It was some minutes before she could pick it up again. Perhaps she had misread it. Perhaps she had somehow mistaken what had been said and turned it into an insult.

Dear Mum,

What on earth do you think you are doing? I thought you were having a two-week break and now you say you're staying there until the summer. What's got into you, have you lost it completely? There's plenty of things you should be sorting out here. What about the house? What about your job? I know you've been upset and all that, but staying in a hut isn't going to make it better. I'm sure it's idyllic but you must remember I have no memories about that place, so describing it in detail does nothing for me. When you next contact me please give me some definite arrangements.

Love,
Stephen

She screamed out of the door and across the valley as if her vehemence could be carried on the wind all the way to England and slap Stephen around the face. 'I know you've been upset and all that.' That bit got to her the worst. She sat down to write him an immediate reply but could get no further than the first sentence, which she changed many times. 'How could you? How dare you. Why are you so arrogant?' She sat with her arms on the table. Through the door she could see the sky, the clouds changing it from blue to grey to white. A band of sunlight falling on the floor, appearing and disappearing with the regularity of dance. She tried on another piece of paper. 'You do not know what this place means to me.' When she wrote this her eyes filled with tears, because no, he didn't know. The distance between them was much greater than anything geographical.

Stephen. He was tall and blond, like Gregor had been, and with hazel eyes, also like Gregor's. He was confident and well-spoken. He was the first to shake somebody's hand. He liked windsurfing and rock climbing. He drove a red Astra.

23

He liked fixing things. He liked the Lake District. He worked for a computer software company. He liked information. He liked facts. He liked order. Yes, she had to remember that, even as a little child he had collected snail shells and put them in neat rows by the hut. Other young men didn't change their socks and lived happily in festering nests of used handkerchiefs and beer cans, she knew that. But Stephen was immaculate. The Heathers was like that now. Big bright prints. Black and chrome Italian lighting. Dark blue cups and plates. A red blanket on one arm of the sofa. We are alike, she thought, and looked round her own hut, although he might not have seen the connection. Pans hanging on the wall and the floor scrubbed, scrubbed, scrubbed. The loft swept and rid of unwelcome arachnids. Her sleeping bag on a red blanket she had found in the bottom of the trunk. By the sink a dark blue tin mug.

Dear Stephen,
I am not mad, but please accept that I need to be here. You do not know what this place means to me and yes, you are right, I can't describe it to you. I will stay here until June, then I will let you know what I'm going to do.

It wasn't enough, but she felt something final about writing it. She had sent her mother a postcard after she left home. 'I will not be back for some time. Do not worry about me. Love, Mireille.'

She put the letter in an envelope and sealed it. She knew what she was saying. Leave me alone. It was something she had never said to him before. She started another letter.

Dear Stephen,
And this time I shall call you Sanclair, because that is your real name and I named you after the village. I

24

know you remember nothing about this place but I remember it. I wish you did remember. When you swam in the Ferrou, you were never scared of the water, you would have crawled right in if I hadn't stopped you. You were so fearless. Nothing scared you. Even a late summer thunderstorm that shook the hut and the rain beating like boots on the roof. You sat there on the floor with big wide eyes and your mouth open, not afraid, but awed. Gregor said, 'It's the sky gods having a party,' and he took you outside to see the lightning flashing in great forks across the valley, and you both came back wet and shivering. I had to stoke the stove up and you were chattering with cold. You said, 'So big!' and stretched your arms out. 'So big!' For days after you looked up at the sky, waiting for another storm. I wish you could remember. We all slept up in the loft and took it in turns to tell stories. Can't you remember Gregor's, about the man with the lame donkey and the boat to the Scottish islands? The blind woman in the Sudan who could tell her family's history for generations? My stories were Red Riding Hood and the Big Bad Wolf, Peter Pan, and the tale of Avelard, the troubadour. When it was your turn you told such funny things, big monsters, sky gods and the old woman with a lump on her nose. Your world was so small. The hut, the village, the Ferrou, your red shirt, your floppy rabbit. Then I would see you playing and I could see your world was endless. A tree was a wizard, a stone was a lump of the sky. You played by the Ferrou, talking to nobody, talking to somebody, a muddled up French and English. Sanclair. You started off here and I wish you could remember because it must have affected you, to be a child in the woods. I will not send you this letter.

CHAPTER TWO

Sanclair, this is no longer a letter for you but I want to keep writing. I want to go back to the beginning. My beginning. These are the facts. I was born in Charing Cross Hospital in 1954, on a Thursday in early December. I was born a month early and this inconvenienced my mother because she missed out on the Christmas parties. I weighed a little over 5lbs. There was some concern for my health, but not enough. My parents lived in Kilburn in a first-floor flat. My father was an architect. My mother was very beautiful. I had a nurse called Pammy. The pram wouldn't go up the stairs so I used to sleep in the hallway by the back door. Pammy told me this. My mother never said much about Kilburn except that it was a low-class sort of area and she was pleased to leave it. I was a quiet baby, said Pammy. I used to lie in my pram and watch the ceiling. When I was six months old we moved to Bath and Pammy came too. We lived in a large house up the Lansdown Road, overlooking the city. There was plenty of space to entertain and my parents did this frequently. If consciousness is the beginning, then this is where I begin . . .

I'm in the nursery and my parents are having a party. The nursery is right at the top of the house. A little bedroom for me, a room where I eat and play and a bedroom for Pammy. The wallpaper is stripy, blue and white, like a mattress. There is an old-fashioned rocking horse. The curtains have yellow roses on. I'm sitting on Pammy's lap and my mother is there. This is unusual, she doesn't come up to the nursery much. She is choosing a dress for me. I have lots of pretty dresses, smocked at the front with tiny flowers on. I'm sleepy. My mother is saying, 'She looks best in blue, pale blue,' and she's wearing blue too, a sleeveless shiny blue dress. She has sparkling shoes and shiny blonde hair. 'This one,' and she gives it to Pammy, who dresses me and ties up the sash at the back. I stand on the floor and they both look at me. 'Oh, poppet!' says Pammy, but my mother is scowling. She tries to smooth down my hair with a brush. I have curly black hair and it won't stay flat. She rubs my cheek with pink-nailed thumbs. 'Why isn't there a lotion to get rid of freckles?'

I think about my parents and I think of film stars. My father is Dirk Bogarde and my mother is Grace Kelly, but she's not tall, she's tiny and delicate. She has that same icy cool. She smiles and turns her head. She is always being looked at. There are so many parties I can't remember which one, but I remember the smell of wine and cigar smoke, jazz music and the mix of voices like at a swimming bath, jumbled and distorted. I hold my mother's hand and come downstairs. Pammy doesn't, she never does. The guests stop talking and say, ahh. My mother says, 'It's the best I could do.' She has rings on her fingers and they are biting into my hand. We stop at the bottom of the stairs and she smiles and turns her head. Then my father rushes up and hurls me up high. I squeal and laugh. He kisses me noisily. I'm all crumpled and my hair gets messy. My best girl, he whispers in my ear and carries me round to the table of puddings and I can have a taste of any one I want. The music's louder. Daddy's laughing with Alan Crawford. I put my head down because I'm sleepy. Alan's cigar makes my eyes itch and Daddy twirls me round and round and I can still see, near the stairs, my sparkling mother.

Hugo is my hero. I'm his best girl, his darling. When he comes back from France he gives me a doll. I have a cupboard full of dolls with clothes as beautifully stitched as my own. He looks like me. He has dark hair, blue eyes and freckles which on him don't offend my mother. When I think about him now

27

I feel different. He could tell me about the history of France and how to put a drain in a house. How to play cricket and what was the best way to land a Spitfire on bumpy ground. But he never asked me what I wanted or if I was happy.

My parents went away on holiday and left me with Pammy. The house was quiet and we ate in the kitchen. It seemed huge compared to the nursery. There was a round wooden table with red chairs. The floor was black and white. The door led into the garden, a tiny town garden with a wall all round. A cherry tree with blossom like pink snow and red bark that peeled like paper. I watched the sparrows splash in the bird bath. I sat on the kitchen step. Pammy called, 'Lunch!' and we had sausages and mashed potato.

I can't remember Pammy's face, but she was pink and fat. She wasn't a nanny but a nurse, and sometimes she wore a nurse's apron with a little watch pinned to it. But that was when I was very little. I remember her in Bath wearing flowery dresses that squeezed across her stomach. Sandals with socks and a white cardigan with pearly buttons. Her bosom was enormous and her cardigan never fitted over it. She smelled of Coty's L'aimant and Imperial Leather soap. She treated me with the briskness and matter-of-factness that nurses were supposed to treat their patients. I like to think that when I was a baby she sang to me and cradled me, because I'm sure my mother never did.

Pammy likes Elvis. When my parents are away we go into the lounge and play records on the stereogram. I'm not allowed in the lounge and neither is she, but we won't tell. Pammy sings along and now I can see her face. Her face is round, her hair is short and mousy, she sings 'Heartbreak Hotel' in a whisper, she knows all the words. My mother is beautiful and Pammy is not, but her lips tremble when she whispers, 'They'll make you so lonely you will die.' Her eyes are closed.

28

This is ecstasy. It looks curious and rather frightening but I want to feel it too. I close my eyes. The music stops and Pammy says, 'Would you like some milk and biscuits?' She looks embarrassed and pinker and smooths down the covers of the easy chairs. They are covered in yellow roses like the curtains in my room.

I remember these times, which in my memory stretch for months but were probably only weeks. We never visit anybody. She reads me stories in a flat voice. *Cinderella. Little Red Riding Hood. Snow White.* I try as hard as I can to see Cinderella's glittering ball like one of my parents' parties, the grinning wolf like Alan Crawford and Snow White singing as she makes sausages and mash for the seven dwarves.

Sometimes we go out, to the park I now know as Henrietta Park but I call it the pretty park. It's filled with blossom and flowers and sunlight. There's another park with swings and slides and a boating lake, but that's too far, says Pammy. We sit on a bench. We sit in the sun and watch the people. She's not a great one for talking. If I ask a question, she says, 'Oh, I don't know,' or 'Don't ask me that.' Am I getting this wrong or was Bath quieter then? Now its so busy and in the summer heaving with tourists, but I remember warm late-spring afternoons in a park bursting with blossom. We watch a man walk right round the park. The shadows are getting longer. He passes by, raises his hat, and says, 'Good afternoon, ladies.' We walk back up the hill, slowly because Pammy puffs and wheezes. I see the paint on the doors. Peeling dark green paint, dark red paint. The windows of the houses are thick with lace curtains. The houses are a gold honey colour, all standing next to each other like old people in a church.

From my nursery window I can see right across the town and it frightens me. We live up so high we might fall down. Pammy sits by the window and looks out as if she has been put in charge of all the people and not just me. At night I want my curtains closed. I can't sleep unless they're closed. I don't want to see how high up we are. In the night I imagine the house is balanced on a rock and any minute it's going to fall down and we'll all be buried. I start crying and screaming, 'It's going to fall down any minute!' Then Pammy comes in, in a flowery nightie, and puts on the light. I want to tell her how scary it is, but I can't. She tucks me in and sits next to me. She yawns and yawns and rubs her eyes. I say, 'Leave the door open.' She pads back to her room heavily, like a bear. I think I can hear her getting into bed. The springs bounce. I think I can hear her snoring. I feel comforted.

I went to school and Pammy left. This is a fact. I don't remember it. I don't remember saying goodbye or tears or presents, but I remember my school uniform. Grey and blue. A grey skirt, a blue blazer, a grey hat with a blue ribbon. Grey socks. It was one of those little private schools there used to be so many of but they got closed down because they were crap. We sat in rows and copied out letters of the alphabet. A,a,a. B,b,b. By the time I went to school I could already read, but nobody paid attention to that. The school had once been a house and the playground was the garden concreted over. The headmistress was called Miss Tanner. There were three boys, but the rest of the children were girls. I had never seen so many children before, shouting, skipping, singing, playing games I had never heard of and didn't know how to play. The boys fascinated me. They had long grey socks, long grey shorts, and in between were plastered knees. They cut their knees and didn't cry. Their shirts came untucked and they didn't care. One had ginger hair and freckles, but orange freckles he wasn't the least bit ashamed of. He stuck his arm next to mine and said, 'I've got more than you.' The other two boys were brothers, Desmond and Peter. They communicated by nodding to each other. Desmond got

30

slapped on the hands with a ruler by Miss Tanner, because he was bold. He stood there, pink cheeked and defiant. It was Peter who wailed. Afterwards in the playground they plotted how they were going to get her. They were going to hide her chalk. They were going to piss in the girls' toilets. They were going to get a black man to look up her skirt. I was silent and insignificant. They didn't notice me. I heard it all.

My father took me to school and my mother took me home. She didn't talk to the other mothers. After all what had she to say to the dowdy women with fat babies in prams, but my father smiled and chatted. They were respectable women, but marriage had made them sport tweedy skirts and cardigans of sludgy green, over-permed hair and unflattering footwear. My mother was as remote as a princess. Sunglasses, and her hair under a headscarf. A cream suit and little pointed shoes. She said the same thing to me every day. 'Did you have a nice time?' It wasn't the sort of question that needed an answer. She held my hand not out of affection but so I wouldn't get lost. She walked slowly, as if she had all the time in the world, turning her head to look at her reflection in shop windows.

I'm in my bedroom at night and I've had that dream again about the house falling down. I'm crying and crying, but then I realise Pammy isn't there anymore. I also realise that no matter how much I scream my parents won't come upstairs. It's a strange thought and a horrible one and it quietens me. I lie there in the darkness but I can't sleep. Then I do an odd thing. I get out of bed, open Pammy's door, and run back into bed as fast as I can. Pammy isn't there, but I can imagine that she is. I imagine I can hear her snoring on the other side of the nursery. I imagine it so much I can hear it. Then everything feels better.

I still do this, don't I, when I'm by myself? I imagine some-body's there when they're not. It's better than being alone.

CHAPTER THREE

She woke up under the sloping roof of the hut to a wet, windy morning. The wind sang through the pine trees. The branches creaked and sighed. She had been dreaming of Felix. He smoked too much and wheezed in his sleep. She didn't open her eyes. He was still beside her in her dream, where she was waiting for him to wake up and start coughing, but she didn't want to wake him up. Dreaming about sleeping. It seemed a peculiar thing to do. She missed him. It was a physical ache that was difficult to smooth away, much worse than the baby, which was like being given a present and having it snatched from her. Missing Felix was worse because she knew him. He infuriated her. He went to bed far too late. He woke up far too late with a 'Fuck! Is that the time?' There was always something he hadn't done, something he should have done two hours ago. Why hadn't he seen a doctor about his chest? Why had he smoked so much and why was his life so bloody chaotic? But in the morning, when she was awake and he wasn't, she felt tender towards him.

Felix was beautiful in an odd way. He had long fair curling hair, masses of it. His face was angles and hollows. His eyes, which were slanting, were grey-blue. He didn't look like an angel because angels don't growl when they're angry and forget to wash. He looked like a spirit from fairyland. A changeling, furious to be living with humans. He would disrupt them whenever he could. He would turn up at her narrowboat and sit by the stove, warming his hands. Long and bony, a philosopher's hands. She knew he hadn't eaten anything and he was tired. He would say, 'Can I read you something?' and out of his pocket came a crumpled bundle of paper, and he read one poem, then another. Strange poems with not much sense, like thoughts don't make sense but have images and words which connect. This planet, love and community, and the goddess, something he saw on the street the week before, something he felt at a party, in a dream. But when he read he put so much into it, it seemed to make him flicker and glow like a candle at night. The closer she stood the more warmth she could feel.

She opened her eyes and she was looking up at the terracotta tiles, lapped over each other, holding out the rain, which was coming down now in a torrent. It would keep her inside. She turned round to the imagined Felix, still sleeping. 'I won't wake you,' she said, because she wanted him to stay peaceful in her mind. She crept down the ladder and lit the stove. She put the pot of coffee on and a pan of water so she could wash. The hut was gradually getting warmer. She lit the oil lamp and it gave out a soft light over the floor and the rough-cast walls. The coffee began to bubble and the smell of it filled the hut. She poured the liquid into a bowl, sat at the table and dipped in bread. Dark bitter coffee and chunks of baguette. A peasant breakfast. Tomorrow she would go to Draguignan.

Friday morning
Felix, this is a letter for you. There's so much I never told you. You needed to talk about yourself. I was going to tell you so many things but in the end there wasn't time. I'm glad I told you about the Ferrou. Do you remember, I said to you, 'You must find a place to go to in your mind,' and you said, 'Like where?' Sad, and grumpy and hopeless. And I said, 'I know this place in France,' and when I told you, I could see you could see it. You were walking up the track and towards the great rock and the pool. I could see you looking into the pool and holding your breath. Afterwards you said, 'Take me

33

there.' I was cautious because this is my special place, but I knew you needed some sort of vision, some sort of future and I said, yes.

You are here with me now in this room, so I will take you to the Ferrou.

I want to find the beginning of this place. I can think of events, but they seem so random. When I first came here I felt, I am meant to be here. I was nine. Vivienne and Hugo were here and Jeanette, chattering away, but they have disappeared in my memory and there is only me standing with such awe and such fear. I looked up at the cleft in the rock, at the sun shining above it and into the pool dazzling me. Firewater. When I touched the water I thought it would be hot, but it wasn't, it was cold.

Here's a memory. I'm in the top class of the prep school. The children in the first class look like babies and I can hardly believe I was that small. I'm as tall as my mother and I feel like an oaf. Felix, you once said to me your mother couldn't see you for what you were. I don't think my parents saw me at all. I was dressed. I was washed. I was given food and talked to, but I wasn't a person. I was a pet, sometimes irritating, sometimes delightful but most of the time forgotten about. When I left home I was angry about this. I was so angry I wanted to forget about them. I wanted to eradicate them. Especially my mother.

My mother sat there at social functions like a sorbet, but afterwards tore each guest to pieces. They were fat, ugly, badly dressed. My father laughed because she was funny; she was a great mimic, she could capture a person's tone of voice, or their posture, and she found it funny too. It sent her into shrieks of laughter. When she laughed like that it terrified me. One day she would laugh about me, I knew it. I could already hear her: 'That Mireille, with the freckles, that beanpole,

34

darling, socks with sandals, did you ever, have you ever seen such a specimen (people were always specimens to my mother)? Have you ever seen such a frump!' I felt ashamed. By my mother's shallowness and also by my father being taken in by it.

Hugo was ambitious. With Alan Crawford he became involved in property development in the south of France. After St Tropez had become fashionable the whole coast from there to Nice was gradually submerged under ugly holiday apartments. My father's name was Devereux, and his grandparents were French. He spoke French, he understood French ways. He saw a way to make money and didn't hesitate. I used to believe I was like my father because I knew I was entirely different from my mother, but now I know I was so different from both of them. What they ate, what they wore, what they bought was of paramount importance. My mother was so status-conscious she would throw away her curtains, have a baby, move house, if it would improve her standing in the eyes of other people. She was an excellent acquisition for my father.

I am silent and shy. I read in my spare time. I am learning to read French and I can speak it. I pray every night. Please God, can I have a friend? I want a friend but I don't know where to start. It's nearly the end of the summer term, it's hot and we have lessons outside in the playground, but Miss Tanner is lethargic and the pupils are half asleep. She tells us we will go on a trip to the Roman baths and all the class go, 'Oh no, not again!' But I have never been. My parents have never taken me. They only take me to places where they want to go. I have been to France more than seven times. I have been to Nice, Cap Ferrat, Toulon, Menton, Grasse, Cannes. When I say these names to my schoolmates their eyes widen. They have been to Torquay, Weston-Super-Mare, Dawlish, Paignton.

When we go to the baths Miss Tanner gives us a long speech about Romans, watercourses, hydro systems. Underground and indoors it's hot and sticky. I can make no sense of the stones. Then we are herded out to the great baths, and there they are. The golden pillars, the greeny water. The steam rising. The water pouring out from the spring into the basin, a constant gush of water. I have seen this before, of course I have, at the Ferrou. Again I feel that shiver. I put my hand into the stream of water, expecting it to be cold, but it isn't, it's warm. Not hot like a tap, but warm like a pond of water on a beach, like a cup of *thé citron* left on a café table. The temperature of tears.

Here's another memory. Going back now. I'm wearing a white cotton dress, white socks and black sandals. I'm sitting on a wicker chair outside a café. The chair has a band of green around its edge. It's an uncomfortable chair and sticks to my legs. I'm drinking *citron pressé* out of a long glass, trying to keep the spoon out of my nose. I'm so hot. I've never been as hot before and we are in the shade. The café is in a street. There are people everywhere, talking, and I don't understand because it's French. A smell in the air of fish and scent from the purple flowers that trail over the wall. All colours are brighter. Hugo is in white, so bright I can hardly look at him. He is laughing. His sleeve is rolled up and his arm is brown. He is talking French. My mother is in the shade, dressed in mint green like an ice cream but one frozen so hard it won't melt. She is wearing dark glasses. She crosses and uncrosses her legs. She is smoking a cigarette, slowly, like somebody who wants to enjoy all of it. Then Hugo jumps up and comes round the table and kisses her forehead. Her expression does not change, but they hold each other's hands and squeeze tight. I can see their knuckles becoming whiter.

My parents are dead now, but they stay young in my mind and I think I now understand their passion. It was about owning. Each wanted to possess the other. Without my father my mother was half a person, bored, flicking through magazines, telling me to sit up straight and not slouch, but when he walked into the room a look came over her face of complete radiance. Suddenly the way she sat and the way she talked was aimed, I can see it now, at dazzling and over-whelming him. In the end there was nothing he could see but her and nothing she could think about but him.

We are due to go to France for nearly all of the holidays. My father is working on a project on the coast. The previous summer they bought the Ferrou and it stays there. One dark pool. One unmodernised hut. They want to build a holiday home, with a swimming pool feature under the great rock. I have seen the plans. I know about building plans because when we return from France we will be moving into the new house my father has designed. He talks about this new house, how it will bring him a great deal of attention. It has a fountain courtyard and a garden, sweeping down a hill. It's all my parents talk about these days. New houses. My mother's going to sell the furniture in Bellevue. It's old-fashioned and that is bad. Everything in my room is also old-fashioned.

It's Sunday morning and I come down for breakfast. My father's up and dressed in his cricket clothes. He's going to play cricket later. They have been discussing the new house. He looks at me thoughtfully, which he rarely does because my mother usually diverts his attention. He says, 'Why don't I take her to see the site? It would be good for her education.'

'Trampling about in mud?' says my mother with a sneer.

'I won't get dirty,' I say, because spending time alone with my father is a treat.

She looks at me as if there is nothing right about me. 'Go on, turn her into an architect. She's such a brain-box.'

We go in the car across Bath. It's not sunny. It's humid and

37

overcast. My father tells me about drainage problems, but I'm thinking about the new house, the magic castle. 'Here we are,' he says, but I don't see anything. A drive of mud, as if a finger has scraped into the earth to taste it. We get out of the car and walk across the mud, which is soft like paste and sticks to my shoes. In front of us is a pile of grey concrete bricks. It looks like an air-raid shelter or a public lavatory. This is the house. My father tells me about the cunning design. It's layered down the hill and this is the first level. It's flat-topped and squat. We go inside. But it's just concrete and more concrete. Wires coming out of the walls, holes in the floor as if its innards are being operated on. I feel cheated. I hate it. I would rather live in a little hut like the Ferrou, even though there is only one tap, because it is golden and private. This place is a prison. My father tells me where the kitchen is going to be and the lounge. We go outside through more mud and puddles of water. There's a view across a smudgy valley. The hill rolls down to a wooden bridge across weed-filled water. I look at the bridge, then I run, right down the hill. My father shouts after me, but I keep running. He catches up with me on the bridge. He is hot and cross in his cricket clothes. 'You silly girl, what are you doing!'

He's not often cross with me and I burst into tears. 'What's up? What is it, my special girl?'

'I don't want to live here. I want to live in France.'

CHAPTER FOUR

Mireille walked into the square. It was the Easter weekend
and the village looked festive. In front of the church bunting
had been hung up, and around the square flowers planted in
wooden tubs. The church was open, ready for the Easter
mass, and from inside came the chattering of the cleaners,
their French dipped in the Provençal accent until it twanged
and resonated like a wet guitar string. Outside, Jeanette and
Auxille were chattering too, their hands, if not flapping near
their heads to emphasise a point, smoothing down their best
clothes. Auxille was all in black. A neat little black suit with
an opal brooch on the lapel. She had tiny lace-up shoes and
silk stockings. She still had shapely legs. Jeanette's hair was
now blacker than ever, almost blue-black. Her dress was red
and tight and her shoes were red and high-heeled. She was
wearing a gold necklace and at least six rings. When they saw
Mireille they waved wildly. Macon lumbered out of the café.

Macon's car was not large and it jolted every time the gears
were changed. Jeanette drove, talking to Macon the whole
way, who didn't listen but fiddled with the collar on his shirt
and held on to the strap of the seat belt every time Jeanette
hurled the vehicle round another corner. Auxille didn't like
cars. She closed her eyes and folded her hands on her lap, but
no amount of discomfort could stop her talking.
    '. . . and I said to Madame Cabasson, your *tarte aux
pommes* is certainly as good as the one I bought in the best
bakery in Draguignan and half the price, but there, of course,
they put it in a little box with a ribbon, a little present. I

suggested this to Madame Cabasson especially in the summer when we have the tourists . . . and her niece Martine is to be married to a policeman . . . I offered to do the flowers . . . in May . . .'

Mireille looked out of the window. The villages of St Clair and Lieux were already disappearing as the car sped round another bend towards the road to Draguignan.

In Draguignan it was sunny and noticeably warmer than St Clair, where the wind still had a sharp edge. It was also crowded. Draguignan has no grand buildings of renown, remarkable museums or many distinguishing features, but the old centre was quaint and still had a mediaeval feel to it. Serious attempts had been made to modernise the town, including paving over one of the main streets, putting in smart new lighting and restoring the façades of some of the old houses. But it remained provincial, attracting people from the outlying villages.

The market was at the far end of town around some gardens. Pots and pans, leatherwork, African goods, cheap dresses, cheap shoes. Jeanette and Auxille held each other's arms and inspected every item on every stall, comparing prices and tutting to each other. Macon had already sloped away to a nearby bar. It was going to be a long day. 'What do you think?' asked Jeanette, holding up a black and white spotty silky dress to her ample bosom.

'I'm not sure of the quality,' said Auxille, examining the hem. The stallholder reassured her it was of the finest quality and drew their attention to other ones, pink and white, red and white, orange and white, green and white.

'I like the green,' said Jeanette to Mireille. 'What do you think?'

'I'm going to buy a *cannise*. Shall I meet you in an hour?'

'Make it two,' said Auxille. 'In the bar with Macon.'

*

Away from the women she explored the lower end of the market, which sold more practical things like hedge-clippers, buckets, nails and, bizarrely, sausages and fresh country salami. Leading up one street was a flower and plant market. She could easily have spent the rest of the day among the oleanders, wistarias, lilacs and rose bushes. Whole bay trees in terracotta pots. Lavender plants. Orange trees, and buckets and buckets of early mimosa. Two gypsy women with faces like pickled walnuts and teeth full of gold were selling bunches of wild asparagus.

Towards lunchtime the market filled up with younger people and became more rowdy. Music was turned up and the stall-holders shouted out their bargains. Groups of young girls identically dressed in tight tops and jeans tried on cheap jewellery and looked as bored as they could. Young men watched them from the gardens, smoking and leaning on their motorbikes. Jeanette and Auxille were sitting outside at a table. Macon was inside, up against the bar, where in France the drinks are cheaper.

'The dresses would fall to pieces. I could make her something for half the price,' said Auxille.

They were drinking coffee and eating sugared waffles out of a bag.

'But look at this. What do you think?' Jeanette unwrapped a large painting. It was an idealised Alpine scene complete with mountain goat and a patch of Alpine flowers. 'To go over our fireplace. Maman saw it. Now, her mother's father was a shepherd who used to go to the high pastures every June.'

Mireille thought it was hideous but Auxille didn't wait for her answer. 'And what have you bought?' she asked, having a good look at Mireille's shopping. 'A hunting knife? A cooking pot? A blanket? Nothing to wear?'

'And this,' said Mireille, and put a lavender plant on the

table. She also had the *cannise*, rolled up like a carpet.

'Maman, what does she need clothes for? She lives in a hut,' said Jeanette.

On the way home Jeanette insisted that Mireille stay with them for the whole weekend and whatever protest Mireille put up about orchids or not having enough decent clothes was loudly quashed. In the end she agreed. Jeanette and Auxille responded with the glee of two spiders finding a large fly in their web. Even Macon found the idea entertaining. They didn't have many guests. Surely this was a reason to celebrate.

The Blancs lived in a flat above the café. In St Clair the old houses were divided up in strange ways, like interlocking puzzles. People's kitchens jutted into other people's bedrooms and, once inside, it was difficult to make out who or where the neighbours were. The Blancs' flat was no exception. The main living area contained the dining table, the sofa and the television. It overlooked the square and was the most pleasant room, although it was small and overstuffed with furniture. A sideboard was positively littered with photographs of nephews and nieces, silk flowers and china ornaments. There was a massive old fireplace surrounded by brown glazed tiles. It was never used as a fireplace, but Jeanette kept her copper cooking pans hanging there. They were never used either, but had once belonged to Auxille's mother. A small patch of old Provence among the spanking new. The kitchen, at the back, seemed to be cut into the rock and had no natural light. A huge beam ran across the ceiling and looked as if it could carry the weight of three houses, not one. The bedrooms were down winding stairs, Jeanette and Macon's with a large bed, a quilted shiny pink bedspread and a brown tiled floor, Auxille's no larger than a cupboard, with one tiny window and an airless lavender smell

42

of old woman. Mireille was to sleep on the sofa, which, when Macon tugged it enough, creaked itself into a bed. During the day the Blancs lived in the café. It was only at night they sat upstairs.

Macon, in front of the television, was nodding into a post-dinner stupor. Auxille and Jeanette washing up, both talking loudly about unconnected topics and Mireille straining to hear them above the noise of the television. Outside young men shouted to each other across the square. A dog started barking, then another, then another. Macon's old hound momentarily twitched its ears.

On Easter Sunday they went to church. Jeanette dressed up in twice as much jewellery as when she went to market. Auxille in black, Macon in a suit, and Mireille with backache and a headache. The church was cold and badly lit. It had been recently painted but still managed to look faded and crumbling. Large ugly paintings of gesticulating saints hung above the side altars. In a chapel the statue of the Virgin Mary held a bright pink Jesus in front of a wall crammed with votive paintings depicting various tiny miracles. A runaway cart that didn't squash anybody. A wheel falling off another and nobody hurt. A baby in a wooden cot and its equally wooden mother praying to the statue in the sky. 1808. 1854. 1873. 1902. Mireille read the dates. The priest, youngish and vigorous, was doing his best to rouse the congregation with his sermon, but they were there, he knew, only to look at each other and gossip afterwards. 1865. 1918. Plenty of those. A soldier returning up a track to be greeted by his family. 1926. 1935. But whoever had painted that one still hadn't learned about perspective. The last one was 1945 and showed the village decked out with flags. They were in the middle of the offertory now. Jeanette was craning her neck to see who had made it to church and who hadn't. Macon was nearly asleep. Auxille was the only one who was holy, whispering through her rosary

43

prayers with a look of detached peace on her face. Mireille looked at the paintings again and one caught her eye. The rock at the Ferrou, badly painted but recognisable by the black split down it. The sun above it and underneath the words: 'Thank you. 1942.' Thank you for what? She would ask Auxille.

But after mass there was no time for questions. Jeanette introduced Mireille to the rest of the villagers, who stayed outside the church shaking hands with the priest and complaining about each other. She described Mireille variously as 'an expert on orchids', 'a journalist' and 'the daughter of the famous British architect'. Having a guest had given Jeanette an exalted sense of status, and, despite her orange and pink dress, bare legs and those red shoes, she still managed to look like an important guest at a garden party.

Then it was lunch! And that was going to take all afternoon. A gigot of lamb, hard-boiled eggs and a *salade sauvage*. Local red wine, coarse but not unpalatable, and Macon even turned the television off. They ate in the closed café, the tables pushed together and covered with the best linen.

'. . . and did you see Madame Cabasson's niece . . .' said Jeanette, serving up. 'Pink cheeked, and how plump she looks. I'm sure she's pregnant.'

'And he's a policeman,' said Auxille.

'And wasn't that the Villeneuve's youngest daughter near the back in green with a smart hat? She must be getting married soon but she will get married in Paris for sure. Did I hear she became a lawyer? Mireille, more salad, it's good for the digestion.'

'Was that picture of the Ferrou given by Old Man Henri?' asked Mireille, but neither Jeanette nor Auxille could remember such a picture. The church fittings were not the reason why they went there.

'During the war there were many miracles,' said Jeanette. 'Our Lady spared many lives,' and she blessed herself to revere this fact.

'But not your father's,' said Macon into his wine glass. 'Your parents were married five years before they had you. Now that is a miracle.'

'Hold your tongue on this holy day!' snapped Jeanette, but Auxille hadn't heard. She was telling Mireille about her grandfather. 'Old Man Henri was a shepherd from the Maures and every year he used to take the sheep up to the Alpine pastures.' She looked fondly at the new painting now balanced above the fireplace. 'But one year he was resting with the flock near the river at Lieux and a village girl came down to wash the clothes (they did that then), and what a picture she was, dark hair, rosy cheeks, a true Provençal, and just fifteen . . .'

Mireille had heard this story before and so had Jeanette and Macon, hundreds of times.

'That's the carpet I bought with your mother's money,' said Jeanette, pointing to a patterned rug on the floor. 'Your mother, I remember her so well. What a lady. *Très gentille. Très sympa. Très élégante* . . .'

'Of course he had to give up being a shepherd, because my grandmother's father said he would never let his daughter be married to one . . . he became a carpenter but he liked the open air too much, he walked for hours in the hills . . . but when she died during the war, an appendix complication and they couldn't get a doctor, he wouldn't live in the village again. He bought the land at the Ferrou and lived like a hermit.'

'Of course, if they had built that house, that mansion, you might have married a French boy, a cousin of the Villeneuves', but that wasn't to be and now the Ferrou is a wilderness. Who can find it? It is forgotten.' She was becoming poetic.

'. . . and he lived like a hermit until he died and he didn't want company, and he didn't want anybody to visit him, but I did sometimes with some goat's cheese and anchovies in season . . .'

45

Mireille listened to both of them. Perhaps the painting made sense now. Thank you for peace and quiet. Thank you for a life away from the rattle of the village. Thank you.

Chapter Five

Wednesday. Afternoon

I didn't get back home until Easter Monday and even then Jeanette was pressurising me to stay another night. But I couldn't. I wanted to get back here. I love the smell of this place, wet earth and plaster and always the pine trees. Opening the door is like smelling a lover when you first embrace him. At Jeanette's I could hardly sleep. The room was so stuffy and the bed wobbled when I turned over. God! Am I so hardy again I need to sleep on wooden planks with a hefty draught under the door? I like Jeanette and Auxille and even Macon. They drive me nuts, but I know they are honest and kind and I appreciate it. I'm writing this in bed because when I got back I was sick. I've had a bad stomach since. I wasn't used to all that food. It seems a shame that Auxille's cooking should land up so rapidly in the pit in the woods. I didn't want it that way. I wanted to feel that their generosity could at least linger in my body and do me good. I'm now on a diet of bread and a herbal brew I made out of lime-flower tea with lemon and celery leaves. It's pretty revolting. I've been too ill to saw up wood and the hut has become cold again. I must remember not to leave here for too long because once the stove goes out the temperature drops rapidly. I want it to get warmer outside because then I can bathe in the Ferrou. I'm longing to do this. Even in the hottest summer the water makes me gasp. I'm thinking about Old Man Henri. He lived here until he died. Is that what's going to happen to me? I have made no plans to do anything else. I'm thinking about history now. Every place has a history. Every person has a history and this place is part of my history and I am a part of this place, with Henri and before him with whoever was the first person who stood by the Ferrou and touched the water. It's a history impossible to trace, but I feel part of the line when I stand there. And I felt it when I was nine.

My parents were bored with the coast. The phenomena of St Tropez did not interest them. My mother would never have been seen dead in bare feet, hipster jeans and a shirt tied in a knot to show off her midriff. She called them 'dirty bohemians' and Brigitte Bardot was a 'silly, dirty bohemian'. I think it was more that they realised they were not young any more. Hugo Devereux, the brilliant young architect, and his beautiful wife. They believed this even though they were in their thirties. They believed it at their parties in Bath. They believed it when The Heathers was being built. But that summer they couldn't believe it because the young had all gone to a little fishing village and were hanging out on the beach.

We went inland in a hired car. It started out as day trips with a picnic packed by the hotel. I had only seen fashionable resorts and I thought all of France was like that. Hotels with shutters. Large houses with tiered gardens and swimming pools. All French people were like my father's clients, who were mostly British anyway, with skin the colour of polished pine and manners as well tailored as their clothes. But we went inland to tumbledown villages perched on the tops of hills, where old women wore black and shuffled by in worn-down espadrilles. A man in navy workclothes and a peaked hat was followed by a small dog. Where the bars were smoky and the only food they served was *croque monsieur*. My mother hated it. She fanned herself with the map. She sat in the car for the picnic because of the ants. She remained conspicuous, with her pastel clothes, golden blonde hair and tiny frame, where all the other women were sturdy, busty in

48

cheap floral dresses. My father loved it. He was an architect and he loved buildings. Squashed-up stone houses. Dark cavernous churches. Forgotten eighteenth-century mansions with crumbling façades and that shabby, shabby grandeur that's impossible to imitate. It was his idea to go further north.

I remember this journey in fragments. It was August and although the heat wasn't as stifling as it was by the coast there were no swimming pools to dip into. The car was an oven and I was a currant bun cooking on the back seat. Wherever we stopped was dry. Even the leaves on the trees were dry and the grass snapped when I stood on it. The ants marched over my shoes and up my legs. The ground smelled strong and aromatic. There were pine trees with huge cones and I collected them. I kept them on the back seat and poked my fingers in between their smooth wooden spires. We drove through canyons and gorges. Past cliffs of gnarled grey rock. Past huge boulders. Past ravines that fell to fast rivers hundreds of feet below. Round scary hairpin bends and up hills to small towns, dusty in the evenings. The smell of cooking filling up the streets. The golden light making the fronts of houses look like gilded books. The hotels were empty. Big uncomfortable beds with stiff white sheets. Huge creaking furniture and shutters with heavy iron clasps.

We're in Rochas. It's a village on a hill where everything is on a hill. We're staying in the only hotel. It's a flat building with sixteen windows. I've counted them. The bar downstairs opens on to a square with a fountain. The fountain doesn't gush but trickles water out of four spouts into a basin thickly green with weed. Do not drink this water, it says. *Eau non potable*. But I did yesterday and now I wonder if I will get ill. The chairs and tables are under a blue and white canopy and that is where my mother is sitting, reading *Vogue* and drinking Pernod. My father is not here. He is looking at land because now they want to buy some land and build a holiday home so we won't have to stay in hotels. He's been away nearly all week. There is one shop that sells postcards and ice creams. There's another that sells bread and cakes, but it's only open in the morning and the afternoon. Rochas is built on a rock. The houses are on one side and the rock is on the other. The streets go round and round like a maze. People hang washing out of their windows and lines go right across the street.

They have windows full of geraniums and canaries in cages. Everything seems to be up in the air. On the ground hot dogs flick their tails in puddles of water from the washing.

I want my father to come back. I have breakfast with my mother, hot chocolate and croissants, then we sit in the square. She reads her magazine. I play jacks and look at the fountain. She drinks Pernod, which smells like aniseed. The men in the bar look at her but she doesn't look back. She smokes a menthol cigarette and drinks more Pernod. We have lunch, a toasted sandwich, and my mother doesn't eat hers. She says the sun takes away her appetite. Then we have a siesta because the sun gives her a headache. I stay in my room and draw pictures. I can't sleep. I open the shutters. There's an iron rail across the window and I lean on it. The men in the bar look up at me now. I go back to bed. The bed's all white. The sheets are the sea and my finger is a boat sailing up and down it. It's getting hot because I left the shutters open. I will get told off.

The clocks are striking four and my mother comes in. She's wearing something different and she smells of perfume. 'You didn't close the shutters,' she says and looks out of the window. The men start to whistle.

'Get dressed,' she says and slams the shutters closed. She brushes my hair to try and make it go flat. Her hair is tied back in a scarf. We have a drink in the bar, lemon tea in glass cups. The dogs are lying in the shade and panting. My mother looks at her watch. It will be days before Daddy comes home.

We go for a walk. There is only one walk, to the church. We walk in the shadows and the houses are like cliffs. A window opens and somebody flaps a duster. We walk up the steps, up the back of the rock.

The church is at the top. There's a small square in front of it with trees and benches but it's boiling hot. The church is black and its door is open like a mouth waiting to swallow us.

Inside it's freezing. I can't see anything even though the lights are on. We walk up to the altar and my mother starts to laugh. 'God, it's tacky in here.' I'm sure you're not supposed to laugh in churches. The altar is covered in statues of angels blowing trumpets, painted gold, and a huge picture of a man stripped to the waist being whipped. The blood is running into puddles on the floor. I hate this picture. It makes me feel sick, but it makes my mother laugh even more. I'm sure we're going to get into trouble.

'Can I have a franc?' I ask her. 'For the crib?' The crib is at the back near the door. It's under glass. It's a model. When you put the franc in, the figures move. The three wise men and their camels start to walk to the stable. The shepherds, too, and the little sheep nod their heads. The star moves up and down. Villagers with baskets of bread pop out of their houses. A train steams out of a tunnel and down a hill and in the stable the baby Jesus waves his arm. I love it. There's always something I didn't see last time. It's a grandpa wobbling on his stick and at his feet is a brown and white puppy. The model whirrs and creaks like an old clock. It's all over too fast.

The noise brings my mother over. She puts in one franc after another. The model makes her laugh even more than the picture. 'A first-century train. Oh my God!' The model creaks and creaks, I'm sure it's going to break. The camels are jerking their legs much too fast. I'm sure the baby Jesus's arm is going to fall off. I want to cry, but I don't want to cry in front of my mother. We stare at the model until it finally stops with a big clunk. Then there is no sound in the church but me breathing and the door pulling on its hinges.

There was a piece of land for sale in St Clair owned by the woman in the café. Jeanette was then recently married, it was Auxille who ran Le Sanglier. We waited for them, at the tables under the plane trees, my mother, dressed in pale green, with a patterned headscarf. She was yawning and fiddling with her sunglasses. Auxille came bustling out of the café.

'Oh, the English architect, and this is your wife! Oh, she is so beautiful, she is so chic, and this is your daughter!' She rushed up to me and put her bony hands around my cheeks. 'Jeanu, Jeanu, come and see a little English girl.'

Jeanette was curvy and healthy like a fresh peach. Her dress stuck to her curves. She had bare legs, brown but unshaven, and armpits full of dark black hair. 'Oh, the little one!' she exclaimed. 'What beautiful skin, and such blue eyes, and such beautiful hair,' and she too petted and fondled me, purring over me as if I were a kitten. I wasn't used to such attention.

'What a specimen. What a tart,' my mother said in English.

'You are such a lucky man to have such a fine family,' said Auxille. Jeanette was now sitting next to me and patting my hand. I looked into her face. I decided I liked her. I felt comfortable with her like I used to with Pammy.

Jeanette had dark brown eyes, darker than anyone I knew. 'Do you like puppies?' she asked. I could just understand her French.

'I don't know,' I said.

'When we get back I shall show you six puppies, they were born yesterday.' Her hand was rough but I didn't mind.

'And you will have more children,' said Auxille. 'Some fine sons, eh?' She winked knowingly at my mother.

'Heavens above,' said my mother, smiling and nodding.

*

We all went in the car, Jeanette and Auxille in the back giving conflicting directions and me squashed between them. We drove back down the hill. Jeanette and Auxille smelled of garlic, sweat and rose water. Their speech slipped into a language I didn't understand. We drove up a bumpy track. 'It's here!' 'No, it's not.' 'It's further down, it's by the farm.' We stopped and we were nowhere. Terraces of olive trees and, behind, the woods going up the hill. 'Now we walk,' said Auxille, and we did, up a tiny path winding round the terraces. Herb bushes and brambles scratched my legs. My mother guarded her dress, but Jeanette and Auxille strode on.

'My grandfather lived here for twenty years and only last month we buried him. He was a shepherd in the old days and used to take his sheep up to Alpine pastures in the summer . . .'

We were in front of a tiny hut, like a gnome's house, with a tiny chimney and a tiny window.

'God, it's a hovel!' said my mother. 'Did the old boy die here?'

'Shh,' said my father. 'We could knock it down. It's a good spot. The view is terrific.'

'*Voici les montagnes!*' said Auxille and we looked, towards the snowy peaks and the clouds resting on them. 'This is where my grandfather used to live.'

Inside there was hardly room for all of us. 'It smells of rats,' said my mother.

'See, there is water,' and Auxille turned on the tap.

'There is a spring,' said Jeanette. 'You will never run out of water.'

'Where is the spring,' asked my father, 'in the woods?'

'No, at the Ferrou,' said Auxille.

'What's a Ferrou?'

'I'll show you,' said Auxille and we walked round the back of the hut through the woods and towards the gully.

'Good God,' said my father and even my mother was quiet.

*

53

I'm standing by the pool looking up at the rock and the split down the rock, towards the great stone basin full of clear water like glass. The sun shines above the rock and into the water, dazzling me. I feel shivery and strange. I feel very young and very old. The water and the sun are all I can see. I put my hand into the water, thinking it's going to be hot, but it isn't, it's cold. It makes me shiver more.

Saturday. Early evening
Today I walked to Rochas. I wanted to get moving again. I felt so stiff and old. I remembered walking there with Gregor once, with Sanclair on his shoulders. It seemed to take no time at all. We had a drink in the hotel and then walked up to the church to show Sanclair the crib. He was about two then. Didn't he love it, pressing his face to the glass and saying, 'Monster!' when the train popped out. A sunny day, don't I remember it, blue sky and wild flowers everywhere. It must have been May. Today it took me two hours, and I shall write this again in case I ever think about walking there in the future. It takes two hours to walk to Rochas. A tough walk along a barely visible track. Deep in the woods. There's no view and the last bit is past the sewage works and a rubbish tip. I don't like Rochas, with its big ugly church and the houses snaking up to it. It has stayed decayed. St Clair was always pretty, sitting in the clouds, and Lieux with its fountains and houses of flowers is in every guide book of the region, but nobody goes to Rochas. I sat in the hotel café and drank Pernod, not outside because it had started to rain, but in the dingy bar room. Was that the same group of men that used to pester my mother? It could have been.

Rochas is dirty. I'd forgotten that. It's not a picturesque decay but one of neglect. The young people have gone away. There are houses for sale, but they won't become holiday homes. The streets are always in shadow because of the rock. It was worse in the rain. I walked up to the church and felt like I did with my mother. The church was being renovated. It was a shell of stone with cement-mixers and scaffolding at the front and that smell of cement that makes me think of so many things: the building site at The Heathers, my father relaying the floor at the Ferrou, Stephen laying the patio in his new house, the bull-dozers and diggers on the by-pass. As the rain poured, brown rivers of mud ran down the hill. The great doors had been taken away and the church looked more like a tomb than ever. I was thinking about my father.

It was the last summer I spent with my parents in France and the one I remember most clearly. Do we all have a time we remember, that holiday, that special holiday when the world becomes magic and exciting and there we are, alone, exploring it? My parents bought the Ferrou but they didn't stay there. They rented a flat in the village. It was the ground floor of a large house owned by the third best Blancs. A sun terrace ran the whole length of it. Grapes grew up the walls and on to the roof of the terrace. Green bitter grapes with large floppy leaves, I was told they would be ripe in October, but I ate them anyway. Below the house was a small swimming pool, which my mother sat by all day long and occasionally slipped into like a lazy snake. If I talked to her she smiled as if she had just woken from a blissful dream. The Blancs upstairs were an elderly couple who did all our washing and cooking with the energy of people who had been energetic all their lives. Only illness or death would stop them. I watched them as they hoed the garden, hung out the washing, and wondered what they thought of my mother whose biggest decision of the day was whether to wear a green or a blue bikini.

My father spent most of the day at the Ferrou. He was relaying the floor of the hut, which was to become part of the new house, he imagined. This was the year of the new houses. The Heathers would be ready for us to move into when we returned. The plans for the Ferrou kept changing. The modern building became more traditional. The mock pool feature more natural, the terraces of olive trees more unaltered.

I walked from the flat down to the Ferrou. Down the track and through the woods. At first I had left markers in case I got lost, white stones, twigs pointing like arrows, but now I knew the way I didn't hurry. I had a picnic lunch for myself and Hugo in a little rucksack. I skipped and told myself stories. I hid under trees and waited to pounce on passers-by, but there were none. I put snail shells in my pockets. I listened to the cicadas in the woods and, far away, the churchbells.

I'm running down the track because I'm late and Daddy hasn't had his lunch yet. He sees me bouncing along the top terrace. I'm wearing red shorts and a white T-shirt now very dusty, but I like it, I feel wild and ferocious like a pirate. He's waving at me. He's dusty too, with trickles of sweat down his face, and his shirt is sticking to him. 'I'm sorry I'm late,' I say, but he says, 'Are you, my special girl? I didn't notice.' He has made a table out of a few planks. We sit on the ground and eat. He looks at the bottled water I've brought and laughs, 'Here is the best water in the whole valley but they think I still need some in a bottle,' and he pours the lot over his head. We both laugh. He says, 'Go into the hut and fill it up with real water.' I turn on the tap. The water comes out with a gurgle then a gush. I fill the bottle to the brim and take it to him. He drinks it. He says, 'It tastes like nothing on earth,' and he hands the bottle to me. I drink it as well and it's true, it doesn't taste like ordinary water because it has a taste, a strong taste, a bit chalky, a bit fizzy. I look at Daddy. His face is brown from the sun, not brown like Mummy but darker, and the freckles are getting bigger like mine do. His hair is dusty. His eyes are blue like the sky. He has a dirty mark on his cheek I don't want to rub off. He shows me the floor he has done. One half is tiled, the other half is still mud. There's a pile of wet cement outside and he must go back to work or it will get too hard. I don't go back to the flat. I go through the woods to the pool. It's a hot day but the water is still cold. Nobody is looking. I take off my clothes and slip into the water. It's so cold it makes me gasp. The bottom is stone and falls away suddenly, so I have to swim fast and panicky. The water gets up my nose and I kick my legs. Then I stop panicking because I'm floating. The water is holding me up. I lie very still and stretch out my arms and legs. I'm floating on the pool. I put back my head and the water sings in my ears.

It was there I learned about water, how it can hold you up, how it can fill you, how it can sink you. When I felt brave I held my breath and sank down with my eyes open. What did I see? What strange shifting half shapes did I see in the twilight of the few seconds I plunged under?

It's early evening now. There are no spectacular sunsets here because the sun sets behind the village. But it rises over the mountains. If I get up early enough I will catch the pink and the gold. I like the evenings. The valley becomes still. Did I imagine it or was that two swallows? It's definitely becoming warmer. The sky is cloudy, holding in the heat, and for the moment there is no wind. For dinner I made omelettes with wild asparagus.

Alan Crawford came to stay and my parents became busy with poolside drinks and barbecues. I wasn't allowed down to the Ferrou on my own, so I sulked in the garden. Alan Crawford had sandy hair and eyelashes. His face was red. I didn't like the way he smelled. I didn't like the way he dived into the swimming pool with a splash. I didn't like the way he and my father were always laughing. I didn't like the way he called my mother 'Viv'. I went to the village. I walked round

57

the streets, looking up alleyways and over walls into gardens. I peered into the church. I hung around the square, kicking dust with my sandals. It was Jeanette's dogs who saw me. She had kept two of the puppies, shaggy spaniels with high-pitched barks. They rushed up and started sniffing me.

'*Bas les pattes, bas les pattes!*' shouted Jeanette, but the dogs didn't scare me. 'Oh, the little English girl. Where are your parents?'

'They are having a party,' I said. 'For grown-ups.'

'Oh, the poor little one.' She sat next to me and squeezed my hand. 'Let us go and see Maman and see if she has any *bonbons*.' She wore an apron dusty with flour. The dogs licked my knees and made me giggle. All of a sudden I felt happy.

Auxille was sitting outside the café darning a sock. The café was empty. It was late afternoon. The air was droopy like the leaves on the plane trees. They gave me sweets wrapped in coloured paper, lemonade in a long glass and slabs of dark brown nougat. Jeanette brushed my hair and put a red ribbon in it.

'When I was a girl,' said Auxille, going back to her sock, 'my grandfather told me the stories of the shepherds.'

She told me stories all afternoon. Stories I'd never heard before, of princes, love-sick shepherds, saints with strange names, lost princesses and troubadours . . .

There was once a troubadour called Avelard and he was the finest minstrel in the region. Princes would pay a fortune to have him sing at their courts. But Avelard belonged to nobody. He came and went as he pleased.

There was a prince married to a beautiful princess and they lived in the grandest palace in the Maures. Now, this prince had the best of everything, the best food, the best wine, the best company at his tables, but he did not have Avelard. And this is what he wanted most of all. One day a thin-faced shabby man appeared at the palace gates and asked to sing at the prince's tables. Grudgingly the guard let him in. After all, perhaps he could at least make the prince laugh. But there was something else about this man, his confidence, his sense of purpose, his piercing blue eyes, that also persuaded the guard.

That night at the banquet the man sat with the servants, ate the poorest food and said nothing. There were plenty of entertainments, musicians, clowns, jugglers, story-tellers. At the end of the feast the prince said, 'Where is this man who has asked to sing for us?' and without a word the man stood up, took up his mandolin and started to sing.

What silence fell over the banquet, for the man sang such sad songs, played such touching melodies that every person down to the meanest kitchen boy was moved.

The prince and the princess were enthralled. They urged the troubadour to sing on late into the night. Finally the prince said, 'Please, please, tell me your name,' and the man said, 'I am Avelard.'

Wasn't the prince overjoyed! He showered the man with gifts and money, but all the man wanted was food and a quiet room. His insistence on simplicity unnerved the prince because he realised he could not buy this person. As the months passed, the reputation of the prince's court grew. The finest minds, the most learned people were to be seen there, and at each banquet Avelard sang to them.

Then one day the time came that the prince most dreaded. Avelard went to see him and said, 'I have enjoyed your hospitality but now I must leave. I am a troubadour and I cannot stay in one place for long.' The prince tried all he could: reason, offers of the most lavish gifts; but no, the man was insistent. He had to leave. This time it was the prince who was unnerved by Avelard's steady gaze.

That night the prince couldn't sleep. He knew if Avelard left, his court would deteriorate, and for his pride and vanity he couldn't let this happen. He devised a plan to keep Avelard in his palace.

The next day, as Avelard tried to leave, the guard stopped him at the gates and said that the prince wanted to see him most urgently.

'I can't let you leave,' said the prince, 'until you have taught me all your songs.' Now, the prince had his own army and the castle was a fortress on a hill. Avelard realised he was a prisoner.

'I have no choice. I have to accept,' he said.

Weeks passed and Avelard tried to teach the prince. The prince was an efficient musician but he had not the understanding or the skill to sing like a troubadour. It would take months, possibly years, to teach the prince all he knew.

Avelard became depressed. He kept to his room, sometimes for days at a time, looking out of the window at the wild, wooded landscape and the freedom that was denied him. It was the princess who realised his plight and came frequently to visit him.

'My husband is a proud man,' she said. 'I know he will not let you go until he is satisfied,' and there was something in her sad eyes that made Avelard realise she was right.

Then one day the princess came to him bright and excited. 'I have an idea,' she said, 'why not teach me? I can sing, I am a fast learner. Teach me your songs then I will teach them to the prince. After all, I have the rest of my life to do that.'

That night the princess put this idea to the prince. At first he was adamant: no, Avelard must teach him; but gradually the princess put forward so many arguments in favour, she was so insistent, so charming, the prince agreed. After all, she was his most rare acquisition.

Over the next few months Avelard taught the princess and found to his astonishment she had the delicacy and intelligence to be one of the finest troubadours. Then the inevitable happened. They fell in love. The more the princess came to know Avelard, the more she despised her haughty, arrogant husband. The more Avelard came to know the princess, the more he realised how much he loved her. 'Come away with me,' he said, 'let us live a life of freedom for ever.'

The time came when the princess had learned all Avelard's songs and a great banquet was held in their honour. The prince sat at the head of the table puffed out with pride at his own cleverness. After all what could be more clever than having his beautiful wife sing to his guests. But after both Avelard and the princess had sung, and after the rapturous applause, the princess whispered in the prince's ear that she felt unwell and needed to lie down. Unwell? The prince was delighted, perhaps this was the first sign of the son he had been longing for. Unperturbed, he continued with the banquet, getting more drunk with his self-importance.

In the midst of this merry-making nobody noticed two hooded figures slip across the courtyard, through a side door and into the dark woods that surrounded the palace. In the morning, when it became apparent what had happened, the prince was filled with fury at his wife's betrayal and Avelard's deception. He sent his army into the forest to find the runaway pair. No amount of public humiliation would be enough for them. But the army came back empty-handed. The princess and Avelard had disappeared into thin air.

The prince was stricken with remorse. He had to accept his own part in the events. He loved the princess but he could see his pride had driven her away. The wise and the learned stopped coming to his castle. It fell into disrepair, then disuse. Then it was practically no more than a ruin with the prince living like a hermit within its empty halls. As he had no heir, when he died his lands were divided and his once grand palace became no more than a heap of stones on the deserted hillside.

But what happened to the princess? Some say she and Avelard lived happily ever after, but some know better what is in the heart of a troubadour. One day, surely, the princess woke up in her makeshift bed under the stars and found that

Avelard had gone, as she knew that one day he would. She was sad, because she loved him and she knew he loved her, but she also understood his need to be free. She could never go back to the stultifying life of the court. From that moment she became a troubadour in her own right. She too began the travelling life, singing in the great courts of Europe.

I love that story. I've told it to myself many times since Auxille first told it to me outside the café. I told it to Sanclair, sitting where I am now, in the doorway of the hut, as the light fades and darkness sweeps across the sky like an inky stain.

CHAPTER SIX

Monday. Afternoon
When the sun comes out it is quite warm. Over the last few days the wind has dropped. It rained several times, mostly in the night. There's a feeling of stillness and moisture around here. I have decided to look for orchids. I drew a map, probably not accurate, of all the terraces, and yesterday and today went searching. On the top terrace near the woods were two patches of early pink. Behind the hut was something purplish, without chlorophyll, I'm not sure what it's called, like a butterbur, and nearer to the gully was a bee orchid hiding in the grass. It does indeed look like a bee, and felt like one too, sort of furry. Some botanical paper this is going to be! Three species and none of them rare.

I have started to give the terraces names. There's the top terrace, the hut terrace, the rock rose terrace, the bee orchid terrace, the fig tree terrace, the washing line terrace and the vine terrace. I put the names on the map. It's a lovely game mapping out my territory, naming my boundaries. It's a pretty map. I used coloured pencils. I drew the hut with me standing outside, a stick person in red and purple clothes. Actually none of my clothes here are red or purple, everything's brown, blue or green. I used to wear such bright clothes. What happened? Velvet and silk, faded embroidery. Midnight blue. Pollen yellow. I look at my jeans and my walking boots and I don't want to wear them. Here is a list of the shrubs and trees I found growing on the terraces. Pine, olive, box, fig, cherry, myrtle, juniper, holly oak, oak, wild pear, laurel, rowan, wild plum, and near the gully wild apple.

Cistus and helianthus on the top terrace, which is the sunniest one. I want to list all the plants as well, but I don't know their names. I shall get a book from Draguignan.

Now the wild flowers are coming out the whole countryside is like a garden. When I was a child I only came here in the summer. It wasn't until I lived here with Gregor that I saw the spring. The flowers will all be dead by June.

But June in England is when summer is at its most beautiful. Roses, honeysuckle, the fresh green of the leaves and long, still evenings. I'm thinking of The Heathers, sitting on the patio and watching the cows in the meadow beyond the canal. That's where the by-pass is now. But before that. Before they even cleared the canal.

When we came back from France we moved into The Heathers. It smelled of paint and varnish. The kitchen had white cupboards up to the ceiling. The bedrooms were white. I have never seen my mother so actively happy. It was a house designed for her. Modern. Spotless. Arid. Sweeps of floor and white walls. Dark brown leather furniture with a steel trim. Metal lamps. Open-slat wooden stairs. Their bedroom had nothing in it except a white bed and a vast skylight, like an abstract painting, but one constantly changing colour. Possessions and clothes were kept behind slatted doors. I can see now how brilliant my father was, because the house is filled with the sky, and the sitting room is one picture window looking across the valley. There's no need for ornament. My room was at one end of the house. My father said that when I left home he would make it into a study. It was pure and bare like a nun's cell. My things were in an oak trunk. There were no curtains but wooden blinds. The windows looked over a fountain courtyard. There was a table by the window.

I liked the fountain. It reminded me of the Ferrou. It was a circle of rocks and I watched the water tumble over them like the water down the split. The courtyard was made out of pebbles. Beyond was the curve of the hill and the sky above the meadow. I kept the Ferrou in my head. When it rained I tried to see the bright sunshine and the dark shadows. When it snowed I tried to see the colour of the terracotta tiles. When my parents held parties I tried to hear the sound in my ears when I held my breath underwater.

This must be one of the last days in St Clair. I'm standing with my father by the Ferrou. He's looking up at the top of the rock. He says, 'I wonder what you can see from up there.' Then I realise he's going to climb it. I'm terrified. I hate heights and I hate the thought of him going up high. What if he slips? What if he gets stuck? But he's already off, up the side of the rock. 'Daddy, be careful!' I wail.

'It's not difficult,' he says and offers out a hand to me, but I say, 'I can't, I can't!'

'Suit yourself,' he says. He keeps climbing up. I wait by the bottom, being as quiet as possible in case I make him fall. I want to cry but I try not to. My legs feel shaky. I can't keep my eyes off him in case he makes a mistake. The rock seems to be swaying. He's near the top. He pulls himself over the last bit, then he stands up slowly and puts his hands on his hips. I can hardly see him because the sun is behind him and is dazzling me. He is a black statue. And I am crying now.

'Well, well, well ... that is extraordinary ...' says my father from the top of the rock. 'In fact that is remarkable ...' He stays up there for what seems like hours.

I watch him climb slowly down. I don't feel happy until I am hugging him.

'Could you see the sea?' I try to sound cheerful.

He seems distant. 'No ... I thought I saw ... but it must have been an illusion ... it was a trick of the light.'

I know how it is. I see things out of the corner of my eye, but when I turn my head they're gone. I thought I was the only person in the world that happened to until my father said that. It was strange to realise I wasn't as different as I thought I was. Sometimes I see people. Especially in bright sunlight. People in the shadows. For years I used to see my father.

It's a Saturday in early June and I'm playing in the garden at The Heathers. Around the house and down the lawn are planted the shrubs and heathers that give the house its name, but I am far beyond the planted garden. I'm on the wooden bridge. I'm looking into the water to see if there are any fish. The other side of the bridge is the old tow-path. I like being here, on the edge of our grounds, thinking if I wanted to I could just walk up the tow-path and away. One way is Bath. I know that. Daddy said he would take me the other way sometime. It's the way to Bradford-on-Avon. The canal used to go all the way to the Thames and London. I'm trying to imagine what it was like when the canal was open and not full of weeds. I imagine a canal boat coming towards the bridge. I shout out to it, and the man at the front, who looks a bit like my father, says, 'Hop on,' and off we go, on an adventure, meeting canal people who are a bit like gypsies. We eat round camp fires at night and sleep on the roof of the boat. My father's office is down the canal towards Bath. It used to be a boat-house. I went there once in the winter. He has a drawing board by the window. Alan Crawford works there too. Since The Heathers was built they have been working all the time. They're designing more houses in France. Today they are playing cricket.

In the water something plops. Perhaps it's a fish, or it could be a frog. The water is green and murky and I can't see the bottom, not like the Ferrou, which looks like the bottom is only two feet away but it's not, it's much deeper than that. I lie on the bridge and look into the water. I can see my face. Sometimes it ripples and I disappear. When it's still again I can see the clouds behind my head.

I haven't had any lunch. My mother was on the patio this

morning. I think she must have fallen asleep. I rub the mud off my shirt and my shorts. She doesn't like me getting dirty.

She's not on the patio, but the doors are open. I can see Alan Crawford walking up and down inside. There's a crying noise coming out. It's coming from my mother.

Alan Crawford knocked the ball for six. It whizzed across the pitch and hit my father on the head. They thought he was all right at first, but then he collapsed. He died on the way to hospital of a brain haemorrhage. All the time I was on the bridge looking for fish.

I don't remember the funeral. I remember the house full of uncles and aunts I didn't know and my mother crying and crying. My mother without her smart clothes and her make-up. People saying, 'You must be brave, Vivienne.' Alan Crawford answering the phone.

My mother wouldn't get out of bed and if she saw me she screamed, 'Keep that child away from me.' Alan Crawford said, 'She doesn't mean it,' but I knew she did.

Alan Crawford had killed my father. I didn't like him, but I felt sorry for him. He was standing on the patio. He was wearing a dark suit. It was a hot day and he was sweating. He wiped his head with a blue handkerchief.

I said, 'I haven't got any clean clothes,' and he looked at me as if it was the first time he had ever seen me. 'We've all forgotten about you, haven't we?' he said and it was true. Everybody had.

Grief does strange things to people. It makes them cruel. It makes them hurtful. Did my mother say it? 'Why didn't you die instead of Hugo?'

I'm going to a new school after the summer. My mother is out of bed. She's sitting on the sofa looking out of the window. I know if I talk to her she won't answer. She's wearing a flowery dress. I remember her wearing it in France. I want to ask her when are we going to France? I want to be in St Clair. I want to see Jeanette. I want to run down the track to the Ferrou. I want to run away. She picks up a magazine and looks at it. She starts flicking through the pages. If my father came into the room now she would smile and laugh and so would I.

I wake up in the night and I've been crying. I was dreaming my father fell off the rock, he was falling down to the bottom of the pool. I can hear voices in the lounge. It sounds like my father, but it can't be, can it? I tiptoe out of my room. It's Alan Crawford and my mother looking at papers. She's dressed up like she used to be with pink lipstick and her hair in a band.

'You can stay here,' he says. 'There's enough money from the developments in France. But of course if you sold . . .'

'I won't leave this house,' says my mother.

'Of course . . .' says Alan, 'but you must understand that to build a house in St Clair is quite out of the question now.'

'We could rent in the village like before.' She lights up a cigarette.

'Viv, you must understand if you want to live at The Heathers you have got to cut down your expenses. Cut them right down.'

'I could sell the Ferrou,' says my mother, and I hold my breath. I'm standing half behind a door.

'It's not worth anything,' says Alan. 'It may be one day, but at the moment there's more land out there than anybody knows what to do with.'

'Are you saying no more holidays?' She blows smoke out through her nose.

'No more holidays in the south of France.'

'You mean if I want a holiday I shall have to take the child to Weston-Super-Mare and go donkey riding?' She picks up the papers and looks through them angrily. 'Surely there must be something else I can cut down on. What's this school she's going to?'

'It's where Hugo wanted her to go.'

'Can't she go to a convent? Somewhere cheap? I'm sure a convent would suit her. I'm sure I could save enough money so I could still have my holidays. She could stay with an aunt . . . they were all offering to help . . .' and my mother smiles and puts her hand on Alan's arm. Her mouth is a pink slit. 'Alan, you like the south of France, don't you?'

Alan Crawford went to America some months later. He now lives near Key West with a young man. My mother needn't have bothered. I went to the convent. I don't know how much money she saved, but she never went to France.

ST CLAIR

CHAPTER SEVEN

Tuesday. Morning

I was dreaming about Felix again. I dreamt we were in the boat and he was asleep beside me. When I woke up the day hit me like a slap and here I am on my own, and that empty all-gone feeling has come back. It's difficult to get up. It's difficult to do anything.

I think now I'm beginning to understand my mother. When the crying stops there is nothing left at all.

When my father died I missed him, but it was as if he hadn't really gone. I saw him in the shadows, behind trees, behind doors. I talked to him. I suppose I invented him, my darling Daddy, my best friend. How happy we would be going off on an adventure together. I know my mother didn't help. I couldn't step forward and break her circle of ice. At The Heathers I'm always in another room. She's on the sofa and I'm by the stairs. She's on the patio and I'm looking through the glass. She's in the kitchen and I'm in the garden. She's in her bedroom putting on her make-up and I'm standing by the door. A lonely child makes up friends. Makes up a whole world, troubadours, castles, deep woods in France and magic spells to make things better. What does a lonely adult do? I remember being about thirteen and realising pretending didn't work. Sometimes it did, but it had changed because I knew I was pretending. I'm writing this because I know Felix has gone. I can dream about him. I can talk to him, but he is not there. He never will be.

Today I will go to the village and do my shopping. There are more swallows today and I thought I heard a cuckoo in the woods.

In the village shop she bought candles, matches and a pad of paper. She had already bought her food at the mini-market. Odette said, 'You've got another letter.'

'From England,' said her daughter, standing behind her like a shadow.

'Go and put out the newspapers,' snapped Odette. Her daughter, Marie, could stack shelves and open boxes, but she couldn't manage the till. Odette shuffled outside and sat on her chair. Her shop would be busy later.

'Eugénie Gués went into hospital last night. They say she will die, and her husband Hilaire he died only in February.' Mireille watched the daughter putting the newspapers upside down in the rack. 'The old graveyards are full, they had to build another on the road to Grasse.' Odette stretched out her swollen legs. 'Everybody's dying these days . . . it's just like the war.'

From across the square Auxille was already waving. 'That's your letter,' said the daughter, beaming as if she had said something very clever.

'Go and put out some more cheese,' said Odette.

Auxille was as gloomy as Odette. She handed Mireille the letter without asking about the contents. 'It's from your son,' she said. 'I recognise the handwriting.' Jeanette peered out of the door, but the café was filling up with people and she couldn't come over. Auxille sat down.

'I'll bring your coffee,' called out Jeanette although Mireille hadn't ordered any. She couldn't make up her mind whether to open the letter there or take it back home. It wasn't a thick letter.

'Eugénie Gués was taken to the hospital last night. Madame Cabasson told me this morning. She went out to call her dog and fell down in the street right in front of Charles

74

Perrigues, which was lucky because he's the doctor's son. It was a stroke and now she's full of tubes.' Auxille smoothed down her apron, oblivious to Jeanette being rushed off her feet inside the café. Two house martins swooped down, chasing each other over the tables.

'And Hilaire only died in February. I remember when they were courting, they married a month after the end of the war. Hilaire's brother Victor was shot in the head by the Nazis. He was only fifteen. They said he was in the Maquis but he wasn't. Hilaire was. He never got over the guilt. Those Germans. You only had to look at them the wrong way and they shot you, and now they're re-buying houses in the village. Two behind the church and on the road to the Col de St Clair, a grand place with a swimming pool as big as the café. I don't want to serve them but Jeanu says we can't blame the younger ones, they had nothing to do with the war. Mind you, some people have always served Germans.' She was sitting with her back to Odette, who was now scolding her daughter about the newspapers.

Mireille opened her letter. The envelope had indeed been written by Stephen, but inside was an air mail letter from India. There was no message from Stephen at all.

'It's from my husband,' said Mireille.

'He was a German, but he was *sympa,* he was *gentil.* He had nothing to do with the war.'

It was on thin blue air mail paper. Tightly written as all Gregor's letter were. She had last written to him in January. She had been very low then.

'My little schoolgirl . . .' he began, 'I was so sad to hear your news. First you write and tell me how happy, then you write and say how full of sadness. Perhaps when you write now you will say how happy. It has been a long time I am in replying because I am just returning from a trip with the Baba to Delhi and he has been giving lectures . . .' Over the years Gregor's English had not improved.

She read the letter rapidly. She was hungry for its contents, but it was the same as his other letters, mostly about the Baba. The Baba was a tiny old wrinkled man. Gregor had been in love with him for over twenty years. He answered the Baba's mail and saw it as a privilege. The Baba and his devotees lived in an ashram in the hills above Bombay. It was supposed to be a place of extraordinary beauty and solitude, though Mireille had never been there.

'Yesterday,' wrote Gregor, 'when the Baba was talking to us a sparrow flew down and sat on his head, it was indeed as if he was a piece of the country like a tree or a rock and the Baba did not stop talking. It was supposed to happen . . .'

Gregor's letters were full of little incidents like this, which he saw as terribly significant, but seemed to Mireille like everyday events that happen all the time. After reading his letters she always felt she had missed something. They wrote to each other infrequently now.

Jeanette brought the coffee. 'And how is your son,' she asked, bursting with curiosity, 'and his charming girlfriend?'

'It was from her husband,' said Auxille. She started theorising about Germans again.

'Maman is so out of sorts!' exclaimed Jeanette. 'Eugénie is ill and she is her best friend, but when she is well, do they ever talk to each other? I have a pile of washing and people will want their lunch soon. But how is your husband?' She wasn't too busy to listen to Mireille's news.

'He's very well,' said Mireille.

'Will he come here?'

'I shouldn't think so. His life is in India now.' She knew she sounded disappointed. She had wanted the letter to be more personal.

'So many years apart . . .' said Jeanette with such a look of compassion it made Mireille want to sob or run away. 'Perhaps you will go to him.'

'To India?' said Auxille, catching up on their conversation.

76

'Who would want to go to India? He had religious fever, now that is different.'

'I don't want to go to India,' said Mireille, clarifying things before Jeanette's imagination got out of hand, but at that moment Dr Perrigues walked across the square.

'Eugénie died this morning. I thought I had better tell you,' he said cheerfully.

Auxille threw up her hands and started to wail. So did Jeanette, the lunch and the washing all forgotten.

'Eugénie! Eugénie!' cried out Auxille. 'I gave you my best crystal earrings when you went for your first dance with Hilaire. Now, who will remember that when I am gone?'

CHAPTER EIGHT

Sunday 1st May. Midday

It's the beginning of May. Today is the celebration of the end of the war and in the afternoon Eugénie's funeral. I shall go to neither event. I am sick of death. Today the sky is that blue blue. I remember it was always like this in the summer. There isn't a single cloud. I'm sitting under the tree by the front door. Just an occasional breeze through the pines in the woods behind me. On the track to the village the wild flowers are spectacular now. Blue anchusas, dark pink gladioli, blue cornflowers, purple irises. Here on the terraces, clover, wild thyme, marjoram, sage, and the grass is as green as it ever will be.

I wrote to Gregor but I didn't say what I wanted to say. It feels I can only say what I want to in here. When I wrote to Gregor I said how beautiful it all was and how I feel so much better. It sounded like pap. We have been writing pap to each other for years. Him telling me about the Baba and me writing I did this, I did that, Stephen did this, Stephen did that. I wish I could write to him honestly. When I was writing I thought, I don't even know what you look like anymore. I've seen a picture of the Baba and I imagine you look like that. A bald head, long white hair, long white beard. Brown wrinkled skin. In my mind you have become the Baba. I want to write and ask you, are you still Gregor?

I feel so many things when I think about Gregor. We were only together five years, but even five minutes with him felt like a long time. So much could happen in five minutes. I've never missed him, which is strange because I've missed so many people, but I suppose with Gregor I felt I had had more than my share. When he left, sometimes I was glad he had gone. Life was quieter. Life was simpler. His intensity wore me out and I had Sanclair then. I'm trying to find a way of describing how it was with Gregor. Things went fast, my mind went fast. I didn't feel that again with anybody, I didn't think I could until I met Felix.

It doesn't feel like time has been even. There have been patches when I felt more, when colours were brighter, the times I remember most accurately. Pictures have stayed so clearly I can step into them again. Suddenly here I am and there is Gregor walking up from the road with a crate of oranges on his shoulders. Oranges, why has he bought oranges? So we can have fresh orange juice for a week, of course. Going to the cafés in St Tropez when Sanclair was still little, and singing for money. Gregor could sing so loud and I'd dance round and round. People did give us money, not to send us away but because they liked it. *Encore! Encore!* And I'd sing too and Sanclair laughed and clapped his hands.

Singing in the square by the café to the British tourists who never guessed I was British too. Singing to Badouin and Julian, Jeanette standing by the door, and even Macon came outside to listen. I played the accordion, Gregor sang and Sanclair banged a little drum. Sanclair, dressed in a gold Indian tunic, like a sun god, and me in bright green with a red scarf in my hair. Gregor wearing white trousers and no shirt, no shoes. Three gypsies, three vagabonds, three troubadours.

There have been patches when time went so slowly it felt like nothing happened. After my father died my mother's life became very small. There were no more parties. There were no more holidays. She spent more time on the sofa. She smoked more. She spent more time in the garden. My life shrank as well. School and home. I cycled to school up the tow-path. I hauled my bike over the wooden bridge and at the top wondered if I would ever cycle to Bradford-on-Avon. I had extra French lessons on Wednesdays. I had piano lessons on Saturday mornings. We started going to the Catholic church, possibly because my mother liked putting on her best clothes, possibly because she wanted to impress the parents of the other convent girls. She didn't become friendly with them. She was too proud to become friendly with anybody.

I found the convent dull. They were fussy about manners and uniforms. I had to wear white gloves and boaters in the summer. White ankle socks and bright blue dresses. In the winter a navy skirt, a yellow shirt and a navy hat with a yellow trim. It was not a school for the well-off. The buildings were old-fashioned. The toilets leaked. The science labs were archaic. The tennis courts needed resurfacing. The nuns had names like Sister Christopher, Sister Dominic, Sister Sylvester. They were androgynous, peculiar beings. I never understood them. To me they were badly educated, ridiculously sentimental and pious to the point of insanity. But I liked what they said about Heaven. My daddy was in Heaven.

By the time I was thirteen I was quiet and studious. I was not shy but I didn't make friends. I suppose I didn't know how to. Home and school. School and home . . .

Cycling home in the rain along the tow-path. Summer rain and the banks are green and white with cow parsley. I'm cycling through the puddles, under the bridges, through the tunnels, past the stagnant water of the old canal. The pond near Widcombe lock. The gardens of Sydney Sussex Buildings falling to the canal. My father's old office, still an architect's studio but now owned by somebody else. Then the long stretch where the railway runs near the canal and sometimes I'm racing against a train. The long bumpy stretch, splashing through the puddles, and my blazer is getting wet and my hat is in my satchel, although I'm supposed to wear it all the way home or I'll get a detention, but who can see me in my bit of wilderness, my only bit of freedom? I push my bike up the garden path and there's my mother on the sofa waiting to scold me because my socks are muddy.

I was fifteen. I sat next to a girl called Caitlin. She was so shy that it wasn't until the Easter holidays on the school trip to Paris that we talked to each other. She could read French but she couldn't speak it. She knew nothing about France. We shared a room in the shabby hotel. In the day the nuns took us to the Louvre, Versailles, Notre Dame, Montmartre, but in the evenings we had to stay in our rooms. Some of the other girls managed to sneak out and meet boys in a nearby café and there was much discussion about what the nuns wore in bed, but Caitlin and I opened the windows and looked out over the rooftops. I told her about St Clair, the hilltops, the pine trees, the blue sky. It seemed like a different country from wet Paris. Caitlin had a pale face, greeny eyes and brown hair, not as dark as mine. She had a whispery soft voice. She had long beautiful fingers. She was one of ten children. She thought I made most of it up because I included troubadours, seven-foot-long snakes and witches in caves, but she wanted to hear more. I told her about Jeanette, Auxille and the Ferrou, she definitely thought I made that up. She was my first friend.

At school we revised together. Girls from the Convent of the Good Shepherd were not noted for their academic achievements, but we were going to go to university. I was going to study languages, be an interpreter and go travelling, and she wanted to study literature. She loved the Romantic poets, she wanted to write about Coleridge. She wanted to go to the Lake District. Her family hadn't been on holiday for years. There were too many of them.

They lived in a large Victorian house up the London Road. It was untidy and scruffy. Caitlin had three older sisters who

81

were always arguing, four younger brothers who were always fighting, and two baby sisters. A toddling one and a crying one in a cot. Her mother was plump and tired-looking, the babies seemed to be stuck to her all the time. The food was mostly stew and potatoes. The children had Celtic names, Fenula, Siobhan, Aisne, Finbar, Collum. Caitlin shared a room with Fenula who wore make-up and chucked her clothes on the floor.

Her father was the bursar at the Catholic boys' school. He was a dapper little man and spoiled his family shamelessly. He let the boys climb all over him. His gave his eldest daughters money to go to the pictures. He gave the babies sweets. He kissed his wife and called her, 'My darling.' He said all her cooking was delicious. He said Caitlin was a genius. I thought about my own home. My mother's complete lack of interest in anything about me. The way my father used to promise to take me places and never did. I watched Mr Costello playing football on the balding lawn with his sons, the toddling girl getting in the way, the older sisters screaming with laughter out of an upstairs window and Mrs Costello sitting in the garden bouncing the baby on her lap. It made me feel peculiar.

But Caitlin thought The Heathers was wonderful. The silence, the clean floors, the beautiful unmarked lawn. My mother's clothes, so stylish and so expensive, and my clothes, I had a wardrobe full. My mother never stopped spending money on clothes. I gave Caitlin a huge bag of dresses I didn't want and she pored over them as if they were jewels. Could she really keep them, oh could she? She only wore hand-me-downs from her sisters. And the piano! And the fountain! And my mother! My mother loved attention and here was this young girl, what a specimen, in the most dreadful dress, probably bought from a catalogue, goggle-eyed because she had never seen a gold-topped perfume spray before. I hated my mother for laughing at Caitlin, dazzling her with gold jewellery, Pierre Cardin suits and Bally shoes. She gave Caitlin French *patisseries* on bone china and Earl Grey tea. She showed her the house, 'designed by my late husband', and the garden, 'landscaped, of course'. Caitlin went home starry-eyed, as if she'd been taken to a fairy palace, but I could hear my mother shrieking with laughter like I hadn't heard her laugh for years. 'Oh do invite your little bog peasant again. Perhaps I'll give her coffee next time. Do you think she's ever tasted real coffee before?'

The bitter taste of my mother, like the blackest of coffees. When Caitlin complained about her rowdy family, her tumbledown house, her mother's awful cooking, I said, 'At least your family love you,' and she said, all green eyes and innocence, 'Mireille, surely your mother loves you?'

She knew nothing else. She had only experienced love.

Monday 2nd May. Morning

I thought summer was coming, but early yesterday evening the wind started blowing down the valley. In the night the shutters and the doors were banging. This is the mistral. The cold wind from the mountains. It's a harsh wind that hurts your eyes and whistles in your ears. It's not a wind I wanted to be outside in. I chopped up more wood earlier and when I came back I was raddled. I was blown to bits. I'm annoyed, I was planning a long walk to the top of the Col de St Clair. That will have to wait. Today will be a quiet day then. The crackle of the wood in the stove. The creak of the door on its hinges. Me, wrapped up in the red blanket with two pairs of socks on.

Caitlin. She was my friend but she annoyed me. She never wanted to do anything. She had spent all her life surrounded by her family and any independent activity set her in a panic. Walk to Bradford-on-Avon? Oh, we couldn't. Go to the shops in Bristol? Oh, we couldn't. Go for a day out to Weston-Super-Mare? Oh, Mireille, we couldn't. My teenage years were like this. Me staying at her house for the weekend and she staying at mine. We read books, listened to music on the record player, not the progressive rock of the late sixties but Debussy, Handel, Mendelssohn, Chopin. After my mother died I helped Stephen clear out her things at The Heathers and in a drawer by her bed were two photographs. One was of my family outside the Sanglier, the last summer we stayed in St Clair. A black and white snapshot taken by Jeanette. My mother smiling brightly in a patterned dress. My father, as I remembered him, white trousers, white shirt, looking older but still handsome and me, as I remembered myself. Tousled hair, skinny legs in shorts and scuffed sandals. Summer 1964. The other photograph was a school portrait. Summer 1971. 'My darling Mireille', it said on the back. I looked at this photograph and was disconcerted because I was beautiful. When I was seventeen I was beautiful and I didn't know it because I thought beauty meant having sleek blonde hair and designer clothes. I had dark curling hair down to my shoulders, shining eyes and an uncertain smile. The freckles I hated just made me look more charming. I was bursting with beauty.

I'm seventeen and I know I'm clever and I know I'm musical. I'm tall and I like cycling and walking. I can speak French and I'm learning Italian and Spanish. I know some German too. I like D. H. Lawrence, Thomas Hardy, the poetry of Eliot and Auden and I'm passionate about Shakespeare. At school I'm a swot and I'm not fashionable, my mother despairs of my dress sense. Clothes bore me. Most of the time I am bored. I want to travel. I want to go on aeroplanes. I want to go up mountains. I can't wait to finish school and go to college. I can't wait to leave home.

This is May and along the old canal the elderflower is out, cow parsley lines the route. The countryside is lacy, frothy, strong-smelling like cats or unwashed underpants. The choked up canal smells stagnant, but I like these smells. To me they are fertile. I'm cycling to school fast because I'm late, because I stayed for too long on the bridge for no reason other than to look at the grey-green fields and the slow-moving clouds, white-grey, grey-white, hanging over the valley. I'm cycling fast, as fast as I can, and just as the path turns by the Widcombe pond I have to jam on the brakes because a man is standing in my way. I don't hit him but I nearly do. 'Didn't you see me?' I shout. He turns, he has long hair, blond and straight, and a beard under his chin. He has a suntanned face. Stupidly, I think he looks like Jesus. This thought makes me confused and I blush. His eyes are calm. He has hazel eyes. He says, 'Did you not see the heron?' He has a foreign accent. He has wide shoulders and is wearing loose trousers and an embroidered shirt. I stare at him. I don't know what to say. At school we are always being warned about strange men and he is strange. 'I have to go. I'll be late,' I say. After school when I cycle back I'm worried and excited in case he might still be there. I know that what I'm doing could be dangerous but I want to see him again. I want to ask, who are you? I get off my bike and walk slowly past the Widcombe pond. I can't see anyone. Then I see that there's a yellow van parked to the side in some bushes. In front of it is a small fire with a kettle over it. The kettle starts whistling. The man comes out of the van and says, 'So you would like some tea? Yes?'

That's how it started. I sat on the grass and above me were elderblossoms. He gave me tea in a blue tin mug. He had brown arms and a silver bracelet. I said, 'Are you a gypsy?' and felt stupid, but he smiled, his eyes still calm, and there was a glint in them, a twinkle of mischief. He said, 'Why? Are you?'

This is Gregor. Half German. His mother lives in Berlin. He never knew his Russian father. His mother married again when he was fifteen and he left home and has not been back since. He didn't tell me this by the canal. What he said was, 'I am a traveller. I'm a seeker for the truth and I will go on travelling until I have found the truth, but what I am finding is that there is not one truth, there are many truths.'

When he said this I felt like I did when I stood in front of the Ferrou. Awed and so shivery I had to put my tin mug down. I had been told there was only one way, my mother's way. Dresses, houses, things, and now incorporated into Catholic stuff from school. One God, one church, one nation, but I knew, I knew, I couldn't believe this. Gregor was looking at me intensely. He had a way of looking that made me feel transparent. He said, 'I think you understand, yes?'

He said, 'I have come to Bath to see the famous hot water that comes out of the ground already warm, you know this place, yes?'

And I said, all flushed, 'But there are other places where the water comes out completely cold.'

Gregor laughed and laughed. 'You are a schoolgirl but already you are making connections. Oh, you are a thoughtful little schoolgirl.'

I felt very stupid. I said, 'I've only been to France. I've never been anywhere else.'

Gregor laughed even more. 'But you travel in the mind, oh yes, you travel all the time.' I blushed and blushed because that was true.

I don't remember what we talked about, but we talked about everything. Everything I had always wanted to talk about but there was nobody to tell it to, not even Caitlin, who believed in God, Jesus, the Virgin Mary, the Holy Family, the Devil and Hell. She was afraid of Hell, but I wasn't. It sounded like an exciting place to me and it wouldn't stop me sinning.

'Do you live in your van?' I asked and he showed me. The little bed, the mugs on hooks, a tin trunk, a leather coat. He had been to Israel, Greece, Spain, Norway, Finland, America when he was eighteen, Morocco last year and recently Ireland and Scotland.

'What do you live off?' I asked, sitting on his bed. There were no windows in the van, but the evening light coming through the back door was warm and soft. It seemed like the only way to live, in a tiny space with an ever-changing view.

He said, 'I can work, I can fix things, I can work in bars, I can make things, you understand, yes?'

'Are you staying long?'

He smiled and took the tin mug off me. 'That is for me to say. I know when it is time for me to go. Now it is time for you to go, don't you think so?'

I wheeled my bike up the garden path towards The Heathers. I could see my mother on the sofa, watching television. Suddenly, she and the house seemed insignificant. I was late. She would be cross with me.

Gregor, I was seventeen and I was bold enough to stop and talk to a strange man. Did you see my boldness, did you see my longing to escape? Did you see that I was as restless and dissatisfied as you had been when you were fifteen, and as unhappy? Did you want to help me? I've never asked you this. Did you want to help me or were you just flattered because a pretty seventeen-year-old wanted to talk to you?

I'm writing this in the hut where we lived together and where I had your baby. Is it true that if I hadn't met you my life would have been so different? You took no credit. You said I made my own choices, you said you didn't encourage me. But you stayed by the canal for nearly two months. You found work washing up in a café. Do you think you stayed because you enjoyed the company of a convent schoolgirl who was a fledgeling who was ready to fly?

I'm standing by the window in my room at The Heathers

listening to the fountain, and I can't sleep because I know something has happened and is happening. 'A' levels, college, jobs, they're not important because I know there is a different way of living and I want it. I want it. It's a longing, it's a hunger and I'm impatient. Through the window on the breeze I can smell the elderflowers, musty and female. I don't want to sleep.

CHAPTER NINE

Saturday 7th May. Evening
The baker's niece got married today. I went to see the end of it outside the church. The mistral is still raging. Her veil blew over her face and all the guests grabbed on to their hats and skirts. The happy couple looked like most young marrieds, awkward and bemused because the parents and in-laws were in charge. This was a Cabasson affair. The mayor was there, a short skinny man in a shiny suit, but you can tell he knows he's important by the way he holds up his head. Everybody wants to talk to him. The baker's wife looked splendid in powder blue. You would have thought she was the bride's mother. I think the bride's mother was another fat lady in a dress that looked suspiciously similar to the one Jeanette saw in the market. I sound like my mother, what a specimen. I didn't join in. Who needs my congratulations? I sat outside the café with Jeanette and Auxille, who weren't invited to the reception but were behaving as if they were.

I saw the Gregsons. I can spot British people. For a start they are usually taller than the villagers. They wear summer clothes when no one else does. Mr Gregson in a pale blue shirt and cream trousers. Mrs Gregson in a lacy blouse and long blue skirt hanging on to a straw hat. I didn't like the look of them. Suave. Opulent. Smug. Their loud voices and bad French coming in snatches on the wind. Auxille and Jeanette wanted to follow the wedding party up to the *mairie*, perhaps they hoped they'd get invited at the last minute. Some chance, that lot are far too snooty. Instead I went to the graveyard to see Eugénie's grave.

89

I'd forgotten about the graveyard. It can't be that I never went there. It has a high wall around it and the entrance is through a metal door. It was sheltered from the wind. There were two cypress trees inside like sentinels. It felt like a peaceful place. The tombs are extraordinary. Big stone slabs like altars with whole families bunged in them and on the top, not real flowers, but china ones. In Britain they'd get nicked but here the china wreaths have stayed. Dark red, blue and purple stylised roses. Sometimes white for a young woman. Sometimes a single flower. I spent ages looking at the tombs. The oldest ones surrounded by metal fences, like hospital beds. Do they sleep peacefully in there, the Cabassons, the Gués, the Blancs, the Perrigues, the Cavaliers? Their bones mingling together, relatives who in life hardly talked to each other. Is there a feud going on under the slabs? The Villeneuves had what looked like a tiny chapel with engraved glass windows and inside were wreaths made of wire and tiny beads. All decayed. No Villeneuve has been buried in the village since 1952. Eugénie's grave was a dug-out one on the ground, shared with Hilaire and next to them his brother Victor. The earth was piled on top. There were no ceramic flowers yet, but pots of geraniums and hydrangeas. Bright bold flowers. On Victor's grave was a photograph behind glass. He was just a boy, dressed in his best suit with the same dark face of the youths who screech around on motorbikes. Old Man Henri was under the cypresses in a grave with five Cabassons. On top was a photograph of his wife and a woman who had died in her twenties. No explanation, but she looked pale and sickly. I didn't feel sad in this graveyard. Most of its incumbents were well over seventy. It seemed a fitting place for them to land up. It was more personal than graveyards in England, not like a graveyard at all, more like an old people's home and for once they're all quiet, for once they're not chattering.

I'm thinking about that wretched crumbling crematorium in

Bristol. It rained the whole time and then it was sleeting. They put the gas heaters on but the chapel didn't get warm. The graveyard outside was overgrown and untended, massive Victorian monuments covered in ivy. During the service I couldn't bear to listen to the Christian stuff so I walked in the rain up behind the chapel. It was like a wood, bare winter trees and dark cedars, part of the original planting. I thought, yes, Felix would like this place, he could walk here and be invisible.

The wind is making the door bang and the lamp flicker. It's hard to see what I'm writing. My parents are in a graveyard overlooking Bath, neat and municipal. The baby is up there too, in a corner with other babies. It's a bit pathetic, rotting fluffy toys and other mementoes, all going mouldy. It doesn't work in England, does it, leaving things outside? They always rot in the rain.

Rain. Wet dripping trees and cycling through puddles up the tow-path. It's July and I'm panicking because when school finishes I won't have an excuse to see Gregor. Nobody knows. I see him on my way to school and on the way home. He works in the evenings. In the morning we have a cup of coffee together and in the afternoon, tea. We talk. We don't kiss, but lately I've been thinking I want to. I like looking at his brown arms. Once he had his shirt off. He's muscled and strong. He has blond hairs on his chest and a line of hair coming up his belly. Coming up from his trousers. I like his feet. He has bare feet often, and they look like feet that are used, not hidden away in socks. He says, 'Here she is, my little schoolgirl, tell me what have you been thinking?'

I've been thinking I want to stay with you in your van. I want to put my head on your chest and listen to your heart beating. I want you to stroke my hair. I don't tell you this.

I was seventeen and I had never had a boyfriend. I didn't want one. I didn't want to dress up and flirt. Caitlin and I, we both knew that in the tussle and tumble of the mating game we would be left last, like not being picked for the netball team. We discussed it often. We decided we were better off. We could wait until college then we would meet boys who were more mature. We liked that idea, 'more mature'. I didn't tell her about Gregor.

We kept doing the same things. Her coming to my house, me visiting her on a Saturday. Meeting after church on a Sunday. But I began to feel this was just the skin of me, the real me had wriggled out and was sliding through the grass towards Gregor. What I found most strange was that nobody seemed to notice they were talking to a discarded skin.

It's August and the trees are heavy and green. The cows move slowly in the fields beyond the canal. St John's wort and willowherb grow by the banks. When I say to my mother, 'I'm going for a walk now', she nods and smiles. She's weeding the garden. She's thinking about becoming a Catholic and Father Connelly from the church is giving her instruction. He's tall and has an angular, craggy face. He's vaguely handsome. I'm sure becoming a Catholic will take a long time.

I run down the garden to the bridge. I'm wearing dark green cotton flares and an orange scoop-neck blouse with drawstring sleeves. My mother hates it. She says it makes me look like a folksy bohemian. But I love this blouse, it's soft, faded and comfortable. I'm growing my hair. I run down the tow-path feeling wild and messy and free like I used to when I ran down the path to the Ferrou. And there is Gregor.

When I leave it's like stretching something that stretches and stretches until it snaps and there I am alone on the patio, looking for my mother. A few hours with Gregor. The other hours in the day have no meaning for me.

I'm in my bed and I can't sleep. It's two o'clock in the

morning and Gregor will be back from work. It's humid and the air feels like soup. I open my window and I can smell water, the water of the fountain, but I want to smell the canal water, especially at night. Cold smelling. Dark smelling. I want to smell Gregor. He smells of smoke and coffee. What does he smell like after a night's work? Detergent? Onions? Bleach? I've never been to see him at night. I can't sleep. The moon is huge and pink coloured like a blood orange. The sky is indigo and faded like tissue paper. I'm not used to going out at night, but I climb through the window. My orange blouse pulled over my nightie, my school shoes and socks. I look odd I know, perhaps I can pretend I'm sleepwalking. But no sleepwalker runs as fast as I do. The tow-path is dark and I can't see where I'm going. The moonlight has turned the world to a grey silver and the water shines. It's an eerie world, still and quiet. I think I can see people, but they're only bushes and shadows. I'm frightened but I'm not going back.

Gregor's van has no lights on, and now I'm worried in case he isn't there. I tap on the window, whispering (I don't dare to shout), 'Are you there, are you there?' Then the door swings open suddenly and he's shining a torch at me. I shield my eyes, and now I think he's cross, but he's laughing. 'What's this, a nighthawk? A ghost? What creature is this?'

I sit on his bed and he's still laughing. 'I couldn't sleep,' I say apologetically.

'You don't work, you don't know what it is to be tired. So now I must talk to you, all night, yes?' He makes coffee and we drink it, sitting on his bed. 'So what shall we talk about my little traveller? What do you want this old man to talk about?'

'I don't mind if we don't talk,' I say with a dry throat and a voice squeezed to a whisper.

'Now what is this?' asks Gregor, turning to me and fixing his eyes on me, and when he looks at me like that I know I have no secrets.

'I want to make love,' I say and in saying it I feel daft because I have no idea how to.

'Well, well,' says Gregor and smiles in a bemused way, and we both look at each other. I hope be knows what to do because I'm shaking like a leaf.

He puts his arms around me and hugs me and my heart skips and does a cartwheel. It feels like I've just come home, to my real home.

This is strange. I can't remember what it was like. I remember sitting in church the next day squeezing my knees together. Feeling blissful, feeling I loved everybody. Father Connelly, my mother, Caitlin, her family and the whole congregation. I was soaring up to the roof with the angels. I remember running back up the tow-path and the sun was just coming up soft golden and the fields were misty. I remember my bed smelled of me and was so soft I fell asleep right away. A candle flickering in Gregor's truck, wax dripping down the side. He held my hand and we listened to nothing.

I've had sex since that was exciting and powerful, I felt like an animal. This was with Julian. With Alan and Tony it felt matter of fact, something grown-ups did, and with Felix it was magical, almost mystical, but I can't remember with Gregor. At the hut in bed we talked a lot, we held hands. I suppose sex was part of it. It was friendly.

The lamp is flickering now, not because of the wind but because it has nearly burned down. There is less banging outside. I think the wind has dropped.

Sunday 8th May. Lunchtime
It's warm. I'm sitting on the rock rose terrace. This morning I made a seat out of planks of wood and stones. This is the driest terrace and the sunniest. It also has the best view of the valley. The seat is reasonably comfortable. I found the wood

some weeks ago behind a house that was being renovated in the village. Perhaps you could say I stole it. Living with Gregor made me more flexible about other people's property. I would never call him a thief, but if he saw something he thought might be useful, he took it. I'm grateful to him for this attitude. On my walks to and from the village I have so far found a length of rope, a wooden crate, a frying pan and a broken candleholder.

Sunday is the noisiest day in this valley. At the farm below they're cutting the grass with a loud machine, whining and whirring. Dogs are barking. Voices of people who sound like they're having a large family lunch. Four cars went up there this morning. I can't see anybody. The trees block the farm. They sound like they are just at the foot of my land although it's more than half a mile away. If I shouted and sang would they hear me? Can they see me chopping wood? Surely they can see the smoke from my chimney. People are so nosy here I'm amazed nobody has come up to look but nobody has. Every time I've walked up to the village along the path I've not met a soul. People have more cars. The land is less cultivated. I'm living in a place that nobody wants to make the effort to discover.

I've lived in other houses, The Heathers, my boat, but this is where my heart is. I felt this when I was ten and that's why I wanted to come back. This is where I asked Gregor to take me.

We're walking to Bradford-on-Avon, up the old canal path. There is no reason to go other than to make the journey. It's late August and the countryside is overblown and heavy. Some of the trees are beginning to turn yellow. Flowers are in seed, willowherb fluff blows on to the water. The clouds are heavy too, white with grey undersides like fat fish, not swimming but floating.

Gregor has shaved off his beard and this, I think, makes

him look more majestic. He wears blue trousers and sandals and a red shirt. I love the colours he wears. Always bright. I have a scarf in my hair and beads round my neck. My mother thinks I'm at the shops. On the way, Gregor sings a Moroccan song he's learned and I sing a madrigal. Then we get silly and I'm singing nursery rhymes, hymns and Christmas carols and he's singing German drinking songs. We're singing like this as we come into Bradford-on-Avon. Golden stone, sweet pretty houses and baskets of flowers. Oh dear, people are looking at us, what dreadful hippies we are, but we laugh more and go and have tea in an old-fashioned tea room by the bridge. We eat as many scones with cream as we can. I don't think I've ever been so happy. Every minute with Gregor is an adventure. But there's things I don't see, other people looking at us, other people judging us.

The next day after church one of the convent school mothers comes up to me when I'm talking to Caitlin and says, 'Mireille, isn't it? Didn't I see you yesterday in Bradford-on-Avon having tea with a strange-looking man?' and she has that smug interfering smile of the perfectly righteous. I'm struck dumb and afraid because I have been lying to everybody all summer, committing the sort of sins they believe I will burn in Hell for.

'Oh no, Mrs Davenport,' said Caitlin, who never lies and couldn't believe that I could. 'Mireille was in town all day in the bookshops and came to see me in the evening with a book of poems she'd found. Mistral. All in French, which we translated together.' Sweet Caitlin, she was so pure, of course Mrs Davenport believed her.

'What would you be doing with a strange man anyway?' said Caitlin.

I shook my head. Gregor had given me the book. One of the poems was called 'Mireille'.

'On Monday let's translate some more,' said Caitlin.

I nodded. I looked around for my mother. She was by the

church door talking to Father Connelly, who looked patient and weary like he wanted to run away.

I was afraid. Not just because Mrs Davenport had seen us. Not just because school was starting in two weeks and I didn't want to go back, but because Gregor started talking about going to India. It was one of the places he had never been to. He had mentioned this many times. The summer was ending. He started tinkering with his van. When I went to see him I sat and watched, handed him spanners, made him cups of tea, tried to understand car manuals, but inside I was shrieking, Don't go, don't leave me. It was the first of September and we were sitting by the canal looking into the water. I was so full up with words and emotions I hadn't spoken all afternoon. Gregor turned his bracelet around on his wrist.

'Now, it is time for you go go,' he said.

'Mother doesn't start cooking until seven,' I said. 'She won't expect me.'

'No, it is time for you to go, because it is time for me to go.'

I opened my mouth but no sound came out. It felt like water was pouring into my mouth.

'I am a traveller,' said Gregor, 'and now it is time for me to go. You must not be unhappy, little schoolgirl. You will forget this rough, crazy German, yes. A few months and you will meet a crazy English boy who will suit you.'

'No!' I shouted. 'You can't go!'

'And stay here? What shall I do, little schoolgirl, talk to you all winter? Make love to you? Amuse you?' I hated what he was saying because I didn't see it as amusement. It was my real life, the rest was peripheral.

'We can . . . we can . . .' But of course I had no answers. I hadn't got that far. I burst into tears. He left me there by the canal and went back to the van.

*

97

It feels like when my father died, it feels the same. The death of dreams. I remember sitting on the wooden bridge that day looking at the fish and the clouds and my reflection and I didn't know it but my daddy was dying. But this is different, surely, because Gregor isn't dying he's going away, and I'm looking at the water, the three worlds inside the water, the leaves on the surface and the clouds and I'm thinking, this is different because I can choose.

I stand up and walk to Gregor. He's sitting by the fire, solemn and serious, not sad, and for the first time he looks old. He's thirty-five, he has wrinkles around his eyes, creases when he smiles. He suddenly looks very very old, like a wise man.

He looks up at me and his eyes seem to have three depths in them as well. I'm tiny on the surface, but I want to be in the furthest depth.

'Little schoolgirl, you do not seem anymore like a girl who wants a man to amuse her.'

'I want to come with you to India,' I say.

He thinks about this. He puts his head to one side and smiles. It's a challenge. He likes a challenge.

'If you change your mind I won't bring you home,' he says.

'And you must tell your mother.' This makes me wince. 'Oh yes, you must tell her you want to leave home. You must be honest. I told my mother.'

'What did she say?' I can't imagine.

Gregor laughs, 'She threw a shoe at me. She said I was ungrateful and she never wanted to see me again. So she hasn't.'

I'm going to meet Gregor at ten o'clock in the morning. It's a Monday. It's a wet September morning. I'm standing on the patio looking at the fields, the black and white cows, the misty hills. My mother is in the kitchen, washing up.

'Mireille, don't stand outdoors, it's too wet, you'll bring

the damp in. When I'm out don't forget to change your sheets. They've been on that bed too long. No wonder your room smells. Open the window and air it. Mireille, are you listening? The Davenports are having a bring-and-buy. I thought I'd take some of your old dresses, you don't wear them, they might do for some of those Costellos. Heavens above, what does she dress them in? I saw the oldest – what's her name, Vymura? Fenicula? – wearing, can you imagine, a yellow trouser suit and she's ginger. What a sight, and Mrs Costello, she's always in a maternity frock whether she's *enceinte* or not, it seems to make no difference. Mireille are you listening?'

Yes, Mother, but what is there to listen to?

'. . . and you're off to the Costellos for the week? How you can stand it there, I don't know, but that Caitlin is unobtrusive, I suppose. Have you packed enough bras?'

Yes, Mother, I have packed all I need.

I turn and watch her flit across the sitting room. She's wearing a navy and cream suit, a handbag over one arm. Her hair is wound up in a bun. She pauses by the mirror to put on some lipstick. Crimson red. She looks at herself in the mirror from various angles. Satisfied, she picks up the bags of my old dresses. 'I suppose I'll see you at church on Sunday.'

Goodbye, Mother.

I sit on the sofa and wait until quarter to ten when my mother, Mrs Costello and everybody else is at the bring-and-buy.

I phone up Caitlin. 'I'm sorry I can't come over after all.'

'What a shame. I was hoping we could go to the library and find some more French poems.'

'I'm going away . . .' My voice starts to get shaky. 'Caitlin, can you keep a secret?' I want to tell somebody now, I do, I want somebody to say goodbye to me. 'Caitlin, I'm going away with a man. Mother thinks I'm staying with you.'

'Oh no, oh dear . . . oh, Mireille, you can't . . . oh no!'

'Caitlin, I am. Please don't tell anybody.'

'Oh, you're not going to do anything sinful are you?'

This almost makes me laugh. 'Caitlin. Don't tell anybody. Please promise.'

'I promise. I promise. But your mother will find out, won't she? What shall I do?'

'Do nothing,' I say. I want her to say goodbye to me. 'Goodbye, Caitlin.'

She is very upset. 'Which man?' she says. 'When did you meet a man?'

I want to go now. I have to meet Gregor.

'He's a gypsy. He's a German. He was living in a van on the tow-path. Goodbye Caitlin.'

I run down the garden and over the bridge. I have a small holdall with a few clothes and my passport. I'm running down the tow-path, splashing in the puddles. I'm running away.

We're on the ferry between England and France. There is no land to be seen. Nothing except water. The ferry lurches and rocks. I start to feel sick and I start to cry.

'So leaving is not so easy, is it?' says Gregor. 'I told you if you change your mind I won't take you home.'

'I didn't tell my mother,' I sob. 'I lied. I told her I was going to Caitlin's. I couldn't tell her. I thought she would stop me, but I wish I'd said something now.'

Gregor is angry. 'You must not lie! You must never lie! You must tell people what you want to do. So what do you want to do now?'

I think about this. 'I will write to her,' I say. I go to the shop and buy a postcard. It has a picture of the ship on it. Blue and white and red with a fake-looking sky and an even faker sea.

I sit down and try to write, but what can I say? 'Dear Mum, I've gone to India with a man named Gregor. I love him. Please don't worry about me. Love, Mireille.'

CHAPTER TEN

Sunday afternoon (cont.)

I did a bad thing running away. I never thought for one moment I would hurt people. I thought my mother would be furious, it didn't occur to me she would be upset, she would be distraught, she would be devastated. It's difficult now to think I could have been like that, but I was seventeen, self-absorbed and headstrong. Gregor never felt any guilt about it, but when I came back to England with Sanclair I wanted to make things better. When the baby died I remember thinking, I know why this is, it's my turn to hurt now.

I remember seeing Stephen standing on the patio at The Heathers, like I used to stand, knowing he didn't know what to say. I thought that's what it was like for Vivienne. I was there all the time and she didn't know what to say. Then I thought, I'm not my mother, I do know what to say. So I went out on to the patio and said, 'Stephen, shall we go for a walk?' How pleased he looked that I had talked to him.

We walked, not very far, down the garden and over the bridge and up the tow-path. It was frosty and the canal was frozen over, but the ice wasn't thick. I think it was the afternoon because I remember the sun going down, red in front of us. We chatted about nothing, everyday things, not the painful things, and he was relieved, I know. He didn't want to talk about the painful things. We walked past my narrowboat, looking locked up and lonely. Past my father's old office and then through the tunnel, and I thought, I'm just strolling up and down my life here.

Then we were by the Widcombe pond and I said to Stephen, 'I met Gregor here, he had a van, over there in the bushes.'

'Really?' said Stephen.

I was sure I had told him that story before, but he hadn't remembered.

'I thought you met him in France?' he said and he scratched his head and looked in the bushes as if there might still be a leftover relic of his father. I realised he had constructed his own history. Our histories are incomplete because our memory is incomplete. I assumed he must know because I knew.

I said to him, 'I was seventeen and I was cycling to school . . .'

We sat on the bench by the lock and Stephen listened. About me and Gregor and how I ran away. 'What a wild thing to do,' he said. 'I never thought of you as wild.' Then he said, 'It makes more sense really, doesn't it?' and I knew he meant about Felix and the baby. But we weren't going to talk about that so we were quiet. We watched the ducks swimming in the puddles in the ice.

I stopped talking about France and Gregor to Stephen because I thought he remembered; but he didn't, he forgot. It's the telling that makes you remember and the story changes each time you tell it. What really happened? What really happened? What I'm writing here about me and Gregor, was that how it was, or is it the story I told to Stephen by the canal?

I'm just strolling through my history. I'm trying to make a story because if I know the beginning and the middle then I can see an ending. I'm forty-two, I want to see an ending.

The valley's quieter now. This is post-lunch snooze time. The sun is as warm as an English summer but not yet that burning heat that pulls me to the pool. I want some sandals. I want some shorts. I want a dress. It looks like I shall have to go to the market in Draguignan again.

Things to buy.

Sandals, shorts, a short-sleeve dress, sun cream.

Espadrilles. Cherries, because they must be ripe now. There's a few in the gully but not enough to pick. Strawberries? Strawberries in May? It's not British, is it? Young artichokes, yes, I'd love those. Asparagus. Olives, black ones with herbs. Goat's cheese. Salami. Brown bread because they don't sell it in the village. Tomatoes. Fresh pasta. Couscous, mushrooms, aubergines, peppers, tapenade, Gruyère, olive oil, a piece of lamb. God, I'm hungry!

Wednesday 11th May. Afternoon

I've bought a hammock! This feels so extravagant. It was 150 francs. It's made out of string and I've rigged it up on the vine terrace on the path that goes to the Ferrou and and I'm in it now. It's between two pine trees. There was a smaller tree, too. I had to cut it down, but if I put my foot on the stump I can get the hammock to swing just so. Now, this is bliss! There's a cuckoo in the woods. It's been warm all week and I've been clearing away bloody sarsparilla from behind the hut. The thorns are evil. I chucked the whole lot down the gully. I want to start clearing paths. Behind the hut is clear now and so is the front. When the first warm weather comes it's better to be outside. Later it will be too hot to work. I bought the hammock in the supermarket.

I went to the village to get the bus to Draguignan and there was Jeanette just going to Monoprix. She's so insistant. Why go on a bus? Why pay more in Draguignan? The supermarket has everything, it's so convenient, it's so modern. They have special offers. So I went.

It was a vast place on the ring road. I hate supermarkets. I hate the artificial air. But it was true, they did have everything. I went bonkers and bought the lot. Sandals, tins, jams, food, creosote, nails, and then I saw the hammock. Jeanette gave me a lift home. I don't think I would have been able to carry all that lot down through the woods. I invited her in, but she had to get back to do lunch. She was curious, I could see it. She thinks I live like a pig in a sty, but in the end she wasn't that curious. The Ferrou to her is just a hut and a pond. She's seen it before.

So I am now a consumer. I've been polluted. The myth of this place is that the locals shop in the village markets and they are all unspoilt peasants. The locals do shop in the markets, but they stock up at Monoprix. It was full of the most ordinary people. Come here, tourists, I thought, and you will see how people really live. They spend the whole morning there, and then have lunch. There were two cafés. Of course it's not much different from a megastore in Britain. Different cheeses, more fish. Big square bars of household olive oil soap. But there's the same bland, controlled atmosphere. You go in there to buy tomatoes and you come out with a sunhat because they're cheap. I also bought a dress. Jeanette helped me choose it. It's in Provençal material with a flounce round the hem. Bright red, no sleeves. I'm wearing it now. I'm swinging in a hammock wearing an almost pretty dress. What am I trying to be, seventeen again?

I've been thinking how I can describe that time I spent with Gregor. I could write down all the things we did but I've forgotten the order now. We were going to India but there was no schedule. We drove down through France and into Spain and then Portugal. Then I think we went back through Spain, France, and into Italy. Then Yugoslavia, Greece and Turkey. It's confused because there was no sequence. We travelled and met people, went back to their houses, stayed in one place for some weeks, stayed in other places for only a night. There's a medley in my mind of dark bars, foreign faces and talking into the night. Sleeping in fields, sleeping under the stars. A tractor pulling us out of the mud. Where was that? Watching a field being ploughed by a horse-drawn plough. I think that was Yugoslavia. Istanbul, buying fresh melons in the street. Swimming in the bluest sea in Greece. Driving over mountains and into the morning, seeing a shepherd with his flock, and he waved to us. He had a black moustache and the widest grin. He seemed brown all over. The fishermen in Portugal cooking fish on the beach. Eating it with our fingers and coarse white bread. A bar in Lisbon, smoky, with sad wailing singing. Beautiful tiles on the outside of houses. Picking grapes. Working so hard in the heat and my fingers sore and blistered. Listening to Gregor, who had enough energy for five people, talking about the meaning of God with an Australian who had a squint.

We travelled until April and by then we were in eastern Turkey, ready to take the Asian part of the route to India. In Europe it was easy to earn money, and if not money, a meal. Gregor could fix things, cars, machines. These were handy skills. We helped build a shed. That was in Spain. I was standing up the ladder handing him tiles, terracotta tiles, like the ones here. I wasn't that high off the ground but I started to feel giddy and sick. I thought I was going to fall off the ladder, so I dropped the tile. There was shouting and screaming because it nearly fell on a small boy who was watching us. I got down off the ladder and lay on the grass and the world turned round and round. The women came close, they patted me and muttered. They smelled of sweat and garlic. I tried to hear what they were saying but it wasn't a Spanish I had learned at school. I sat up and one gave me a drink of water. She patted my head and smiled. Then she rubbed her stomach.

I was pregnant. I told Gregor. He put his head to one side and said, 'Yes, yes, that was always a risk.' And I hadn't thought about it at all. I supposed he knew what he was doing. I realised then he didn't know everything. Things could go wrong. Things had gone wrong.

'What shall we do?' I said.

'Do?' said Gregor. 'We're going to India and baby makes three.'

He told everybody we met. Were you delighted, Gregor, your little schoolgirl, your little protegée was having your baby. Did it make you feel big? Here was something you hadn't experienced before, fatherhood. Now you could find out all about it. But I was sick. My mouth tasted of metal and my head felt like a bag of cotton wool. I slept more in the back of the van. That winter we moved south towards Turkey, but it was hard to find work and I didn't feel like working. The nights were cold and we often didn't eat. Gregor was used to this but I wasn't. We sang in bars and cafés, but there weren't any tourists to give us money. I remember rain and cold winds, bleak hilltops and closed up villages. Sometimes, a clear sky so blue it hurt my eyes and at night a whole universe of stars.

In eastern Turkey the people were hostile and suspicious. Children threw stones at our van. Nobody was smiling anymore. We were by the border under the slope of Mount Ararat, a perfectly shaped mountain with snow on top, in a terrain of rocks and desert, sharp biting air.

Dark-suited men with donkeys, hooded women and tangled-haired children who followed us asking for money. It felt so foreign. French, German, Spanish, nobody spoke these languages. We had to haggle over prices. Food was scarce. What did these people live off? Bread and goat's meat? We were waiting to cross the border but I was full of despair. I didn't want to have my baby by some roadside tea house with villagers standing and watching. I was six months pregnant. The baby turned and kicked inside me.

I pleaded with Gregor. Let's go back to Spain. Let's find a place by the sea and wait until the baby's born. Please, let's

106

find somewhere familiar. He didn't change his plans for anyone, but I cried for nearly two days. What I was afraid of more was that he would leave me. Then in the night he got up and started the van. I was asleep. I woke up and we were moving. 'Where are we going?' I said, thinking he was trying to sneak me over the border.

'I don't know,' said Gregor, 'but I'm going to find you a house to have your baby.'

It's April and we're still in Turkey. We're in Cappadocia, near the cave city and the hot springs of Pamukkale. The countryside is extraordinary. Boulders on top of weathered spires of rock. Miles and miles of twisted rock formations, but the land is green and it's spring. The caves and the rocks are pulling at my memory and I'm thinking of the Ferrou, the great rock with the split. We've been staying in a peach tree grove for a few days and the trees are in flower. Beyond us is the strange moonscape of Cappadocia and I'm thinking, trees and rocks and a little hut below a village. Water in the tap. Food in the market. Jeanette and Auxille coming out of the café. I'm looking over the beautiful weird landscape thinking of the Ferrou, and the baby inside me moves and stretches as if it too can feel my thoughts. I want to go home. I wake up Gregor, who is asleep like a bear in the van. 'I know where we can go,' I say.

'*Was ist? Was ist?*' he mumbles. He turns over and grunts, then he sits up.

'Schoolgirl, let the old man sleep!'

He looks at me. He has not seen me so excited and animated for months.

'I know where we can go,' I say, 'I know where the key is. There's a little hut in France. I know how to get there.'

We arrived in early May. We didn't go to the village but straight to the hut. I remembered the way, the turns and twists of the road I had not been down since I was ten. We walked up through the terraces. I can see myself, pregnant, clambering up the path, excited, but nervous in case the hut isn't there anymore, and Gregor in front of me, turning round to help me.

Then I see it. The rock and the hut on the rock and we're walking along the terrace towards it. It's just as I remember, it's just the same. If my father was there waving at us I wouldn't be surprised. I'm crying now because it's what I want. Gregor's already looking for the key. I tell him it's under a stone at the back and he's found it. He's opening the door. He enters the black space and I daren't go close in case he's disappointed, but he comes out all smiles and stretches out his arms to welcome me. He's hugging me and I'm crying. He's saying, 'See, we have found a home, now you must start smiling.' But I'm not sad, I'm relieved and happy. I'm so happy.

Is this the same night? Gregor's made a fire and brought the bedding up from the van. We're sleeping on the floor. We're making love. Yes, I do remember this. I'm naked and pregnant and it's all a bit awkward, arms, legs, and my big belly, but we're making love and I feel blissful. Gregor's beard is tickling me and he grunts in my ear like this: huh, huh, huh. I'm holding his shoulders. His shoulders are hairy too, and his back. He feels like a carpet and the baby inside me feels squashed up and slightly surprised at this intrusion because we haven't done this for ages. I hold on to Gregor and it's like a strange dance where he doesn't miss a beat once. Huh, huh, huh. I hold tighter and it feels like we're tumbling round and round in space.

Is this the next day? We're sitting outside the café and here is Jeanette, older and plumper, but I recognise her immediately, and there are Auxille and Macon. I look at Jeanette and she

108

looks at me and I say, '*Jeanette, c'est moi, Mireille!*'

She throws up her hands and shrieks, '*Maman, viens ici!*' and we're all shaking hands and hugging.

Gregor and Macon, later, drunk as lords and singing, and Auxille too, starts to sing, one of the songs her grandfather taught her. Gregor listens, slaps the table and shouts '*Splendide!*' and we all join in the chorus. We're all singing late into the night. Is this what really happened? It's what I remember. It's what I want to remember. Gregor, I've forgotten so much. You are the only person who would remember and you always said to me, don't look back, keep going forward. Have you forgotten as well? If I asked you, what would you remember?

I showed you the Ferrou on a day as hot as this, but by the water it was shady and cool. You bent down, cupped your hands and drank. Then you stood up and looked at the great rock.

'Now I understand, little schoolgirl, why you wanted to come here.'

Mireille left her journal and walked through the woods to the gully. No birds sang there. The pool was as still as a mirror. She knelt by the side and touched the surface lightly with her finger tips. Ripples ran across, breaking the reflection into fragments, but, underneath, the water was as still and dark as it had ever been. It was too cold to swim.

CHAPTER ELEVEN

For the rest of the week Mireille worked clearing paths along the terraces. By Friday it was possible to walk unhindered up into the woods, to the Ferrou, by way of the hammock and down into the gully. The sun was high in the sky and the noises from the farm had stopped. The sun made the countryside static. With the spring rain and wind there had been a feeling of movement, of change, as clouds fell and lifted, hiding and revealing, but the sun made the air hang. It was only the progression of it across the sky that altered the view, creating shadows from different angles. With the sun, anything in the shade was darker and anything in its light was intensified to the point of being almost dazzling.

Mireille worked in the sun. Freckles joined up across her shoulders and face. She wore shorts and a loose shirt. Her hair had lost its straight-across cut and was curling now towards her shoulders. It made her seem both younger and older at the same time. Younger, because she had a youthful figure and a way of moving that was still like an adolescent, whose legs and arms have a will of their own, and older because with whiter hair and browner skin she was like an old peasant woman.

Late afternoon and the sun moved towards the village. The shadows in the valley were the darkest green now, nearly indigo, and the light was as golden as treacle. Mireille threw the last of the clearings into the gully. The water would rot down any debris; it was the only place to put garden rubbish. Fires were out of the question. When it was dry the land was like a tinderbox. She had never seen a forest fire and she didn't want to.

At the hut she took a tub of water outside, stripped off and washed herself down. The water stung, she had bramble scratches on her arms and legs, but it was wonderful to be clean. Inside the hut she stuck her head under the tap and washed her hair. She had learned to live like this with Gregor. How to keep clean with one tub of water. How to cook a meal in one pan. Wash clothes when it was sunny. Collect rainwater in buckets.

Dressed in her pyjamas she sat at the table. On it were jam jars full of wild flowers and their smell filled the hut. She had had enough of outdoors for one day.

Friday 13th May. Early evening
The orchids are nearly over. I noticed this today when I was clearing a path up to the woods. I am going to have to make up another excuse. So much for my scientific survey. I didn't even find out the botanical names. But in the village it seems to be accepted I'm staying here for a while. If people don't want you around they soon let you know. I don't know why I've been working so hard. It feels like I've settled in. Money isn't a problem yet, but by the end of the summer it will be. I must remember it's possible to live on next to nothing. This is how I lived with Gregor and I don't remember ever being hungry. I don't remember going without anything. I don't remember feeling poor.

Gregor loved the hut. We made it like it is now, with a bed, pots and pans and a table.

I'm very pregnant and hanging the washing outside today. Gregor's making some stools out of pine wood. There's salad, bread and salami on the table.

Gregor hasn't had a home for years, only his yellow van, but here we are cooking, eating, sleeping, finding things for the hut. This is our little home and we are as happy as squirrels in a tree.

In the evening we go up to Le Sanglier and chat to Macon and Jeanette. Gregor's French isn't as good as mine but talking to Macon it doesn't matter. '*Ça va?*' '*Bien!*' '*Encore du vin?*' '*Eh alors!*' Macon says there might be some work, he could do with some extra help. Gregor is German, but he's only half German and he knows how to drink. I talk to Jeanette. Auxille is in the kitchen making dinner. There's always customers at La Sanglier. Jeanette wears a white apron over her dress. How lucky I am to be having a baby, she says. She and Macon, well, they tried, and there was nothing wrong with her, it made her depressed at first, but now she's busy with the café and Maman will let her do the cooking soon. But it's a shame because she has no sisters and Macon's family, they aren't the best of friends, it would be nice to be an auntie.

Perhaps my baby will be a boy. Then won't my mother be pleased?

Gregor says I mustn't tell lies but I have told another one. I told Jeanette my mother knows I'm here. That she said we could live in the hut. Gregor doesn't know this. He can't follow Jeanette's twanging French, and Macon has no interest in the ins and outs of families. Jeanette talks about my parents a lot. How stylish and elegant they were. When she talks about them I want to cry because my father's dead and I have run away from home and my mother will probably never talk to me again. Jeanette says I must write to my mother and tell her the news in the village. She would love to write herself but she knows her handwriting is poor and it is an embarrassment to her to write to a woman as chic as my mother, and isn't she concerned that her daughter, still so young, is going to take a baby to India?

I nod and smile and drink my wine. Gregor and Macon have been joined by a Gués, a bus driver who lives on the road to Lieux. There's going to be a *boules* match on Sunday, perhaps Gregor can come and watch, and does he know anything about carburettors? He doesn't look too German. Odette is closing up the shop. She looks across the square at Gregor, then at me. Unsuitable husbands, pregnant young girls. She's seen it all before.

I was going to have the baby in the little hospital in Rochas. I had been there several times already. The doctor poked and prodded me, but I wasn't scared because Gregor was there. The hospital was old-fashioned with metal-framed windows and echoing corridors. There was a large cedar on the lawn outside. Nobody was quite sure when this baby was due. I had been given three different dates. I wasn't afraid of giving birth because Gregor would be with me. When he was in Alabama a black woman had gone into labour on the bus, and had her child at the back of a diner on the highway. He had held her hand the whole way through. 'As soon as she saw that baby, she forgot the pain, oh yes, that is how it will be for you.' And I believed him.

I enjoyed that last month. I felt dreamy and detached. I stayed at the hut basking in the sun like a melon, huge and ripe. I swam in the Ferrou, the water taking the weight away from me until I felt light and agile again. In the hut I filled the tin trunk with all the things I would need. Nappies, little baby clothes. I knew nothing about babies, but I don't remember this bothering me. I don't remember anything bothering me.

It was midsummer day 1972. Gregor left the hut early in the morning. He was working with Macon at the farm by the château. I think they were building a wall. I had my breakfast outside. I remember this because it was a hot day. The sky was completely blue, pure cobalt, even in the morning. I could see the mountains, so clear, it was as if I could see every peak. I sat there for hours. Then, I suddenly felt energetic. I had done nothing more active over the last month than walk to the Ferrou and back. Yes, I would clean out the hut. I swept the floor. I washed the floor. I aired the bedding. I

113

scrubbed the table. It was wonderful to be so busy, but it was odd, it was like it was happening to somebody else, like it was when I was looking at the mountains. I put the mattress back on the sleeping platform.

There's sweat running down my face and down between my breasts. My belly feels tight and uncomfortable and there's a wetness between my legs. I think it's blood, but it's not, it's just wetness, perhaps it's sweat. I'm so hot now, all I can think about is being cool. The hut isn't cool, the only place that is cool is the Ferrou.

I'm walking to the Ferrou and it's taking me a long time. My back aches. My legs don't seem to work. I'm getting pains now like cramp, like period pains but worse. When they come I have to stop and lean against a tree. I want to put my feet in the cold water. I want to lie on the grass. I know I have to get there.

I splash myself with cold water. I want to swim but I feel so heavy I know I'll sink to the bottom. I thought I saw my father at the top of the rock. The sun is shining into the pool. When I look at the water I see the sun. I know it's started now and I'm scared. I'm scared to look up at the rock. I'm on my hands and knees on the grass and each time the pains come it feels like I'm falling off the rock. I just have time to scramble up then it starts again.

And now I'm splitting. I'm splitting in two and I'm sure I'm dying. I do look up, at the wet split down the rock and I'm crying. I'm crouching by the water which is still and the sun has moved. It's no longer a pool of light, it's a pool of dark. Then it starts again . . .

Sanclair was born by the side of the pool. Nobody knows this. I didn't tell Gregor and I've never told Sanclair. This is my secret. He was born and I thought he was dead because he didn't cry. I was frantic. I was going to dunk him in the cold water, placenta and all, because I thought it might revive him, but then I looked at him and he looked at me. He had such clear eyes. He had fair hair and he was breathing with a sort of gurgle. I picked him up and wrapped him in my skirt. He was still looking at me, taking it all in. He looked so old and wise and young and new and so utterly and completely beautiful. It felt like I was holding a piece of the sun. I've fallen in love twice in my life and that was the first time. This is my secret.

I must have walked back to the hut because then I'm in bed. I've cut the cord with a kitchen knife and tied it with my shoelace. I don't know what to do with the placenta so I've left it on the table. Sanclair is crying now, loudly, and I'm laughing. 'What a noise you make.' He hasn't got a name yet. I put him against my nipple and he starts to suck. Then Gregor comes back.

It all goes crazy and we're laughing and crying at the same time. I forget to tell him it happened at the Ferrou. Somehow it doesn't seem to matter now. What is real is this squeaking bundle of pink whose cries are becoming louder. Gregor thinks he ought to get the doctor because the baby is here two weeks before anybody's dates.

He comes back with old Doctor Perrigues, who enters the hut and exclaims, 'I didn't think people still lived like this!' He redoes the baby's cord. I need a few stitches. He says we must keep as clean as we can. He says the baby is a fine size. He wishes us well and takes the placenta away. And now it's quiet. Gregor is cooking. The baby is asleep and I'm so tired I want to sleep as well.

It's strange writing this when I had a baby only six months ago and my belly still feels soft and sometimes my nipples are tender. That birth was so different. I was in hospital wired up to a machine because the heartbeat was irregular. The winter baby. Sanclair's eyes were full of the sun and the blue sky, but that baby had dark eyes like the bottom of the pool. He had dark hair. He looked at me once and it was like looking into nothingness, like looking into infinity.

Saturday morning

Last night I dreamed I was at Bellevue. It's not a place I dream about much. But I dreamed I lived there with Felix. He was in the sitting room smoking dope with his friends and I was in the kitchen cooking. Somehow we had become respectable. Dog-ear and Paignton wore suits and Rosebud was in a little cocktail dress like my mother used to wear. I think we were going to have a dinner party. Yes, and Pammy was there too, because we had a baby. Pammy came down the stairs to show us the baby who was all dressed up in an old-fashioned embroidered nightie. In the dream I started to think, but this isn't real because I haven't got any babies. This baby looked so real. It had pink cheeks and dark hair and was wide awake, looking at me with blue eyes. I wanted to hold it and kiss it and cuddle it. I put out my arms and Pammy gave me the baby. I put its cheek against mine and I smelled that fresh skin baby smell. They have such soft skin. I felt so happy. I wanted it to be real.

Shit.

I'm sad this morning. When I woke up I started crying. I'm feeling better now but floppy like a rag. I've just read what I wrote last night and it didn't seem real either. Surely, surely I didn't really have Sanclair up by the pool. That is so fantastic. Then I walked all the way back to the hut? When I read it, it sounded ludicrous. All these years I haven't questioned it, but now I'm living in the reality of it. The brambles, the rocks, the ants. I think I must have dreamed it. I think I must have made it up. I lived here for four years with Gregor. I think of them as the four happiest years of my life, but when I try to remember, it slips away. I remember vivid patches, but in

116

between I can't find anything of substance. I see the same pictures again and again. Me and the baby. Me and the baby. Laughing. Singing. Happy. In the sun.

Gregor was right when he said, don't look back because when you do the pictures you remember are just like reflections in water. One poke of reality and they start to quiver.

I have to describe the pictures, because that is all I have now.

We call him Sanclair, after the village, and he is a child of the air. He has blond hair and pink skin and I am besotted. I stare at him for hours. I feed him until no more milk can possibly dribble into his mouth. I hold him for hours. I don't mind that Gregor works, because I have my baby. I don't want to go to the village. I don't want to go anywhere. I'm happy at the hut washing nappies and cooking.

In the winter I chop wood and stoke up the stove. Sanclair is a sturdy, plump baby sitting on a mat playing with pine-cones. He wears two jumpers because of the cold, but his cheeks are pink and he's always smiling. I wait for Gregor to come back. At night we all sleep together and tell each other stories.

In the spring there are flowers everywhere. I show Sanclair a rainbow. I don't know if he can see it, but he laughs anyway.

In the summer we spend the hot days by the pool. Sanclair is crawling now. He's not afraid of the water. I swim with him. He splashes and giggles. His skin is golden brown now and his hair is quite white. He has hazel eyes like Gregor's. He can say mama and papa.

I'm sitting outside the café. Sanclair is crawling over Macon's dog and laughing. The dog is unaffected and lies there in the sun, panting. Sanclair has never been so close to a dog before and he's not afraid. He's not afraid of anything.

117

Jeanette is talking to me but I'm not listening, because I'm watching Sanclair. I'm worried in case he pulls the dog's ears and gets bitten, but he's stroking the dog and cuddling it gently as if he understands.

'Mireille, you're not listening,' says Jeanette and I turn my head as though she's tugging it with a lead and I don't want to come. 'I said, you're much too thin, your cheeks, look, they're hollow. Gregor, does she eat properly?'

'She eats all day!' laughs Gregor.

'Then she must stop breast feeding that child. Look how big he is, and how thin she is. He's not a little baby anymore, he'll be walking soon.' They both look at me. I don't know whether I'm thin or fat. I don't know what I look like, but their attention makes me uncomfortable. 'She's a baby herself. Look at her, worn out looking after her baby. If only her mother were here, young girls need their mothers.' Jeanette suddenly hugs me, pressing me into her squashy bosoms. 'Look at her, look at her, she's a bundle of sticks!'

Gregor is serious. 'Yes, I suppose you're right. But she has been so happy, yes?'

'She won't be happy when she gets ill.' Jeanette squeezes me tighter. She scolds me, wagging her finger. 'Stop breast feeding, you'll get ill! You can't look after your baby if you're ill.'

I have not thought about myself and I know this, but I love feeding Sanclair. These days he crawls on to my lap and pulls up my shirt, but I love the suck and the tug, the dreamy tug on my nipple as his eyes close and he sucks himself to oblivion. I love it. It's better than sex. It's more close and intimate.

Auxille has joined the conversation now and she starts pinching my arms as if I'm the Sunday chicken, and recounting tales of dying young girls and grief-stricken husbands. I burst into tears. I want them all to go away. I want my baby.

That night in bed Sanclair has sucked himself to sleep and I'm still tearful. Gregor hates it when I cry, he hates to see me unhappy. We have reached a compromise. I will feed Sanclair at night, in the day I'm to push him away. 'It's true,' says Gregor, 'it's just a habit now.' He will spend more time with me, he will look after me. Somehow this doesn't cheer me up.

It's the middle of August. Sanclair is starting to walk. Gregor has spent most of the summer repairing the terraces. He does this in the morning before it gets too hot. I know he needs to be busy. I know he needs something to occupy him and being with me and Sanclair is not enough. It's the hottest part of the day. He comes and sits with us by the pool. He has been tinkering with the van again. I don't mention India because I don't want to go there now, but I wonder if he's thinking about it. He lies on the grass and looks up at the sky between the trees. Sanclair climbs on to him and bounces on his chest. Oof, oof, says Gregor and Sanclair laughs. I know Gregor loves him. I know Gregor loves me, but it's not the same.

It was Auxille, strangely, who changed things. We went to the café in the evenings so Gregor could drink with the men and Sanclair could be fussed over. Jeanette was doing most of the cooking then, so it was Auxille who could chat. I didn't mind her talking, she didn't barrage me with questions and if she did ask a question she never waited for the answer.

Auxille tells me stories of Old Man Henri. She tells me again the story of Avelard and the Princess. Sanclair climbs on to my lap. He falls asleep as I stroke his hair. He's listening to the story too, the sing-song French which I don't want to stop. Gregor and Macon are also talking, about saucy village girls and cheeky farmers. Gregor's French will never be brilliant but he can tell a rude tale.

'And now you must sing,' says Auxille. 'Nobody sings these days.' So I do. I sing the songs I learned at school.

'Greensleeves.' 'Linden Lea.' 'Danny Boy.' 'The Unquiet Grave.' Sanclair is completely asleep now, curled up like the tiny baby he used to be. Auxille taps her foot and nods her head. Gregor and Macon listen, as do the other customers in the café. Jeanette comes and stands in the doorway. It's getting dark and there are candles on the outside tables. It's early September. I left home two years ago. I'm singing, 'The King of Love My Shepherd Is', and thinking about cycling to school up the tow-path. It seems a life away.

When I finish, people clap. A woman gives me some money, she says keep it for the baby. Other people give me money. Perhaps I still look thin. Perhaps my skirt is torn. Perhaps I just look too young to have a toddling baby on my lap. Gregor picks up the money and says thank you. He puts his arm around me to show that he cares. He sits next to me. 'We must learn some French songs,' he says.

CHAPTER TWELVE

Monday 16th May. After lunch

– O Magali! se tu te fas	'O Magali, if thou wilt play
Lou pèis de l'oundo,	At turning fish, beware!
Iéu, lou pescaire me farai,	For I the fisherman will be
Te pescarai!	And fish for thee.'
– Oh! mai, se tu te fas pescaire,	'Oh, and if thou thy nets
	would'st fling
Ti vertoulet quand jitaras,	As fisherman, then stay!
Iéu me farai l'aucèu voulaire,	I'll be a bird upon the wing
M'envoularai dins li campas.	And o'er the moors away.'

Yesterday I walked in the hills. I sang that song as I walked.
Above the village a small road leads to a farm called Clos
Maroui. It's a messy place with broken-down trucks and a
half-built extension, but they have a vineyard and twelve
terraces of olive trees, old, wide-trunked and twisted. It's the
highest farm. It was lunchtime. There was nobody to hear me,
of course, they were all eating. Behind the farm the road loops
into the hills, called the Bois Communal de St Clair, but there
aren't any trees, just a few stunted oaks, gorse and broom, all
in flower. I was walking through yellow. Once above the pine
trees you can appreciate how spectacular this countryside is.
The valley of the Rioux way below me was just a dark
shadow, and the village looked like something balanced on a
pebble. I tried to work out where my hut was, but up there
distances are distorted. The mountains looked nearer and the

roads were merely brown streaks zig-zagging down. The track I walked on was stony. I was glad I had my boots. Black and yellow butterflies. Bright blue ones. An occasional small bird flipping across. It was breezy up there. The sun was burning, though, and I stopped for a while and sat in the shade of a rock. There were no human sounds at all. It was a lonely place.

I could see the road to Grasse quite clearly, running along the flat grassy plateau beyond the village. There's another farm down there. The *domaine*, where they press the wine and the olives. This is the wealthiest farm and it belongs to the château. I couldn't see the château. It was hidden behind a line of poplar trees. I could see the pool, though, a shining square in the grey stone of the terraces.

On the way back I tried to walk up to the château, but there's now a huge gate on the road, an enormous wrought-iron thing. It was locked with an electronic security alarm. The whole place was like a fortress. I was disappointed. I was tired by then. Coming down from the hills took at least two hours and I was still a mile away from the village. I was never friendly with the Villeneuves, but I wanted to see the château. It used to have ornamental gardens, I remember them planted with roses. The front had sixteen windows. It's built out of grey stone with orange blotches of lichen. The terrace runs right round the house. The pool was at the back. A stone pool with water flowing into it from a stone lion's mouth.

The Villeneuves still own the château, but I know that they hardly ever stay there. It was the same when I was with Gregor, it was rented out, but it always seemed empty, half decayed.

Today the wind has blown up again, not the mistral, it's not fierce enough, but one that sends thin streaks of cloud into the sky. I know how it will be now. The thinner clouds will follow, tumbling into the valley and then it will rain. But this won't happen until late afternoon. Now, it's midday and

I'm in the hammock again. The military are exploding shells in the hills and it sounds like thunder. There's still a cuckoo, but it seems far away.

We spent that winter learning songs, as many as we could find. Auxille knew dozens. Gregor was excited about it, we would be new troubadours. He was a man who needed a vision, he was a man who had to be doing something, and I participated. As soon as the tables and chairs went outside Le Sanglier, we were there. Jeanette and Auxille thought it was wonderful. There was no other café they knew of with such an attraction. We dressed in bright clothes we found in the market and Sanclair too, with his little drum. Perhaps the locals thought we were daft, but they still came to listen, and we were serious. We went to the library and found old books of songs. If there was no tune we made one up. When people listened to us it was with a strange wistfulness as if they were remembering something they only half knew, some snatch of a line their grandmother used to sing.

– *O Magali! se tu te fas* *La pauro morto . . .*	'O Magali, and if cold clay Thou make thyself, and dead . . .'

– *O Magali! me fas de bèn! . . .* *Mai, tre te vèire,* *Ve lis estello, O Magali,* *Coume an pali!*	'Thou healest me, O Magali! And mark how, of a truth, The stars, since thou did'st drop thy veil, Have all grown pale!'

It was then that Macon's father gave me the piano accordion. He was a shrivelled drunk, unlike his strapping son. He came up to the café after we had been singing and put the thing on the table. 'For you,' he said, with no ceremony or explanation. It was beautiful. It was inlaid with ivory and had fine metalwork on the sides. I tried it out and it sounded clear, it had been well looked after. I thought he meant for me just to try it out, so I gave it back to him. He shook his head and smiled. He had a drunkard's smile, over-emphasised and insistent. He didn't take it back. There was an awkward moment. Macon, who had been watching, called out from the café doorway, 'Do you not accept my father's generosity?' 'Of course,' I said. I was amazed. I turned to the old man. He smiled again. 'Thank you very much,' I said.

I'm practising on the accordion outside the hut. I've nearly got the hang of it. Sanclair is playing with stones and shells. I don't think he's listening but when I stop he says, '*Encore, encore.*' I try another tune and he hums as well. These days we are wrapped in music. Gregor is on a job with Macon. After it's finished we will go the coast. There's plenty of money to be earned there.

We sing in cafés in St Tropez, St Raphael, St Maxime. We sing wherever we can. Two strange bohemians and their little white-haired child. He bangs a drum and sings as well, obviously happy and radiant, cute and charming. When people give us money he bows and says, '*Merci, mesdames.*' He's a complete star. He loves the singing. He loves the travelling. He loves the beaches and the sea. He loves the people. At night we camp in the back of the van. Sanclair wants to see the stars. He wants to hear the waves at night. He wants to know what the fishermen are doing. He wants to know if there are sea monsters. Gregor answers his questions as if he's an adult and not a small boy who doesn't want to go to sleep.

It's July and it's hot. The nights are hot too. I sit by the open doors and play my accordion. The sea laps on to the beach. This is an unspoiled piece of coastline, but further down are the blank blocks of holiday flats my father helped to build.

It wasn't like when we travelled before. Then I felt sick and tired and uncertain, but that summer I felt I was doing what I wanted to do with the people I loved the most. I was on a mission too. When I sang, I felt love and people loved us. I don't remember ever being turned away, I don't remember people treating us harshly. We were singing out our hearts. It didn't seem to tire me.

Sanclair, I'm so sad you don't remember this, how brave and confident you were. Three years old, golden child. You never cried, you never complained. When the singing was over you were a little boy again, playing in the dust with the other children, talking a mixed-up high-pitched French and English, but children communicate anyway, whatever their language.

I remember an English couple sitting outside a bar in St Raphael. Elegant and well dressed, not young, in their early fifties. The woman wrinkled her nose, and I could hear her say to her husband, 'What a disgrace to drag a child around doing that.'

Sanclair went up to her with his drum. He said, '*Aimez-vous les chanters, madame?*' He smiled, put his hand on her arm and said '*Très belle, madame!*' with such wonder, and didn't she melt.

'Oh how kind!' She fumbled in her purse and gave him fifty francs. He bowed like a little prince. And wasn't she charmed.

Sanclair, Gregor's son. Learning to be kind. Learning how to look people straight in the eye. Learning to be interested. Gregor never shouted at him, was never impatient, and I sang songs and cuddled him when he wanted to be a baby. I don't think it was a bad upbringing.

For most of the winter Gregor went back to the coast, working in bars, working on the boats. I had no fear he wouldn't come back. Before he left he taught me how to drive, and I learned on the road that leads to the farm. Gregor was a patient teacher, he made me go over each manoeuvre again and again until he was sure I knew what I was doing. I think he wanted me to be more independent, he wanted to know that when he was away I would be able to cope. Gregor's little schoolgirl, still naive and protected, wrapped up in her child, her music and her little home. I think he wanted me to grow up.

That winter was peaceful. Sanclair, now a little boy, didn't need my full attention. He played outside every day. Even in the rain. There were places he sheltered and he didn't come back until meal times, sometimes blue-lipped and shivering. He'd stay by the stove until he was warm and we'd play songs or I'd read him a story, but I could tell he was waiting to go outside again. He was an outdoor boy and he stayed like that. I read more. I could drive as far as Draguignan and go to the library. I read Mistral again, but this time his Mireille wasn't the romantic heroine I remembered her to be. She was downtrodden and pathetic, dying miserably on the beach. I couldn't identify with her anymore. I preferred to read Pagnol and Daudet, at least they made me laugh.

I want to see a picture of how I was then, but there are no photographs. I remember myself like this. My hair is long, right down my back and curling. I wear an odd mixture of clothes. A peasant skirt, thick tights and walking boots. Embroidered shirts and jumpers. I wear a sheepskin coat when it's really cold. I tie my hair up sometimes with scarves. I can chop wood and make fires. I talk French nearly all the time. When Gregor comes back the stillness and quiet is shattered into a thousand pieces, it's hard to concentrate on anything except him and what he's doing. When he's away, if I feel lonely I go to Le Sanglier and talk to Jeanette. Sometimes I play music and sing. Not for money particularly, but because I like to. Jeanette says my mother must be proud of me. She doesn't ask me so much about my mother now. I told her I phone her every time I go to Draguignan. I've been saying this for three years. Jeanette believes it. Gregor believes it and sometimes I think that I believe it. I've made up a version of my mother for myself. She's cold and distant. She doesn't want to see me. She's not interested in Sanclair. No, she's not proud of me.

It was May, about the same time of year it is now. For some weeks Gregor had been home. There were new tenants at the château and he had been working up there with Macon. It was a Sunday and I was going to meet him at Le Sanglier. I walked up the track to the village. I had my accordion on my back and I walked with Sanclair. There were wild flowers the whole way and we picked a bunch to give to Jeanette. A blue sky and light breeze, like it is today, changeable weather, but for the moment radiant. At the café Jeanette took the flowers as if they were dipped in silver, kissed Sanclair until he squealed and promised him sweets and biscuits and chocolate milk. Auxille was full of the woes of the village. She had fallen out again with Odette over the price of a slice of pâté, but I didn't want to hear about it. I said, 'Shall I sing?' There weren't many customers but I sang anyway. I didn't play the accordion, I was waiting for Gregor, but I sang at the top of my voice, a song I'd made up about Avelard and the princess. They became troubadours. The prince awoke to his own foolishness. Avelard left her, so she dressed as a man and called herself Mellano de la Queste. The castle became deserted and the wilderness took over. It seemed as if my singing rose up from the square and was soaring round the bell tower on the church like the swallows. I stopped, and Sanclair came with me to collect the money. He had chocolate milk down his front. We didn't collect much. On the last table were two men, an older man and a younger one. They were not locals, because they both wore straw hats. The younger man wore a cream suit. They looked wealthy. I stood for a while by their table.

'Well, did you ever see such a fine-looking peasant?' This was the younger man. He spoke English and at first I almost didn't understand because I hadn't spoken English for months.

'Looks deceive, Julian,' said the older man. 'Look again, tell me what you see.' And they both looked at me.

'She's young and fit. Bright eyes, cheeky mouth. Give her a wash, she'd do for me.'

He smiled. He thought I didn't understand him. He had pale skin, dark hair and the bluest eyes I'd ever seen. He crossed his legs. He had black ankle boots and silky socks. He was rake thin. He had elegant hands. He dipped one finger in his wine glass and then sucked it. I think I blushed.

The older man laughed. 'Julian, you do not see things properly. You see what you want to see. This girl is English.'

The younger man stared. 'Surely not. She jabbers away like a local.'

'Look, she has blue eyes. Look, she has, how do you say . . . spots.'

'Freckles, Badouin. She has freckles.'

'She is too tall for a girl from the village.' He turned to me. He had a white beard. He was dressed in a pale blue tunic and loose trousers. He had a large gold ring on one hand. 'You're English, aren't you? You're the girl who lives in a *cabanon*.'

'Yes,' I said. Sanclair pulled at my shirt. He didn't understand what they were saying.

'And this little cherub is her son.'

'Well, I never,' said the younger man. 'She seems too young. So . . .' he was baffled. 'So why is she . . .' He looked me straight in the eyes. 'So, why are you singing in cafés?'

'It's what I do,' I said.

The older man laughed. 'Young lady, please join us.'

He was Badouin. He was a painter and he had rented the château for the summer. He was well known although I had

128

never heard of him, and the younger man was Julian Greville-Newton. His father was a patron of Badouin's. They bought me a glass of wine and a sorbet for Sanclair.

'So you live in a hut?' said Julian.

'She lives with that German.' Badouin took off his hat. He was completely bald.

'What, the crazy one who works with the drunken oaf? What, that great lumbering hairy German?'

Badouin laughed. 'My friend is a blunt man, my dear. You must excuse him. Julian, you embarrass our guest. She is a charming young girl, nicely bred and then she runs away with a German, has his baby and now they are so happy, he tells me, and she loves to sing.'

'It's a strange world,' said Julian. He scrutinised me further and moved his head closer to mine. He smelled of perfume. 'You're not shy, but you're reserved. I can see that now. What goes on in that quiet head of yours?'

I could only think that he was clean. His clothes were spotless, and so was he. His nails had half moons on them. His shirt had gold cuff links. His skin was almost translucent.

Sanclair finished his sorbet and said, 'Shall we sing some more for you because I like to eat this.'

Badouin smiled. 'Don't they make a picture, Julian? The young Madonna and her little sun king.'

'Paint them.'

'No, I shall stay with rocks and trees, but I shall remember. You should learn to draw, Julian, then you would see things. See his brown eyes like his father, and his mouth, like his mother, what do you say, a cheeky mouth. This little man is not afraid of his world, and she is not afraid either, are you? Tell me what you see, my dear.'

Nobody talked to me like this except Gregor and I was embarrassed, but they were waiting and Sanclair looked up at me and licked his spoon again, he wanted more sorbet.

'I see that you have a gold ring as thick as a strap, and he

129

has gold cuff links. You both have straw hats, not cheap ones, but real ones of the creamiest straw. Your clothes have been ironed. I can see that you are both rich.'

They laughed and Sanclair laughed even more when they ordered more sorbet. Then I saw Gregor, walking towards the square with Macon, both of them dusty with plaster. Gregor had his shirt off and it was true he did look massive, a bronzed, muscled, hairy thing with hair down to his shoulders and a blond beard. He bounded over to us and Sanclair shouted, 'Papa, hurry up and sing and these people will buy you ice cream.'

'If they can buy me ice cream, they can buy me wine! Come on,' he said to me, 'play that box of yours.'

Gregor may have looked boorish, but round a table with a group of people he was king. There is no topic he can't discuss and now it's art. We have sung and sung and the table has filled up with wine bottles. My head is swimming. Sanclair has fallen asleep on my lap. Jeanette and Auxille have realised who the people in the straw hats really are and they are flitting about like bats. Macon has joined us and he too has an opinion about modern art. Piccasso and Matisse, they're all right but they can't draw, and that's the problem. Badouin and Gregor are locked into a duel, classicism versus romanticism and at the moment romanticism looks like it's going to win. Only Julian is quiet, touching his finger tips together and crossing and uncrossing his legs. He is watching Gregor.

Again he leans over to me and says in my ear, 'Your German is quite a character, isn't he? I can see why you like him, but tell me, is he a complete animal in bed?'

The sun has gone in like I thought it would. I shall go inside and light a fire now, because I know it's going to rain.

CHAPTER THIRTEEN

Monday 16th. Early evening

The rain started about an hour ago and it's coming down quite hard. I didn't bring the hammock in. I suppose it will be all right. I was thinking I don't have many memories of rain here although it rains hard in the spring and the autumn. I have memories of storms because they are so dramatic. I would like a storm because it used to feel that the hut shook in the thunder and I could almost hear the lightning snapping.

It rained the night we had dinner at the château. The roads were wet and the drive to the château was full of puddles. It was just dusk. The château was lit up downstairs and seemed to be glowing. I remember I felt nervous and inadequate. What had I got to say at dinner parties?

The windows of the château are reflected in the puddles in the courtyard like shining cat's eyes. Sanclair is restless and fidgety, he wants to see the big house. When the car stops he is the first out and runs up to the grand front door, then he stops and stares upwards. He has never seen a house so big and here's Julian to welcome us. He's wearing a dark blue velvet suit. He hugs me to him and he already smells of wine. When he hugs me he seems to press his groin into mine, but before I can object he's shaking Gregor's hand and saying, 'Well, this is the country cottage.'

We walk inside. There are candles everywhere. The rooms are empty but huge. There are pink silk curtains at the windows falling into tatters, gilded chairs and Badouin's paintings leaning up against the walls. He paints with a draughtsman's precision, rocks and trees, craggy corners of Provence. Each blade of grass seems to be separate. The effect is of an amazing intensity. A single olive tree has iconic status. A rock formation is a twisted mass of colour. Even in the candlelight I can see this. He paints a world without people, constantly in bright sun. A parched, lonely planet, blue, terracotta and brown.

Badouin is watching us. He wears the pale blue clothes he always wears. Julian offers him another drink but Badouin waves him away. Julian leans against a gilded armchair and watches us too. I try not to look at him but look instead at Sanclair, who is standing in the middle of the room looking up at the ceiling with his mouth open. On the ceiling is a painting of cherubs going up to heaven. In the soft candlelight it does indeed look real.

'What happens when it rains?' asks Sanclair. 'Don't you all get wet?'

'It's a trick,' says Julian, 'it's not real,' and picks him up. They are dissimilar. Thin pale Julian and rosy blond Sanclair. I'm anxious, but Julian isn't interested in Sanclair. He is doing this for my benefit. He spins Sanclair around until he giggles, then puts him down and looks straight at me. I suddenly feel he is dangerous. I look to Gregor for support but he has seen none of this.

Julian smiles, conspiratorially. It feels like we are alone together. 'I think it's time to eat. I think it's time to meet our students,' he says.

The students are Shula and Miriam. They are American art students. They do the cooking, tidy the studio, look after Badouin. Badouin has explained none of this, he never explains anything, but they are spending a year with him. Shula is tall and dark with tied-back hair and big teeth. Miriam is plump and pink, she has crinkly ginger hair and ginger eyelashes. She wears a sari. They like to talk. Shula is particularly interested in Provençal culture. She is doing a

132

dissertation on folk art, and what does Gregor think of the region's votive paintings? And Miriam loves pottery, darlings, she lurves it, and antique faïence ware, darling, isn't it so gorgeous, and is that your son, and isn't he just so gorgeous, and can you play that accordion thing, now that is so fascinating . . .

The dining room has one large table with silver candlesticks. The walls are all mirrors. We have artichokes, then a beef stew, salad, cheese, cherries and strawberries. Tapenade, wine, port, more wine and then more wine. *Tarte aux pommes*, more cheese, more wine and then we must sing. Sing for our supper like Tommy Tucker. Gregor can begin because he doesn't get as drunk as me. I heave my accordion up and hope I get the notes right, but once I start it's OK and we're singing. Gregor on the bass line and me with the melody, stretching it as far as I can, to the ceiling and back, round the table and back. Sanclair is asleep on a sofa now, and twitches like a cat when we sing as if he's singing in his sleep. Shula's smile is fixed to her face, Miriam is winding a curl of hair around her thumb. Badouin has closed his eyes and Julian is staring at me from underneath his dark eyebrows.

And we sing.

I can see us reflected in the mirrors. I can see myself from all angles. I'm not used to seeing myself. I'm fascinated.

It's later and I'm asleep on the sofa with Sanclair. I'm dreaming we're at the hut curled up under the roof, but Gregor is waking me. They say we can stay here, there is a bed upstairs, what do you say, sleepy schoolgirl?' It's nearly morning and I'm too tired to protest. He picks up Sanclair and I follow them upstairs to a room with a large draped bed and windows letting in the pink and grey morning. I flop on to the bed and he puts Sanclair next to me. He's not going to join me, he wants to talk with the men downstairs, who don't seem to need any sleep. I take my clothes off and cuddle up to Sanclair. He rubs his nose but doesn't wake up. I'm sleeping again. The door opens with a click. I think it's Gregor, but it isn't. Nobody comes in. I'm too tired to care.

When I wake it's already lunchtime. The others are by the pool. Shula and Miriam in their swimming costumes revealing their bodies to Badouin, who doesn't give a damn. Badouin and Gregor are discussing something, I think they're on to God now. Sanclair, naked as a fish, is flipping himself into the water, shouting, 'Watch me, watch this!'

I sit next to Julian. He's in the shade of a table umbrella, still in his midnight blue velvet. The rain has blown away. It's sunny now, but humid.

'Will you join the nymphs?' he says to me. 'I won't. I hate sunlight.'

'I didn't bring a costume,' I say.

'Do you think that matters? It would be refreshing to see a decent female form.'

Miriam and Shula in their bathing suits are not glamourous specimens, as my mother would say. Shula is all knees and elbows and Miriam doesn't have any knees, but dimpled creases and other lumps where there shouldn't be any. I wrap my skirt around me. I would love to swim. I really would.

'Why do you wear such unattractive garb?' asks Julian, handing me a drink. 'I'm sure that underneath you have a most elegant body. Little pert breasts like apples.' He purses his lips. He has full lips and they twist easily into a sneer. '*On va manger*. Would you care to nibble a *pissaladière*?'

We eat lunch by the pool. Afterwards Badouin and the students go inside for a rest. That leaves me Gregor, Sanclair and Julian. We move to a patch of shade on the lawn. 'If it gets hotter, I'll die,' says Julian. 'I'm from Norfolk. I'm not used to the heat.' He talks about himself. He describes his father as a pig-farmer. I'm sure he's something more grand than that, and more cultured. He has a private art collection. Julian is the youngest son. He says his brothers are something in the City. His sister is married to another pig-farmer. He has a soft voice and it's sending Gregor to sleep. Sanclair has gone back to the pool and is trying to stop the water coming out of the lion's mouth. Julian studied languages at Oxford, worked as a teacher for a bit, couldn't stand it and now he's bored. He thinks he'd like to do garden design or antiques, but he's not sure. Or open a gallery. That's his father's idea. I'm not used to talking to men of my own age and Julian is a curiosity. He is so mannered. Each gesture seems rehearsed. From his wavy hair to his Cuban boots he has not forgotten a single detail. Gregor is asleep now and snoring.

'Does he do this at night?' asks Julian. 'When he mounts you, does he make a noise, a grunting noise?'

'I think I'll swim now,' I say and go to the pool. I take off my shirt and sit by the side in my pants and blouse. Sanclair swims over and splashes me, my blouse becomes wet and wetter and sticks to my front. I slip into the water and start to swim. I'm aware Julian is watching me. I'm very aware of it.

I was both attracted and repulsed. Gregor didn't lust after me, his behaviour towards me was always, paternal, protective. Sometimes I felt he would rather spend the night telling me about Morocco than making love. I didn't mind this. I found it hard to see myself as a body, as attractive even. But at the château I was the most attractive woman and it was visible. When I walked into the dining room and saw myself on the walls, framed by ornate gilt, in my wet blouse and knickers. Dark hair, blue eyes, long legs, long arms, my wet clothes clinging to me. I stopped in the centre of the room by the long table, still littered with last night's dinner. There were flies buzzing around the debris, blobs of candle wax on the table cloth and there was Julian leaning against a doorframe. 'I was just looking for a towel,' I said, embarrassed. I was making a puddle on the floor. I could see my footprints all round the room. 'It's an attractive sight, isn't it?' said Julian and walked towards me, but I ran because nobody was keeping an eye on Sanclair.

*

135

I was just looking round this hut. How safe it feels here, how safe it feels now. The stove is roaring, the rain's tapping on the tiles, the lamp is lit on the table. It smells fresh here. It's tidy. All my possessions are where I can see them. I've always liked small rooms. I feel there's nothing hiding round a corner to surprise me. I like the outside right up to my window, but inside I like it small. The château was huge. It didn't have many rooms, but they were built to a grand scale, lofty and full of light. I used to feel dwarfed by them. I didn't want to go there much. I wanted to stay here with Sanclair and Gregor on this little bit of land, but Gregor loved the château. He loved the shabby grandeur and the late-night parties, the discussions that went on until morning.

He didn't notice that Julian always sat next to me, so he could run his hand down my thigh as if it were accidental. I don't think Shula and Miriam noticed either. They were too busy with their talk and impressing Badouin. Badouin noticed. I sometimes wonder if he planned it all, as meticulously as his own art, adding people like another colour to make the final perfect picture.

Julian knew what was going on. He was playing the game. He competed with Badouin as to who made up the rules. He urged Badouin to invite us back.

When I chose to stay behind it wasn't Gregor who persuaded me, it was Sanclair. Sanclair adored the château. It was full of hiding places, cupboards, rooms that led into rooms, faded furniture, threadbare carpets, mirrors, tricks of the light and a dusty smell of disuse. It was a magic castle to him, I could see that. Shula and Miriam spoiled him. They fed him tit-bits, they laughed at everything he said, they played with him in the pool. Shula even painted a picture of him. I took it back with me to England and it's still at The Heathers. Like a naive painting. Sanclair in his gold tunic with his drum in his hand. White blond hair, brown eyes and a background of the lawn at the château. He sat for it so well, like a

136

Velasquez prince, holding his arms out stiffly, standing on an old wine crate.

Is there a time when you lose your children? When you realise they've moved out of your care and protection and they start to have a life of their own that doesn't involve you? I've heard people say this happens when their children start school. I felt it happen at the château. My little boy, who was content to play outside at the hut, or sing with us in the bars and cafés, but always at night came back to be my little boy, now didn't see me for days. He didn't even sleep in the same room as us at the château anymore, but in a room next door. At the hut he wanted his own bed. Why can't we live in a big house with windows all round? Why can't we sleep all the time at the château?

Sanclair is by the pool, sitting at a table with Julian. Gregor is working at the *domaine* with Macon. Badouin is painting inside. Shula and Miriam are making lunch. I'm only here because Sanclair wanted us to be here. Julian is all in cream linen, as creamy as a lily flower. Sanclair is naked and golden, a string of beads round his neck and he's drawing a picture with chalks on a piece of thick paper.

'So what is this, your lordship?' Julian calls Sanclair 'his lordship'.

'It's my pool,' says Sanclair. 'I have a pool in my house as well.'

I know he means the Ferrou and I sit up. I have been lying by the side of the water. Somehow I don't want Sanclair to tell Julian about the Ferrou.

'I thought you lived in a shed. How come you have a pool?

'It's not as big as this one. It's got trees and a rock.'

I sit at the table. Julian eyes me up and down. Shula has given me a swimming costume, a blue one with flowers on.

'Look at my picture,' says Sanclair and hands it to Julian. He looks at it one way and then turns it round. He's obviously not used to looking at children's drawings. 'Very abstract,' he says.

'It's my pool,' says Sanclair, but Julian is staring at me.

'Is there more wine?' I ask.

'In the cellar. I'll get it. White. Dry. It should be chilled by now.'

I smile at him. He moves quickly, he's eager for my company.

Sanclair gives me the picture instead. 'Look, it's my pool!' and I look. It's the Ferrou. He's drawn the water and the rock with the split. He's drawn it all in purple, no wonder Julian couldn't see it.

Sanclair looks at the château pool critically. 'Our pool is better, isn't it, Maman?' he says in a whisper. I love him so much I think my heart will burst.

Here's another memory. Shula has taken us to see Badouin working. He works in an upstairs room. We must be quiet and not disturb him, but Badouin smiles effortlessly as if he is used to entertaining people when he's painting.

'He paints from memory,' explains Shula. 'As a child his family lived near Moustiers and he paints the scenes he remembers when he used to go walking in the hills. He wants to present the ideal Provence, the ageless landscape that will remain even when the people have gone. That is why the buildings he depicts are ruined. He is showing us the timelessness of nature.'

We watch as Badouin mixes paint on his palette. Whatever colour he puts on becomes a shade of brown. He is painting an outcrop of rock, bent pine trees on the summit and below, a thin river. In the distance is a ruined church. It makes me think of early Renaissance paintings but without the angels and wistful Madonnas. Badouin is painting in natural light. The canvas is about three feet wide and four feet high. It is the only picture he will complete this summer.

'Every year he comes to this region. Many of his buyers live on the coast. Later we will be organising an exhibition in Cannes. I'm sure you will be invited to the preview. Badouin is very generous.' Shula smiles in reverence.

Miriam nods in agreement. 'He is just so talented . . . in the States they call him the modern Poussin . . .'

'But of course Poussin's landscapes are imaginary. Badouin's exist,' says Shula.

'When I see them I'm right there. I mean, I was going to Lieux the other day' (she pronounces it 'Lee-oo') 'and I saw this tree and I mean it was just Badouin.' Sanclair sneezes suddenly and Miriam says, 'Shh,' gently.

'Painting is too long. I would take a photograph,' says Sanclair.

'His lordship is a modernist at heart,' says Julian. 'Despite his rural upbringing.'

'Shh!' says Miriam, this time more insistently.

Badouin mixing colours. Precise and controlled. Tiny drops of paint blending into each other. A fine-tipped brush. He has all the time in the world.

That night at dinner he turned to Miriam and said, 'Do tell us about your guru. I would like to know more about this Indian you worship.'

At the mention of India Gregor put down his fork and looked at Miriam with that same look of concentration I remember he used to turn on me when I was a schoolgirl by the canal. At the mention of India I felt a ripple of unease and looked at Sanclair, who was standing on a chair, helping himself to more salad.

CHAPTER FOURTEEN

Tuesday 17th May. After breakfast

I don't know what the time is but I slept late and it's still
raining. I shall write this, then wash some clothes. I can put
them round the stove to dry. I want an uneventful day. I shall
look at the map and plan another walk. I shall write out a
shopping list. Last night I was woken up by loud breathing
round the back of the hut. I thought it must be some drunken
git from the village come down to have a peek, so I yelled,
'Get lost and go back to your mother!' I felt safe, there are
two great big bolts on this door. But he didn't go away. Then
I started to get scared. I got the torch and yelled again. I tried
peering through the shutters, but I couldn't see anything only
hear this ghastly, raspy breathing. I shouted 'Go away! I've
got an axe!' which was true, and 'I've got a gun!' which
wasn't.

I don't know how long it all took but it felt like hours, and
there I was in my pyjamas trying to squint through a hole in
the wood. It's funny what you think about in the middle of
the night. This was the ghost of Old Man Henri. This was the
evil spirit of La Ferrou slimed up from the bottom of the pool.
This was my angry dead baby, this was Felix, my mother, my
dad. They were all out there. Everything bad in my life,
everything I've felt guilty about glued together into one hairy
monster outside my door.

I've never felt so alone in my entire life. What did it matter
how much I hollered or cried? Nobody down here could hear
me. I felt so stupid. I've put myself here far away from
everybody. Who would know if something happened to me?

In the end I went to bed and didn't I want somebody then, somebody just to say, there, there, it's all right. But I couldn't sleep. I was sure I could still hear noises. I thought about how many times in my life I had not been brave. I'd run away and lied, so I didn't have to deal with things, and wasn't I doing that again here, hiding away? For once I wanted to be brave and bold, and I got out of bed.

I was shaking like an earthquake. I had the torch in one hand and the axe in the other. I somehow managed to open the front door and I went outside. It was still raining.

It was a pig. A wild boarlet with its nose in a bag of rubbish I'd left round the back. Too greedy to stop chomping onion skins and cabbage leaves to mind my banging and shouting. When I shone the light on it, it froze. Stupid ugly fat thing. Can wild boars look guilty? I'm sure this one did, and frightened. We stared at each other, wet monster and victim. It wasn't a big wild boar, only half grown. I think a full-size one would have been terrifying, but I started to laugh and little piggy squeaked and squealed and the last I saw was its fat bottom as it scrambled up the terraces running back to mama. Aren't I brave? I shall put a notice over my door: Mireille, pig-scarer. Aren't I stupid? There I was in my pyjamas in the rain, flipped out of my wits for hours by a snuffling porker. I was laughing and crying. I had to make myself a cup of hot chocolate before I calmed down. The dawn was just breaking. It was nice sitting there by the stove feeling like a dragon-slayer.

I went back to bed and slept like the just. And now I don't know what time it is and it's still raining.

What came up last night was how guilty I feel about Julian. I sorted things out with my mother, but I never apologised to Gregor because he didn't know. I think to this day he still doesn't know and it's too late to tell him now, it's all ancient history. Gregor, I didn't do it to get at you. It wasn't lack of love, but I knew you would go to India. I wanted something for myself that wasn't you.

Miriam was a devotee of the Baba. I had heard about gurus. I thought they were wealthy characters who drove around in Rolls-Royces and had young girls fawning over them. The Baba wasn't like that. He preached poverty, simplicity and the natural order of life. In fact he didn't even preach. He made no effort to publicise himself. He lived in the hills above Bombay. A Californian man called Frank Stein discovered him whilst searching for the truth back in the sixties. He was impressed by the Baba's modesty, intelligence and humour. Frank stayed with the Baba for seven years and then went back to California to tell the world about him. A small following started up in America. There was a group in France near St. Paul de Vence, one in Italy and two or three in Spain. He wasn't that well known in England. To be a devotee seemed to me quite simple. The disciples wore Indian clothes, had a picture of the Baba round their necks and meditated twice a day. They ate freshly prepared food, didn't watch television and were opposed to violence. It was so simple as to seem almost pointless. Miriam explained this over three days at the château. When she talked about the Baba her eyes went misty and she lowered her voice to a whisper. It was as if she were in love and she had never met him. Frank Stein had written down the Baba's sayings and published them. She had read them all.

'The Baba hopes all his followers will come to him and receive the blessing,' said Miriam at dinner. 'When they are ready they will come to him. I'm not ready yet, but I hope I will be.'

'So how do you know when you are ready?' asked Julian, who had been following all this with amusement. 'Does your hair start to curl, does your skin change colour?' He peeled an apple with an ivory-handled knife.

'The blessing will change your life. You have to be ready,' said Miriam with no hint of irony.

142

'How so?' said Gregor, who was getting more interested in the subject.

'Because he tells you what you need to do with your life. He shows you the path.'

'He tells you what to do?' The idea sounded preposterous to me.

'He shows you the way,' said Miriam.

'How?' I said, still incredulous.

'You spend three months in his company in stillness and meditation. The Baba's gift is to see the special light in all of us. Then at the blessing he reveals your life's path.'

'That sounds beautiful,' said Shula.

'What does he say?' asked Julian, eating his apple. Badouin was smiling.

'You might need to be a shoe-maker, or a gardener, or work with animals, it just depends.'

'To have your life's path revealed to you, must be, yes, extraordinary,' said Gregor.

'What if he's wrong?' I said, but nobody answered.

I'm at the hut with Gregor. It's late at night and he's reading to me from the Baba's book, *Children of Light*. He's reading this . . . 'you all have within you enough light to dispel the darkness in the world. Why do you then object when I help you find the path that leads to your light?'

I feel angry. Surely I know my own path. I've run away from home, left my mother, lived with Gregor and had a baby. After all these changes surely I know what I am doing with my life.

The Baba's words still irritate me, even now when I don't seem to have a life anymore but repeated little events, sleeping, waking, writing, walking, shopping. I don't feel I have any light inside me at all.

I have to write about Julian.

Miriam, Shula and Badouin went to Cannes to set up the exhibition and Gregor went with them. I knew he would visit the settlement at St Paul de Vence and I knew I couldn't stop him. In a way I was glad to see them go. I was sick of the Baba. Shula was now meditating with Miriam every day and Gregor was reading nothing else. He tried to get Jeanette and Auxille interested, but they had their good Lord Jesus and his Virgin Mother and that was good enough for them. Even Julian was becoming involved. He had no path and the idea of being given one was appealing. He didn't go to Cannes. He said he would fry on the coast. It was August. I stayed at the hut, fed up and despondent. Staying by the Ferrou, listening to Sanclair chattering to himself as he splashed among the rocks. August is a grumpy month down here. Sticky and fly-blown. The grass dry as pubic hair. The sun as tiresome as an old joke.

I went to the village, but the café was chock-full with tourists on their way to the Gorge du Verdon. Jeanette and Auxille were so busy they could only wave and shout, 'Are you going to sing?' 'Not today,' I said, and Sanclair already wanted another ice cream.

Julian came strolling up under the plane trees. He crossed the square to greet me. I didn't avoid him because in the dappled sunlight he looked a picture of cool. Cream linen, straw hat, he was everything I wasn't.

'Not gone with the beach party?' he said and tipped his hat.

'I didn't fancy it.'

'So you're marooned as well?' He took a watch out of his waistcoat pocket and looked at it.

'Time for a post-prandial drink?' He surveyed the seething café. 'Not here. Too many grockles. At the château?'

We walked to the château up the old road, tree-lined and full of pot-holes. I didn't talk to Julian because Sanclair jabbered the whole way as if he hadn't spoken to anybody for a month and Gregor had only been away a week. At the château we sat in the drawing room. Sanclair was still in full flood. 'Shall I sing, shall I tell you a story, shall I show you my new dance?' Julian poured me a drink and I gulped it down quickly, so he poured me another. On the terrace the farmer's wife from the *domaine* was watering the flowers. Oleanders in tubs, hibiscus, geraniums.

'Madame Blanc . . .' said Julian, 'that gives me an idea. Come with me, your lordship. I think I know how to entertain you.'

I watched them through the window. Madame Blanc patted Sanclair's hair. They were pointing to the farm. Sanclair was jumping up and down. Julian gave Madame Blanc some money. She refused, then stuffed it in her apron pocket and led Sanclair away.

I rushed out on to the terrace. 'Where's she taking him?'

'Calm down, agitated mother. Your son is going to the *domaine* to see the new puppies. I think he might even stay the night there . . . they're good sorts the *domaine* Blancs. Now, would you like to swim?' Julian's mouth pursed itself into a smile. I could have run down the road and fetched Sanclair back, but I didn't.

I'm naked and swimming in the pool. Julian is watching me. My dirty, sweaty clothes are in a pile, but I'm fresh and wet, diving under the water, diving down to the stone bottom of the pool, green with algae, and the water singing in my ears is saying, enjoy your body, enjoy how it moves, how it feels. When I come up for air the water from the lion's mouth is spurting on to my face.

Enjoy your body. I'm sitting half dressed in the room of mirrors. It's getting darker and Julian has lit the candles. I can see myself in the mirrors. I'm flirting. Flipping my hair back, lowering my eyes, waving my hands when I talk. I don't usually behave like this. Pouting, wriggling, sticking my breasts out. We are both getting drunk. I'm flirting with Julian and flirting with myself.

Julian hasn't touched me, but he's watching me like a cat in the grass watches a bird, like a snake watches a frog, like an eagle watches a rabbit. I wonder at what point I will freeze. I'm getting drunker.

I'm standing by a bed and it's not the one I usually sleep in. The moon shines through the windows on to the bed and onto me in the bed, spread out on the bed and surely something's got to happen now. Julian is on the other side of the room. He's still dressed and I'm not. I don't know where my clothes are. I'm falling asleep.

Then he swoops. It's like a stab. He's so thin there's nothing to hold on to. He's all energy and push and thrust and prick, it's like I'm being nailed to the bed and this is weeks of lust coming out; but I'm not frozen, I'm hot like lava, like bubbling mud. He's all bones and smooth skin like a slippery fish, a hot fish, hot tongue, hot prick and I love how my body feels. I love it.

Julian standing by the window in the morning. Glaring at nothing under his dark eyebrows, leaning on the ripped silk pink curtains, gathered into bundles and swathes. A hot sweaty morning and his skin is as pink as a baby's foot. He's naked and hairless. Thin and wiry like an Elizabethan aristocrat. He has a moist pink just-fucked dick. I can't stop wanting him.

All week. We are decadent. In the room of mirrors we watch ourselves making love on the velvet chairs. We have done it in every single room in the house. In the wine cellar. In the old stable. Twice in the bath. On Badouin's bed. In the kitchen. I'm drunk all the time on wine and sex.

Sanclair has stayed at the *domaine*. He wants to sleep there with the puppies. He comes and sees us in the day, running across the lawn with Madame Blanc puffing after him. She's loving it. He's brought a puppy to show us and it's jumping and bouncing too. A little brown and white smooth-haired hunting dog, chubby and yapping. 'He's mine now,' says Sanclair. 'When he's older we will hunt wild boar together.'

Madame Blanc fans herself with her apron. 'I have not been so busy since my sons were children and this one is like three. Questions, questions. He speaks French so well you would not think his papa is a German, and what an appetite!' Her face resembles Auxille's but she's rounder and more rosy-cheeked. Her hair is usually tucked into a scarf, but now it's all over her face. She sits on one of the chairs by the pool. Julian gives her a drink of mineral water.

'Give Maman a rest and let Grandmère do some work,' says Madame Blanc.

Julian and I look as if we haven't moved from the side of the pool since they last saw us.

'Watch me, I can dive right down to the bottom! Watch me! Grandmère, can puppies swim?'

'He calls me Grandmerè,' says Madame Blanc shyly. 'I asked him who his *grandmère* was and he said he didn't know. He didn't even know what a *grandmère* was. When I told him, he said I could be his *grandmère* . . . No, no, puppy is too little and we musn't let dogs swim in this fine gentleman's pool, they might do *pi-pis* in the water.'

'I do *pi-pis* in the water and nobody minds,' says Sanclair. He splashes the puppy, which squeaks and yaps and shakes itself.

'What a fine strong boy he is!' laughs Madame Blanc. 'And when does Papa come back?'

'They all come back on Sunday,' says Julian.

We're making love again upstairs on Julian's bed, ferociously, maniacally. I would feel better about this if I loved Julian, but I don't. I would feel better if I wanted to stay with him, but I don't. I would feel better if I didn't want Gregor to come back, but I do.

*

We're sitting in the room of mirrors, waiting for the others to return. Sanclair is already asleep upstairs with his puppy. Madame Blanc has cooked a chicken and it's waiting in the oven. I have made a salad and Julian has chosen the wine. I have not drunk anything all day and I feel dry-mouthed and sick-headed. Julian wears his dark blue suit. He sits in the candle-light like a peacock. He strokes his lip. He says, 'When your hairy German shags you tonight, will you think about me?'

'Shut up, Julian.'

'Will you cry out in ecstasy like you did this afternoon, I wonder.'

'Shut up!'

He lowers his voice to a velvet whisper. 'And next week and the week after when you're back in your shed washing his underpants in cold water, will you remember how I took you in the wine cellar?'

I can hear a car coming up the drive. Julian moves closer to me. 'You arch little wench, your German is never going to know, is he?'

I wanted Gregor to walk through the door and see immediately I had betrayed him. I wanted him to shout, 'What have you done?' I wanted him to be suspicious and ask me why I was at the château and not at the Ferrou. But it wasn't like that.

They all came through the door and Gregor was the last. He saw me and hugged me. 'I have so many things to tell you, yes, I went to St Paul de Vence. I saw a film about the Baba. Miriam and Shula and Badouin, they saw it too. I think our lives have been changed, I must tell you, yes.'

We ate our dinner and everybody was talking, not about the exhibition but about the Baba.

'He is just the most fabulous man I have ever seen . . .' said Miriam.

'He radiates wisdom and tranquillity . . .' said Shula.

148

'His eyes are so deep and wide . . .' said Miriam.

'How do I say this? I felt when he spoke, yes, he was speaking just for me . . .' said Gregor.

'Julian, I have to tell you, he does have the most extraordinary effect,' said Badouin.

'What a pity I didn't go. Things have been dull around here.' And he shot me a mocking glance.

In bed I wanted Gregor to hug me and hold me and make love. I wanted to be back in our little safe hut, but Gregor wouldn't stop talking.

'Yes, I must go and see this man, this Baba. I must see him for myself. Yes, we must all go to India . . .'

I pulled the sheets around me. 'Gregor, I don't want to go to India,' I said and then I knew it was all over.

I want to stop writing this and start my day. It must be lunchtime now. I've been picking at the bread on the table and now there's none. That was a stupid thing to do. I'm not going to walk to the village in this rain. If it doesn't stop tomorrow I'll have to, I'm running out of food. I wish I had a car now.

I wish I had a car so I could drive up into the mountains and breathe that clean, pure air. I wish I had a car so I could go to Castellane. I've never been to Castellane. I wish I had a car so I could go anywhere. I wish I could stop feeling I have to keep writing this. I wish I could stop feeling bad about what I'm writing. When I write it, I remember how it felt. I was feeling then that awful sense of inevitability when something is finishing, is ending and there's nothing you can do about it. It feels a bit like giving birth, that oh-my-God-here-we-go feeling. Knowing it's going to be awful but at least with a birth you have a lovely baby at the end of it.

Sometimes.

I'll put that a different way. With a birth you hope, you believe, there's going to be a lovely baby at the end of it. What it felt like at the end of that summer was like giving birth to a dead baby.

I don't remember many details about the last month. I know I didn't go to the château. I stayed here with Sanclair and the puppy, called Dou-dou. I know what happened. Badouin offered to pay for everybody to go to India and he would go too. He had had a good exhibition. He was feeling generous. I know that Julian decided to go as well. Perhaps he didn't want to be left out. I know all these things. I'm trying to remember. I can see myself hanging up the washing and Sanclair playing with Dou-dou on the rock rose terrace. It has been raining but the sun is now out and the grass is becoming just a bit green again. Over the hills clouds are gathering. The yellow van is parked down on the road. Where is Gregor?

I'm in bed and Sanclair and the puppy are both in the little bed on the floor. I'm not asleep. My feet are cold. I'm thinking about Julian. I'm thinking about the room of mirrors and watching ourselves copulating on the chaise longue. I'm thinking of the grand table, the silver candlesticks, the bowl of fruit on the sideboard. Gregor is there and he's not with me. I climb down the ladder and light the lamp. Sanclair wakes up, all sleepy. He says, 'Ça va, Maman?' and I say, 'My feet are cold, I'm going to find some socks.' He says, 'Dou-dou and I can warm you,' and he picks up the drowsy puppy and climbs up the ladder. Under the sheets Sanclair is as warm as a hot-water bottle and the puppy sniffles in my ear. Sanclair starts to snore now, very softly like the wheeze of an accordion. These are comforting noises.

Gregor is going to India for three months, then he will be back. Is this the last day? Is this the last week? He's playing with Sanclair and the puppy by the Ferrou. It's still warm enough to swim but the leaves on the trees are turning yellow now and the days are shorter.

They're splashing and shouting. If Gregor shaved off his beard you could see how alike they look. Something about the way Sanclair laughs sounds like Gregor. An easy laugh that isn't cynical or sneering. They're out of the water now and sitting in the patch of sun. Sanclair knows his papa is going away but it doesn't mean much. He's been away before. Gregor is drying Sanclair down and he's squeaking like the puppy. Then Gregor puts his hands on his hips and looks up at the rock, which at the moment is casting a shadow across the pool. My father looked at the rock like that. The sun is rising above the rock, soon it will be shining right into the water. I know what Gregor is thinking.

'Yes, that would be most interesting . . .' says Gregor and walks towards the rock. I get up and rush towards him, but Gregor has already started the climb. He holds out his hand to Sanclair like my father did to me. I was too scared to accept, but Sanclair isn't.

'Oh, be careful!' I wail, an unwelcome voice, and they pay no attention. I watch them. Gregor bare-chested, going first, going slowly towards the split and then up it. Sanclair behind him looking very small, in red shorts and sandals, pushing his hair out of his eyes and looking up. Don't look down, Sanclair. I'm as scared as I was when Hugo climbed the rock and now there's two of them. The two people I love the most. I watch as they move. Gregor slow and methodical but Sanclair as agile as a monkey. He swings himself up. He has no idea of the danger, it's just exciting.

Then they're at the top, both of them. Gregor picks up Sanclair and puts him on his shoulders. I can hear Sanclair shouting, '*Regardes les montagnes! Regardes! Regardes!*'

The puppy next to me starts barking and Gregor's laugh is booming out across the valley. 'We are on top of the world. We are on top of the world!' He puts Sanclair down and they are holding hands. I can see their reflections on the surface of

151

the water, as still as a mirror. I want to be up there with them, but I know I could never climb the rock.

When they come down I'm waiting for them. 'I'm going to go up there every day!' says Sanclair.

'Not on your own, never climb on your own,' says Gregor.

'Maman can come with me,' says Sanclair.

'I don't like heights,' I say apologetically. 'I feel dizzy. I get scared.'

Sanclair is puzzled. 'But you get as high as the mountains. You get higher. You get as high as the clouds.'

'She likes the ground and the water, don't you, my little schoolgirl?' He hasn't called me that for weeks and we look at each other. Our eyes connect. He's sad to go too, but how many times has he moved on? How many people has he left?

'This is a special place here,' says Gregor, 'and I will always remember it. Thank you.'

Old Man Henri said that on the votive painting. Thank you.

Chapter Fifteen

The rain stopped and evening was coming down into the valley. The grass and the trees were heavy with rain. The paths down the hillside were wet streams of mud, gurgling into drains when they reached the road, and darkness followed them. The clouds drifted apart like thin material wearing thinner, and in between were bright stars, at first one or two, then gradually more, until there were only a few threads of clouds and a whole embroidered lining of starry night. The valley was quiet. A pheasant clucked, disturbed in the forest, a dog barked at the farm. Behind the trees the hut was invisible. Just the thinnest chink of light escaped through the shutters, but there was no other indication that the hut wasn't as black and as lonely as the rock it sat on.

Tuesday. Evening
Tomorrow I will go out, rain or no rain. I'm beginning to feel stir-crazy. Sanclair used to play in the rain and didn't care if he got wet. I've done everything I needed to do and now what is there to do? What is there to do down here? I didn't think I would feel like this. Bored. No, I'm not bored, I'm restless. I want something to happen. A big event. A little event. Perhaps I'm not as solitary as I thought I was. When I lived on the narrowboat, at first the other canal people annoyed me. I could hear them, talking, playing music, cooking. Then I got used to it. I could tell which noise was whose. That was Barney and Rosebud calling for their cat. That was Jim on his bike. That was the Bigbys pumping out the bilge. And the bonfires where Barney's crew used to hang out playing

153

strummy guitar music and that damned didgeridoo. God, it used to drive me nuts! Now I listen and I hear nobody.

They all went to India. They had a leaving party at the château and I didn't go. I don't remember saying goodbye to Gregor. I remember sitting here as I am now, at night with the lamp on the table, listening to the door creaking, to Sanclair and the puppy snoring, to the wind in the trees. Listening for the sound of people, but there weren't any people.

I remember the colours of that autumn, the yellows and the golds and the first chill in the air. Chopping up wood for the stove. Carrying shopping up from the car. Doing things that Gregor had done with ease but which seemed to take me three times longer. Getting colder at night. Singing in the café but for fewer and fewer tourists. How would I make money? How would I live for three months right into the winter until Gregor came back? Feeling hungry. Despairing at Sanclair's appetite. How could I feed him? How could I feed the dog? Jeanette, Auxille, Odette, they all watched me, sympathy mixed with nosiness to see what would happen to me.

I was sitting outside the café on one of the warmer October days, wondering if I had enough money for another coffee, when Jeanette came to talk to me.

She showed me a photograph. 'Look, I found it in a drawer when I was throwing out old things. I thought I would become thinner as I got older, like Maman, but that is not the case. But perhaps it is better to have good bosoms.' Jeanette's good bosoms were hoisted up for the world to see. She was in her thirties then and still outstandingly attractive. She had not lost her curvy plumpness. Only her hands were ageing, cracked and wrinkled from too much washing-up. She gave me the photograph. It was a black and white snapshot of my mother and father and myself outside Le Sanglier. Looking at it was like a slap round my face. My glamorous parents. My mother smiling, my father relaxing in white and me, ten years old, skinny and scowling with messy hair. Three people long gone. I gave the picture back. I didn't want to look at it.

'Oh no!' said Jeanette. 'Send it to your mama. Tell her how pleased I was to find it. I have so many photographs she can keep this one. A souvenir of St Clair.'

I looked at it again. My mother with that hard, bright smile. My father suppressing a laugh. What were they saying to each other? 'Hugo, darling, that French tart wants to take a picture. Do you think she knows how?' 'Shh, Vivienne, not so loud.' 'Come on, Hugo, sit up straight, all she really wants is a picture of your trousers . . .'

My mother in a cream, blue and red suit, taking jumble bags to the bring-and-buy. Another autumn.

Sanclair came and sat next to me. 'Is that Papa in India?'

'No, this is your grandmother.'

'Madame Blanc's my *grandmère*. Can we go to the farm?'

'This is your real grandmother. This is my mother. This is my father and this is me.'

'That isn't you. You don't look like that.'

'A long time ago.'

Sanclair looked at the picture closely. 'Your mama is smart. Your papa doesn't look like my papa. Can we go and see them? Will they give me presents?'

'My papa is dead. My mama lives in England.'

'I didn't know you had a mama and papa . . . why are you crying?'

I couldn't stop. I wanted to see my mother. I had run away and left her alone and now I was alone. I deserved it. Jeanette hugged me. She was the nosiest person in the world apart from Auxille, but at that moment she didn't ask me any questions and I was glad she didn't.

'Young girls need their mothers,' said Jeanette. I wondered if finding the photograph had been so accidental, but I didn't care. She was hugging me and comforting me in a way my mother never had.

155

That night I wrote to Vivienne. It took me ages. I wrote, 'I'm sorry I ran away. I now have a little boy called Sanclair. We have been living in the hut. Gregor has gone to India for three months. Please write to me c/o Le Sanglier, St Clair,' and I sent her the photograph.

She did write. The answer came on an expensive card with roses on the front. All it said was, 'Darling Mireille, please come home.'

She stopped writing. She opened the door and stepped outside. Away from the beam of light from the door she could see the clouds had lifted. She looked up and between the branches of the pine trees curved a whole sky full of shimmering stars.

'So big!' she said and stretched out her arms.

LIEUX

CHAPTER SIXTEEN

Saturday 21st May. Afternoon

I'm writing this in the square in Lieux. There are two cafés next to each other. One is more expensive and has red table-cloths and I'm in the other one. The chairs and tables spill out around the fountain. Here, as in St Clair, plane trees make the square cool and shady. It's hot now and it's been like this all week. Lieux is the prettiest village of the three. It's on a hill, but it's built round five different squares each with its own fountain, and when it's quiet, like it is now, there is always the sound of water. Channels of it run down the streets. Just down the road is a public drinking fountain where the locals fill up their bottles. There's an elegant white statue, which is possibly Roman, and an engraved plaque from the last century in the most pompous French, telling everybody about the medical benefits and the curative properties of the water. Lieux is a smart little place. The houses have wrought-iron balconies filled with flowers. At the windows are white lace curtains and the doors are huge and heavy with great brass door knobs. Old people retire here for their health. Wealthy people have holiday homes here. A tiny spa town. There are are two excellent patisseries, a *feu du bois* baker's, a butcher's, a greengrocer's, and a store selling local produce. The church is grand and inside there's a golden ceiling. Right on the top of the hill is a ruined castle and a high wall runs round the village, a reminder that this place has riches worth protecting. Lieux makes me laugh. It's only a step away from dingy Rochas, but there's more gold jewellery in the square than in any of the shops in Draguignan. I'm sure that by

August it will be just like the abbey square in Bath. All tourists with cameras.

Today there was a market on one of the lower squares and now I'm loaded up with essentials like strawberries, artichokes, tapenade, olives, cheese, local honey and rye bread. Jeanette thought I was mad coming here, she says the prices are dreadful. I'm waiting for the bus back. It'll be here in two hours. I'm in no hurry.

All this week I've been out walking, nowhere in particular, just up and around the tracks in the valley. Four days of sun and the rain has completely disappeared. The cherries are ripe on the trees now. I found a whole orchard by a deserted farmhouse and helped myself. Red sweet cherries, delicious and forgotten. Roses are flowering on the walls in the villages. Dark pink and red roses, heavily scented. Summer has started.

I didn't come here much with Gregor. I think it was too expensive for us. Our crazy singing would have gone down like a lead balloon. Lieux is beautiful, but it's as much fun as a rest cure. Some of the people here look as if they were fossilised before they even knew how to smile. My mother liked it here.

I drove back to England at the beginning of October 1976. With the mattress in the van so we could sleep in the back. I thought I would be away for a few months. Sanclair cried because we had to take Dou-dou back to the farm, but we will be back, I said to him and Madame Blanc, and Jeanette and Auxille, Odette, the post office, the baker's. We'll be back when Gregor comes back.

It took a week to get to England. As I drove off the ferry England looked so quaint. Men in uniforms telling us where to go. It all seemed small and petty. England was dry. There had been a hot summer and even in October the grass was still scorched and trees prematurely yellow and fading. I wanted it to be green, misty and moisty. I had had enough of the sun. Sanclair, who had been asking questions all through France, slept the whole way from Southampton. As we got nearer to Bath it felt like I was the only one returning home. The prodigal daughter. The bad girl coming back to mother. Sanclair was still asleep. It was about four o'clock in the afternoon and I knocked on the door of The Heathers. There was a long pause before my mother opened it. We looked at each other, I think in disbelief. She seemed to have shrunk. She seemed so small. She was wearing a pale green silk shirt and her hair was up, but it was grey and there were deep lines on her face, across her forehead and at the sides of her mouth. The change hit me like a mallet. She wasn't beautiful anymore.

She put her hands to her mouth. 'Oh Mireille, you're so tall. You're so like Hugo!' and she burst into tears.

We sat in the sitting room. The view hadn't changed at all. Not one tree. 'I'm sorry I ran away,' I said and I was crying too.

'It was all my fault,' said my mother. 'After Hugo died, it was so awful . . . I just couldn't . . . I just couldn't . . .' and her tears fell on to her silk blouse like raindrops. She was still elegant, she would be that until the day she died, but the spike and the steel in her that had hurt me so much had crumbled. 'When you left, it was like the end of the world . . .' she sobbed. 'There was nobody at all . . . The Costellos have been very good to me.' She dabbed her eyes with an embroidered handkerchief. I had expected her to slice me up with some curt remark about my peasant skirt or my walking boots, but she was squeezing my hand and gazing at me with wet eyes. 'I'm so glad you're here. I've prayed for you so many times. How long can you stay? I've made up a bed for you in your old room . . .' I was the object of my mother's affections. It was strange and overwhelming.

'And where is your baby?' she asked, composing herself slightly.

'He's asleep in the van.' I went to get him. Sanclair was wrapped up in a red blanket. I shook him gently. 'We're here,' I said, 'at Grandma's.'

He woke up and blinked, then he smiled, jumped up and looked out of the window. 'Is this the house? It's so long and flat. Does Grandmère milk goats like my other *grandmère*? Will I sleep in a big bed like at the château?' I held his hand and we walked into the house.

My mother was standing by the window. She had made an attempt to tidy herself. With the light behind her she looked like my remembered mother, stiff and proud and poised and on edge. When she saw Sanclair she exclaimed, 'Oh, he's not a baby, he's a little boy!' and for a moment I thought she was going to rush forward and hug him.

Sanclair walked right up to her and looked her up and down. 'Are you my *grandmère*?' he said in French. 'You don't look like a *grandmère*. Have you got presents for me?' Then he saw the view out of the window. 'Is that your farm? It's so big, and you've got cows, can I help you milk them, and I can make cheese. My mama and me, we sing and when we sing you must give us money. Shall we sing for you now?' He pressed his nose to the window 'Your farm is very big,' he said thoughtfully.

I was looking at Vivienne. I thought she would be horrified by his manners, but across her face was the same enraptured expression she used to reserve for my father. Seeing it again made me feel peculiar, like I was shrinking and disappearing to a far corner of the room.

My mother sat on the sofa. 'Sit next to me,' she said to Sanclair, in French, and he did, as fearless as he could be, and how much I loved him then.

'I had to leave Dou-dou behind, you can't have dogs in England. But when I get back I'll take him hunting. At the château I had a huge bed and I went swimming every day. I can jump in backwards. Papa went with the château people to India and that's much further away than England, it's the other side of the mountains. India's hot all the time, so hot even in the night . . .'

My mother very gently stroked Sanclair's hair as if she had forgotten how to be tender. He didn't stop talking, he was used to women fussing over him. I watched them. I felt tearful and emotional, not just because Sanclair had completely won my mother over but because I knew, from then on, I would never be her favourite.

It's later and we're sitting on the patio as the autumn day becomes a translucent crystal evening. A mist is forming over the fields and there's a smell of wet and water coming up from the canal. The sky has turned from blue to pink to almost greeny blue. I'm playing my accordion and singing the old songs, singing down into the river valley and up the canal to where I first met Gregor, to where it all started. Sanclair is singing too, he hasn't got his drum, so he's clapping his hands, and my mother wrapped up in a travel rug is tapping her elegant foot. And I'm singing, hoping that somewhere on the other side of the world, Gregor is singing too.

I wake up in my little room at The Heathers to the sound of the fountain. Early morning and I must get up soon and go to school, but surely that's not right, surely I've done all that. And I was dreaming I lived at La Ferrou and I had a baby, and it felt so real, but if it was, then why am I here? I look round the room and it's all the same. I'm seventeen again and I've got to get up and if I'm late my mother will snap at me. Then the door opens and Sanclair creeps in, half asleep, and I remember it all. I'm so relieved I start to cry and Sanclair says, 'I want Papa,' and he starts to cry too. He gets into my bed and we sniff and sob over each other and I say comforting things like, 'When we go back, Papa will be there, and he'll be by the hut waving at us, and after supper he can tell us about India and we'll tell him we went to England and stayed in Grandmère's white house, and she gave us chocolate cake and showed us photographs of Maman as a baby, and Doudou will be there when we get back, and he'll be so big he'll jump up and knock you over . . .' Sanclair is nearly asleep and so am I, listening to the fountain trickling outside the window.

When I think of The Heathers I always feel sad. It's the place of disappointments. The happy family that never was. The mother and daughter who could never talk to each other. The short stay that turned into half a lifetime. I stayed twenty-one years in Bath.

Sanclair got used to it. There was so much to learn about. Mud on carpets, toothbrushes, how showers worked, English winters, buses, clean clothes, haircuts, knives and forks, keeping quiet in church and speaking English all the time, except sometimes to me the last bits of French. My mother explained things to him, patiently, never once raising her voice like she used to with me.

'No, Sanclair, we don't wear our gumboots in the sitting room because of the mud.'

'Can't you brush it away like Maman does in our hut?'

'No, Sanclair, mud doesn't brush off carpets . . . Let me show you where you can leave your boots. On a piece of newspaper in the kitchen.'

My mother had lost her harshness, but it was Sanclair who transformed her into a loving being and I suppose that was his gift. Everybody loves Sanclair. I have to remember this when I've been so angry with him. Everybody loves him. He cares about them too, but nobody gets much time. He does remind me of Gregor.

At The Heathers I wrote to Gregor. I said we would stay there until he returned and he wrote back, the first of many letters. How wonderful the ashram was, how remarkable the Baba was, how beautiful that part of India. His love to me, his love to Sanclair. I've kept every single one and they're in a drawer at The Heathers. One day I will give them to Stephen. The first few I read out to Sanclair, but by Christmas he was so absorbed with Christmas trees, presents and candles, and the shops lit up, Papa in India was a faraway concept.

It was strange to be back in Bath. Sometimes it felt as if I'd never been away, but sometimes it felt I had been away for a hundred years and there was nothing anymore I could connect to. My mother had become a Catholic, and if anything her life was even smaller than I remembered. She took cuttings of her garden plants for the church shop. She went to a prayer evening at the Costellos' on Thursdays. She had tea in the Pump Room on Tuesdays. She helped in the church shop on Fridays. She went to church on Sunday. I went too, not because I'm a Christian but because I liked to sing. The snootier members of the congregation treated me with cold politeness. I had left my mother to disintegrate in her own misery and I was never forgiven, but the Costellos accepted me.

The Costellos were disturbingly unaltered. They had had one more child in my absence, a last little boy called Dermot, and he was the same age as Sanclair and, like Sanclair, immensely spoilt, but he was as tearful as Sanclair was fearless. We went to tea there. Dermot had every toy under the sun. It was Star Wars then and he had two spaceships and all the figures. Sanclair in France had played with sticks and shells. I think Dermot was scared of him. Dermot was a head shorter than Sanclair. He was pale and thin. He cried if he didn't get his own way, which wasn't very often, and was frightened of Sanclair trying to get him to jump down the stairs. Mr Costello called Sanclair the Sun King and recited poetry at him, which made him shriek with laughter, and Mrs

Costello gave us scones and soda bread and fruit cake until we were so full we couldn't eat dinner if we tried. My mother sat there in her little suit as if she were in a tearoom and not the Costellos' dirty kitchen with washing hanging up near the ceiling and the inevitable stew bubbling on the cooker.

One girl was at art school. Fenula was a model. Two were working as teachers. The boys and the younger girls were all doing well at school and Caitlin was just married. She had never left Bath. She had trained to be an English teacher but before her first job she'd met Simon. They had got married in June. It was Caitlin I was most embarrassed to see because I had left her to pass on the news of my disappearance. She had been blamed for not telling anybody sooner. She was my friend and I had abandoned her. I went with Sanclair to visit her and her husband. They lived in a new house hear Combe Down. Caitlin was just pregnant. Her appearance hadn't changed but her house was full of spanking new everythings she had to show me. New curtains, washing machine, a fitted kitchen, carpets throughout. She still had the same soft voice. I used to talk about art and poetry with her, but now she was showing me the inside of her fitted wardrobe. Sanclair jumped on the beds and ran round the house shouting, 'I'm Darth Vader!' He dropped most of his lunch on the floor and showed her how he could do a double somersault. Caitlin had been brought up with rowdy children but not in her house. She started to feel queasy and had to lie on the sofa, so Sanclair sang her a song to make her feel better. At one point when everything was quiet she said to me, 'Mireille, why did you run away, were you really that unhappy?' and I saw a glimmer of the Caitlin I used to know, but what could I say that she would understand? She had never wanted to go anywhere, so I just said, 'It was impulsive. I never meant to hurt anybody.' I hoped she would understand that.

Simon came home from work. His opening line was, 'So, you're the hippy.' He barraged me with questions like, what was my moral stance about marriage? and was I ashamed to have an illegitimate child? and was it right for me to be living off my mother when I had caused her so much distress? and was a liberal upbringing of children a complete mistake? At that point it did look like it because Simon said to Sanclair, 'Shh, you be quiet when grown-ups are talking,' and he said, 'Why? Grown-ups don't say anything interesting,' and sat on the floor and glared at Simon. Simon was the assistant manager of a bank. He was used to getting more respect. Caitlin started to feel worse and Simon said perhaps she ought to eat something because in pregnancy it was important to be well nourished, and after this we left. I knew I wouldn't be seeing a lot of Caitlin.

I'm glad now I did go back to Bath. The things I had found so awful when I was seventeen I realised weren't so awful. They were just normal. Normal people. Little lives. Even my mother. If I'd never gone back I think she would have stayed a monster in my mind, but now I saw her as somebody weak. She was vain and petty and insecure and proud and a snob, but she wasn't a tyrant. I could see how much she needed people. She was generous and accommodating to us. She didn't want us to go. I could see why. She was lonely.

Several times she asked me, 'Why did you run away? You had everything here.' She accepted she had been an inadequate mother but to her, material stability was as important as human relationships. When I described to her travelling with Gregor and living in the hut she asked questions like, 'Where did you wash?' She wasn't angry that we had been at La Ferrou, and that surprised me because I thought she would be. She said, 'I think Hugo would have liked you to be there. He loved that place . . .' and she went very quiet. La Ferrou was the future she never had. I suppose we were her future.

My mother with her wound-up hair, her elegant clothes,

167

her cigarettes, her television, her religion. These were all props distracting her from her great big emptiness. I know this feeling. The feeling of being hollow, of being a vacuum. I felt this when I moved back to Bath. Clothes I didn't want to wear, a life that didn't fit me anymore. Part of me didn't want to go back to France. I could see we had outgrown the little hut but I didn't know what the next step was. I was waiting for Gregor.

Just before Christmas he wrote to me, the longest and most informative letter he has ever written. Badouin had gone back to France with Shula. Shula had decided she was a Christian after all. Their time in India had been a holiday, an interlude, nothing more. Julian had got dysentery, spent some time in hospital and had been flown home at his father's expense. He had hated India. The heat, the flies, the poverty distressed him. But something had happened to him, said Gregor. After he came out of hospital he went to one of the Baba's lectures, which he had previously refused to do, preferring to hang around with prostitutes smoking hashish. Julian had fallen out with Miriam. She called him a parasite, probably an accurate description, and his lifestyle was getting on everybody's nerves. But when he was ill, said Gregor, he thought he was going to die and it scared him. 'When he went to the Baba he was like a little boy going to his father, and after the lecture we went and knelt in front of the Baba and he blessed us, and the Baba looked at Julian, who was still weak and said to him, "Go home now, young man, back to your farm."' Gregor thought this was fantastic. Go home back to your farm. Did the Baba really know that Julian's father was a pig-farmer? It sounded like good sense. It sounded like a metaphor, go back to nature, look after yourself. Gregor thought it was the most outstanding thing he had ever witnessed and it convinced him that the Baba was indeed a spiritual teacher of the highest order. And Julian, too ill to be cynical, did as he was told for once and went back to

Norfolk. When I read this it made me laugh. The prodigal son and I was the prodigal daughter. Just a few months ago we had been the decadent lords, the sex-gods, drunk bodies stuck to each other, as pagan and careless as satyrs on a frieze, and now we were back with our parents, saying, 'Look after me, love me, forgive me.' I thought about Julian then, thin and weak, I couldn't imagine how he could be thinner, languishing in his velvet suit in front of a log fire. Wondering what on earth to do next. I wanted to write to him but I knew I had been nothing for him, an experiment, an experience and he had been the same for me.

Bored Julian. He got into the organic movement. He took over his father's farm and now runs it as a show-case for these methods. He's become a spokesperson for organic farming and I've heard him on the radio several times. He was featured in a Sunday newspaper. He still looks rakish. He wears country-gentleman clothes, waistcoats and pocket watches. He has the same voice, fluid and velvety like a brandy chocolate pudding, and the same blue, blue eyes. He's married now with children. I wonder if he hires pretty farm girls and makes suggestive comments to them behind the compost. I'm sure he does.

At the end of Gregor's letter he said he was so impressed with the Baba he was going to stay with Miriam and take the blessing. During this time he was allowed no communication with the outside world, so this was the last letter for the next three months. He hoped I was well. I was to tell Sanclair his daddy still loved him. I read this letter after breakfast. There was a Christmas tree in the sitting room. Sanclair had helped Vivienne make the decorations. Little silver stars and golden moons. They had strung up paper chains across the room and all sorts of other baubles I knew my mother thought 'terribly vulgar', but she wanted Sanclair to enjoy himself. They were playing snap. She had been showing him new games in an attempt to keep him indoors because he preferred to be in the garden all day whatever the weather. It distressed her to see him soaking wet and muddy.

'So how is your boyfriend?' asked Vivienne. She referred to him as if he were a reckless youth and not a man capable of knowing his own mind.

'Snap!' shouted Sanclair, 'Snap! You didn't see it!' He was wearing all new clothes and he had a new haircut, but his hair was still white blond and shining in the light. I wanted to tell him first. 'Papa's not coming back just yet.' I said to him in French. He always listened when I spoke to him in French. 'He's staying in India for another three months.'

I hoped he wouldn't ask me, 'What are we going to do?' because I didn't know. I had told Vivienne we would be leaving after Christmas. Sanclair looked at me. He was waiting for more information, but Vivienne had understood. 'Mireille, what are you going to do?' she said.

I shook my head.

'Why don't you stay here?' she asked quickly, as if she had rehearsed this answer.

'Can we, can we?' said Sanclair.

'I think we should think about it a bit longer . . .' I said.

My mother did think about it for a bit longer, two minutes. Then she said. 'Well, of course you can stay here another three months, but, Mireille, I think you'll have to get a job.'

Sanclair picked up the pack of cards and was looking through them. He had his back to me. 'Why doesn't Papa want to come back?'

The clock has just struck four. My bus will be here in twenty minutes, That's just enough time for another coffee. The waiter has been watching me all afternoon. He's lean and dark, a young man with an insolent scowl. Perhaps he thinks I'm a rich American. Another time and I would be flattered, but I feel immune to the attentions of young men.

Chapter Seventeen

Sunday 22nd May. After lunch

Hammock time. I didn't want to do anything today but enjoy the sunshine. This morning I picked herbs on the rock rose terrace and then had lunch. The valley is unusually quiet for a Sunday. Perhaps the people from the farm have gone visiting, I've not heard a sound.

Last night I was thinking about Bath and that winter. We were heading into the depths of a British winter and I'm still thinking about it, which is odd because here I am heading towards a southern French summer. Hammocks, sundresses, sandals and long drinks of lemonade, but I'm thinking about frost, woolly jumpers and gumboots. Hot chocolate last thing at night and porridge for breakfast. The canal freezing over and a light dusting of snow over the garden at The Heathers. Snow, sleet, slush, mud . . .

I sold the van. I felt awful about doing it because it was Gregor's home, but I had no money. It wasn't worth much. When the man towed it away I cried because I had grown up in that little yellow van and Sanclair cried too, possibly because I was crying but also that was the last bit of his daddy. He didn't talk much about Gregor. He stopped asking me if I had any letters and if I ever mentioned him he would look at me impatiently until I changed the subject. Funny little boy, did you think your papa had abandoned you? I felt he had abandoned me.

I got a job. I worked in a pub up Walcot Street. I worked some lunchtimes and most evenings and my mother looked after Sanclair. I swapped my peasant skirts and bohemian blouses for jumpers and jeans. I was twenty-three. I looked no different from any other hippy-type young girl. There was folk music in the pub on Fridays and sometimes I sang and played my accordion. I stopped singing the French songs because nobody could understand them but learned ballads and West Country tunes. All the troubadours travelled incognito, I told myself.

Avelard dressed as a beggar and the princess dressed as a man and I was pretending to be a local barmaid, but I wasn't, I was a troubadour looking for the truth. Travelling in my mind and in my heart, like Gregor.

Even now when people start talking about what they did at college, or their teenage years, I keep very quiet. There's a pool of experience I never swam in. There are no points of reference. Television programmes, pop groups, films. Even when I'm with people who have had children what can I say? Sanclair was brought up in the wild, he played outdoors in the rain, I cannot tell you what brand of nappies I bought. I know what an exile feels like, except I was an exile in my own country. It's only here that I fell truly at home, but for everybody else, I'm the outsider.

If it had been just me I would have come back here with or without Gregor, but it wasn't just me. There was Sanclair. Five months is a long time for a little boy. Gregor's next letter came at the end of March. It was a short letter on the thinnest of air mail paper. It said, 'I have received the blessing. I know my path. I am to stay here and write letters for the Baba. You must understand how happy I am becoming. When you are ready, come to see me.'

When I read this I couldn't speak. I ran out of the house and down the lawn. My mother and Sanclair were in the garden looking at the daffodils. I ran over the bridge and up the canal. I was crying, I was so angry. The countryside was just coming to life again but I was so angry I could have blasted the lot away to its roots. I got as far as the Widcombe pond and I wanted Gregor to be there so I could shout at him, 'Why did you let me go with you? Why didn't you leave me alone?' but there was nothing there except water and the bushes and the bushes reflected in the water and the depth of the water itself.

I'm walking back to the house and I'm looking at it from the other side of the bridge. From down here it's long and flat and all windows. I wish I hadn't sold the van because now I want to jump in it and drive away, and the money I get from working isn't enough to go anywhere as distant as India.

Running down the garden comes Sanclair in his gumboots. He's got a trick, he can slide down the last bit of garden, and here he comes, shouting, 'Wayhey!' He jumps on his mud slide and lands up right near the bottom of the bridge. 'Did you see that, did you see that?' he shouts to anybody. He stands up and sees me. 'Mum, did you see that?' We are standing on different sides of the bridge. 'Grandma's making biscuits, then we're going to the shops. Aren't you going to work today?'

He's my son and he's happy here, I have to remember that. I cross the bridge to meet him.

I'm on the hammock in my sundress and sandals, rocking it with one foot. When I was twenty-three I thought my life had stopped, but I had felt that when I was ten. I knew what to do. You just bury yourself. It was easy to be buried at The Heathers. I don't feel like that now, I feel everything has just started. I'm going onward not backwards. I'm writing this because writing this is going onwards.

It was easy living at The Heathers. My mother was delighted for us to stay indefinitely. I said we would eventually get our own place when I'd saved up enough money, but it was difficult to get to that stage. I wanted to go travelling but I didn't want to go to India. I was still furious with Gregor. Sanclair started nursery school and loved it. He was always a favourite with teachers. He was witty and bright and loved to please, his boisterousness was forgiven. I kept working in the pub. I was twenty-three. I had never been to college. I had no training.

Why is it always winter when I think about that time? Sitting by the picture window looking out over a frosty garden, the little zig-zag footprints of sparrows on the patio. Cycling to work down the tow-path and the canal is being renovated, scooped out, relined, but it's raining and the machines are like dead monsters, frozen and skeletal. Taking Sanclair to school, watching him run off and join the other children. He disappears in a mass of coats and woolly hats. I can't pick him out. In my room at The Heathers there's an embroidered blouse I don't wear anymore and a string of amber beads. I take them out and look at them. The blouse is faded, perhaps I should throw it away. I smell it, it seems to smell of pine needles. The necklace is valuable, Gregor gave it to me in Turkey. Perhaps I should sell it. In each bead is a broken insect forever fossilised in the golden resin.

I'm sitting by the picture window watching the evening coming up in a mist from the river valley. I'm playing my accordion. My mother is at a prayer meeting. Sanclair is on the floor drawing a picture. He likes drawing. He draws the insides of cars and imaginary machines. He's eight. He's wearing a red cable-knit sweater and maroon corduroy trousers. His hair is still blond but more golden now. The light from the lamp falls across his face on to an expression of intense concentration. I stop playing. He looks up and says, 'Oh, don't stop. I like that one.'

'You used to sing it when you were little,' I say.

'Did I? How did it go?' and I play again and sing the words.

174

Sanclair listens, with his head on one side, listening hard. 'It's not proper French, is it?'

'No, it's Provençal.'

'I don't remember.'

'Daddy and I used to sing in cafés. You used to sing too and bang a drum.'

Sanclair laughs. 'I don't remember. Was I a baby?'

Surely he must remember. It can't be that long ago, can it? 'Don't you remember France?' I ask.

Sanclair wrinkles up his nose. 'I had a dog . . .' He looks at his picture. It's the cross-section of a spaceship, he's going to start drawing again.

'What do you remember?' I ask him in French, anxious now, but I don't want to show it.

'I remember . . . I remember . . .' When he talks French to me it's as if he's talking in a dream. I'm glad he doesn't learn French at school yet, because when he does I'm sure this will go.

'. . . There was a big house with candles . . . some ladies made me a *gâteau* . . . and an old man was painting . . .' he continues drawing, 'and a big swimming pool . . .'

'That was the château. We didn't live there. We lived at the Ferrou, a little hut. It had its own pool, a rock pool.'

'Yes, and the water ran out of the lion's mouth.'

He doesn't remember. It feels as if that part of my life has been rubbed away. 'What did your daddy look like?' I'm close to tears, but Sanclair isn't upset at all. He's drawing spaceships.

'Oh . . . Papa? . . . He was . . . he had . . . he had a yellow van and we sold it.'

I start playing again.

– O *Magali, se tu te fas* *La pauro morto,*	'O Magali, and if cold clay Thou make thyself, and dead,

Adounc la terro	Earth I'll become, and
me farai,	there thou'lt be,
Aqui t'aurai!	At last, for me.'
– Aro commence enfin	'I half begin to think,
de crèire	in sooth,
Que noun me parles	Thou speakest earnestly!
en risènt.	Then take my ring of glass,
Vaqui moun aneloun	fair youth,
de vèire	In memory of me.'
Per souvenènço	
o bèu jouvent!	
– O Magali, me fas	'Thou healest me, O Magali!
de bèn! . . .	And mark how, of a truth,
Mai, tre te vèire	The stars, since thou did'st
Ve lis estello,	drop thy veil,
O Magali,	Have all grown pale!'
Coume an pali!	

Outside it's dark. I can't see the garden. I can't see the river or the fields. I can only see us reflected in the window.

Here's another memory. This is our first winter at The Heathers. It's February, freezing cold, icy and sharp and I take Sanclair to the Roman baths. He's bored with it. Lumps of Roman stones mean nothing to him but then we see the great baths and Sanclair says, 'Oh!' Our breath hangs in the air like the steam rising from the hot water. 'Oh, it's a bath. It's a bath swimming pool!' and he rushes up and puts his hands in the water. 'It's hot!' He laughs, a bright laugh of joy. 'Maman, our pool wasn't hot was it, our pool was brrrr.' He stands up and looks around. 'Where are the trees? Our pool's got trees.'

When he was older he forgot about our pool. It's strange I

minded more about that than that he forgot about Gregor.

Gregor kept writing. At first I didn't reply because I was angry. Then he wrote, 'I have found my happiness here. I am so happy I cannot tell you, but the only thing that is making me sad is that I do not see you and Sanclair for so long.' He had never promised consistency or commitment. He had met plenty of people in his life and left them behind without a thought. He did think about us. I started writing back.

This is me in my twenties. A job in a pub. A job in a café. A job in a bookshop. A young mother at the school gates. A singer at the folk night. A red bicycle and a stripy woollen hat. Summer holidays with my mother in Teignmouth, Dawlish, Torquay. Sanclair making sandcastles on the beach. Sanclair playing football with Dermot in the Costellos' garden. Me cycling up the tow-path as the canal is slowly restored and the water comes back. It's now navigable all the way from Bath to Bradford-on-Avon.

Sanclair got a scholarship to the Catholic school up the hill. I decided to become an English language teacher. I studied hard. I had to take the course in Cheltenham. There are plenty of language schools in Bath and I think I've worked in most of them. I had a boyfriend called Alan. He said if I played my cards right I could eventually become a course director. But I wasn't ambitious.

Alan was ambitious. He owned a second-hand bookshop, not the sort with piles of paperbacks on the floor but the sort with rare illustrated books with gilded covers. He called himself an antiquarian book-dealer. I met him because for a while I worked in the bookshop next door, and this did have piles of paperbacks on the floor. Alan had a house in Freshford. He had an ex-wife called Melissa he couldn't stand. He was a serious man. He was older than me and I suppose that was the attraction. I didn't have any time for men my own age who just wanted to smoke dope and drink beer. Alan was passionately interested in books, food and cycling. We went on long bike rides together and had a cycling holiday in Wales. He cooked exquisite dinners, little parcels of fish in exotic sauces. He only ate tiny portions. He wasn't much taller than me, and like me lean and wiry. He had curly black hair, going grey, brown eyes, olive skin and a big nose. He said he was fitter than a twenty-one-year-old and he was probably right. We went out for a year.

There were two things wrong with our relationship. He didn't like me singing and he couldn't get on with Sanclair. He came to the folk club, once. He liked opera, which I can't stand. He tried with Sanclair but he was so stiff with him. He lectured to him all the time about how to look after bikes properly. I tried to keep them apart.

My mother thought he was ideal. 'What a nice man, polite and so knowledgeable, not good-looking, but I suppose that doesn't bother you, Mireille, and good quality clothes, proper leather shoes, not something cheap.' She encouraged it. She let me go and stay at his house while she looked after Sanclair. Committing a sin was acceptable if you were going to find a husband. I had to describe every single room to her.

When I stayed at his house I could understand why his wife left him. Everything was precious.

Even the food in the fridge was rationed. The books and the furniture were too valuable to be used. I liked him best when we were cycling, racing each other up hills and then freewheeling fast down the other side. Having a picnic in a field far from anywhere on a Welsh hill, with the wind blowing up underneath us.

We split up after a row about Christmas. He wanted me to spend Christmas with him, but I wanted to be with my mother and Sanclair. He's still in Freshford. He got married again and his new wife helps in the bookshop. They haven't got any children. He says hello if he sees me, but he's distant.

I think he thought I was an odd-ball. I haven't had many boyfriends. I'm not like my mother. I don't feel incomplete if I haven't got a man. In the end she had Jesus and she had him for ever. I didn't want married bliss like Caitlin, washing machines and wall-to-wall carpets. I wanted to be inspired. But inspiration doesn't mean stability. I discovered this with Gregor.

I'm swinging on a hammock in a patch of sunlight and a warbler has started singing in the woods. A fluid, floaty tune, it sounds wistful. There may be warblers in England but I've never heard them. I've heard robins and blackbirds, wagtails down by the canal and sometimes seagulls over the valley. Magpies, chattering in the conifers and the cooing of wood pigeons, not shabby ragged things like feral pigeons but glossy handsome birds with a sheen to their feathers. I once saw a goldcrest and there were greenfinches and linnets.

It's autumn and there's a squirrel on the lawn at The Heathers. Sanclair is watching it through binoculars. They're Tony's binoculars.

I went out with Tony for four years. That sounds like a long time, but he was hardy ever there. Tony was also a TEFL teacher and that's where I met him, at the second school where I worked. I saw him in the coffee break after a bad morning with a group of Spanish girls. He said, 'Look, they don't want to learn English, they want to go dancing and get laid.' We were friends after that.

Tony was good-looking. Short hair, blue eyes with a twinkle in them and one of those rugged chins with a cleft. He took nothing seriously. His job, his life, it was all one big gas. He had worked all round the world, but mainly in the Far East and he kept going back there. Indonesia, Thailand, Laos, Cambodia.

Tony lived in a friend's flat up the Newbridge Road. He

had few possessions. I liked this about him. He borrowed things and kept them, but he was also generous and he gave things away. He gave Sanclair the binoculars and they weren't cheap ones. He gave me his hi-fi when he left for Australia. Our relationship was like this . . . He'd come and work in Bath for about six months, save up enough money and then go travelling. When he was away he never wrote but then I would get a phone call. 'Hey! Guess what! I'm in Amsterdam/Paris/Prague, and I'm coming home!'

I liked Tony. Wherever he had just been he was always full of it, then he would get caught up with life in England and the holiday was forgotten. He liked bike-riding and football, drinking and playing pool. He liked films and we went to plenty of those. He came to the folk club and played guitar.

My mother said, 'He's not the marrying sort,' and no he wasn't. We got on best if we saw each other infrequently. More often than once a week, and we'd both get snappy. He was a restless man and I love silence, but he liked Sanclair. Within minutes of meeting they were outside playing football. We had a holiday together in the Gower and they were out all day surfing and in the evenings jabbering on about surf-boards and wet-suits. I left them to it. I walked up the long beach where the wind sweeps the sand stinging across the sand dunes and the wild ponies shelter in hollows. Tony had no love of nature, the elements were to be conquered and the world was full of entertainments. I wonder what he found in the East, but it wasn't beauty.

He left for Australia the year Sanclair went to university. When they said goodbye it wasn't like father and son. It was more, 'Yeah, see you around one day.' Like brothers who like each other but never remember birthdays and always forget to write.

Tony's playing the guitar in the folk club. He plays well, not just strumming. He's playing the John Martyn song, 'May you never'. He's wearing a blue check shirt and old jeans. He looks good in faded blue. His face is calm and although he's performing, for once he's *not* performing and is almost unaware of the audience. I have never seen him look so peaceful, not even when he's asleep, not even when he's having sex, because even then he's judging my response to see if I'm entertained enough. Asleep he has that half smile as if he's thinking up another joke. Tony's playing the guitar. I'm looking at a private side of him he will never share with me.

Autumn. Sanclair has gone to London to study computers. Tony has gone to Australia for an indefinite length of time and I'm at The Heathers. It's raining. My mother's at church. I decided not to go this time. I wanted to sit here by the window and play my accordion.

Mireille put down her notebook and lay back on the hammock. The sun was shining on her now, warming her, like the touch of a hand, and she lay there and let it. This was the hot afternoon sun with the bite of summer in it, getting unbearably hot as she lay there swinging.

The warbler sang its liquid song like trickling water, or was it water trickling into the gully? She listened again. It was water and it was unusual to hear it from so near the hut. She walked towards the gully. The rain had swelled the stream and it was now pouring down as if the hills were over-full sponges. She walked towards the Ferrou. The pool was as still as ever, but the water pouring out of it was a small waterfall over the stone and down the rocks. Perhaps when it was raining the water was cloudy, but now it was clear.

She dipped her hand in. She could see her face in the water and her grey hair suddenly surprised her because she had been thinking of a younger her, and she was still there in the past, aged thirty-five by the window at The Heathers. Too old to be young. Too young to be old. She looked away from the

181

water, away from her reflection. Standing by the Ferrou she could be any age, 35, 22, 18, 10. She could be ten years old in her own private place.

And as she had done when she was ten, she undressed and stepped into the pool.

Chapter Eighteen

Monday 23rd May. Morning

Felix, I've been thinking about you. It's early morning but it's already warm. I'm having my breakfast outside under the tree. I've taken the table outside. You would like that, you seemed to live in the outdoors and houses were places you only went to sleep, and not even that sometimes.

I saw you yesterday. When I swam in the pool. I dived under and when I opened my eyes I saw you, just your face for a moment and your hair swirling in the water. Then you opened your eyes. Dear Felix, so much can happen in a second. When did I last see you look at me like that, sometime in an early morning, waking up and you were there. You never got up in the mornings but you opened your eyes, and even if you didn't smile your eyes did. I saw you happy. I couldn't hold my breath any longer and I shot to the surface. I once said to you I would take you to the Ferrou and yesterday I saw you.

Today I'm tearful and tired. I couldn't sleep much last night. Isn't it what we all want when somebody goes, to see them again, just once? I used to see my father, sometimes so real I felt I could touch him, but he was never looking at me.

All the water in the world connects and this little pool runs into the gully, runs into the river, runs into the sea, and the canal water meets the River Avon at Bath, and the Severn at Avonmouth, and becomes the ocean. I'm thinking of water around the earth as flowing and shifting as the wind that blows into this valley. On a day like this when there is no breeze and the air is still, it feels like time has stopped, movement has stopped, but what movement is here that I can't see? High up, the air streams over the mountain peaks, and beneath my feet, moisture moves underground towards the river.

Thursday 26th May. Afternoon

I think it's Thursday. These last few days have been strange. So much is happening a day feels like a week, but nothing is happening that anybody else could see. I'm moving from one terrace to another, walking in the woods, sitting by the pool, eating when I want to, sleeping when I want to. It's like being a child, when a day was so long and an afternoon was forever.

I swam in the pool again. I didn't see Felix. I didn't think that I would, these things don't come to order. I used to see my father so often. I've never seen my mother.

She disappeared so gradually that when she did die it felt she had already gone. I noticed it first when Sanclair was at college. She started sleeping more in the afternoons. I thought it was because she missed him. We both did. The Heathers without him was a white, static place.

In the evenings the television gave the illusion of chatter and animation, but we were both silent. My hair started to go grey, a few strands at first, but in three years it was grey all over. I felt old. My mother said I should dye it, but I didn't want to. It seemed pointless, who would I be fooling? I was old. My son was at university. My lover was gone and I was left to look after my mother and do the garden for her because it made her feel so tired.

At university Sanclair changed. I thought at first it was the pressure of studying and the worry of having to support himself that caused it. He talked more about job prospects and career moves, he seemed to be obsessed with finding a well-paid job. All through school he had been easy-going and even when he was taking his 'A' levels he was more concerned with surfing and his bike than with exams. But he was a bright young man and he did well. At university he glimpse of success and it overwhelmed him. He said, 'I don't want to land up having to live with my mum when I'm thirty-five.' That hurt me, because I had stayed in Bath because of him. You can't expect children to be grateful but I never felt so distant from him as the year after he left college. He changed his name to Stephen and this underlined it as well. He wanted nothing I wanted. I wanted adventure, excitement and journeys in the mind. I wanted to be close to the growing world. I wanted experiences I could remember for ever. I wanted to try and feel the strange magic of the Ferrou in the most deathly-boring routines.

He wanted a job. He wanted a house. He wanted a car.

He started work with a computer firm outside Bristol and within a year had bought a starter home near Yate. Vivienne and I went to see it. It was a boxy little house decorated in shades of white. The garden was a pile of mud because Stephen was laying a patio. He had a large music system and a large telly. His bedroom had a bed with a red duvet. It depressingly made me think of The Heathers, but The Heathers had been designed by an architect around the view and the light. This place was jammed in with other little boxes. The view was of next-door's washing line.

Sanclair/Stephen. I wanted him to be what I thought he was, extraordinary. And he was. He was an extraordinary little boy and right through his childhood everyone who met him loved him. Even at the Catholic boys' school when I saw the teachers at open day they would go misty-eyed and say, 'Well, you know . . . Sanclair's unique . . .'

This is Stephen. Tall and blond with hazel eyes. It's Sunday and he's come over for lunch at The Heathers. On Saturdays he goes windsurfing, on Sundays he plays rugby and he's come straight from there. Just showered, he's wearing an

Arran jumper and jeans, his hair's wet. It's cut in a way that flops over his face so he keeps flicking it back. He kisses Vivienne and asks her how she is. She's fine today. She wants to show him a new mahonia she bought for the garden. He can have a cutting. 'Hi, Mum,' he says and I smile. He doesn't ask me how I am. He doesn't ask me if I've heard from Gregor lately. Vivienne attends to the lunch. We sit by the view. He looks at his watch. What I want to do is get my accordion and sing, but I haven't done that for a long time now. He looks me up and down. I know he thinks I'm frumpy. I went to see him at college. I met him in the bar, he said, 'I knew it was you. I saw you walking through the door and I thought only my mum could wear such frumpy old gear as that,' and he laughed. It was a hard laugh I wasn't used to hearing.

'So how's the job?' I ask him and he yawns and stretches and tells me about sales targets, five-year plans and an expansion programme. It's funny, the way he pokes the air when he talks is just like Gregor. Are gestures learned or inherited? I wonder what he has learned from me? Vivienne says, 'Lunch is up,' and I help her serve. She's made far too much. She has the appetite of a sparrow. It's a whole leg of lamb. It will take us all week to eat it. Stephen looks at his watch. He eats and talks about windsurfing, rock-climbing and the lads in the club. Vivienne listens and smiles as if he's revealing the wisdom of Solomon. Stephen eats two helpings and declines a third. We leave the dishes and sit by the window for coffee. Vivienne is tired. She puts her feet up on the sofa. Stephen sits on the floor. On the other side of the canal the cows are lying down. Does that mean it's going to rain?

The valley is going to be dug up soon for the by-pass and I feel the impending loss of this view.

'What do you think about the by-pass?' I say to Stephen, who has been listening to my mother telling him about the ins and outs of the Costellos. Dermot is in retail and is doing quite well.

186

'You've got to get from A to B. Batheaston's a bottle-neck.' He looks irritated that I've brought the subject up. He laughs. 'Mum, are you going to become one of those protesters? I can just see you in your wellies and your stripy hat!' His laugh reminds me of how Vivienne used to laugh.

'It'll be a shame about the view,' says Vivienne. 'Hugo built this house for the view. I wrote a letter to the council but they never replied.'

Stephen stands up. 'Well, I had better be off. The lunch was excellent. Thanks, Grandma. Bye, Mum.'

We stay by the window. The light is fading and it's not even three o'clock. It's November and the trees are bare. The garden is all colours of dingy yellows and browns.

'You didn't give him the mahonia,' I say to Vivienne but she's asleep.

I hated that winter. I hated the rain and the mud. I hated the sleet and the cold when I cycled to work. I hated work and the bored teenagers sent to England by their wealthy parents, and the same lessons over and over again. The gloomy house converted into the language school, painted all sorts of cheerful colours but the downstairs toilet smelled and the staff room wasn't big enough. And I hated the other teachers, who liked to pretend their work had a meaning when of course it didn't. They were there, just like me, because somewhere along the line they had failed to get the big prizes. And I was fed up with the folk club, the same backward-looking traditionalism, the same tunes. I had £5,000 in the bank and I was restless.

I wrote to Tony but he didn't write back. I wrote to Gregor, but he wrote saying the Baba had been unwell and the whole ashram had been in a state of anxiety for a month and now they were all facing the inevitable, that the Baba would die one day 'and then what would we all be doing?' Yes, indeed. I still didn't want to go to India. This was the money I had

187

saved over the last twelve years. I didn't want to waste it. I looked at holiday brochures. I looked at flats in town. I looked at cars. I even looked at motorbikes, but I couldn't spend the money.

It was April and the apple trees were in blossom in the gardens of Sydney Sussex Buildings as I cycled to work. The canal was a lively place now with hired craft and was navigable all the way to London. People moored narrowboats in small groups from the Widcombe pond to Bathampton. There was a line of them just down from the wooden bridge. About seven, some carefully painted, some tatty, some barely habitable. I passed them every day. Sometimes there was a person emptying water or tying up a bicycle. The gardens on the other bank were vibrant and the sky was a patchy blue.

The third houseboat from the end had a 'for sale' sign on it and a telephone number and that sign was there for two weeks. On the second week I stopped and looked. The boat was painted dark blue with fading pink borders. The windows were tiny. I peered in. I could see a little kitchen done up in an old-fashioned style with a lacy table-cloth and flowery cushions. There was a store and a polished-wood floor. A little gingerbread house. A doll's house, like my own hut still in France that I never went back to. And I thought, yes! I want to live here! I want to be a little old woman in a little tiny place and Stephen and my mother can go on having Sunday lunches till the end of time. Yes! I want to wake up and light my stove. Yes! I want to wear long johns and socks in bed. Yes! I want to be alone and cranky with nobody telling me I'm a frump or I'm not smart enough and nobody asking me what I'm doing or what I want for supper. Yes! I want to be alone.

At home I phoned the number. The boat was owned by an old man from Oldfield Park. He used to have holidays on it with his wife, he said, but now she was dead he couldn't manage it on his own. 'It's not la-di-da' he said, 'there's a leak in the roof. 1930s Sheffield, with a Seffel two-stroke. Seventy-foot. There's a water-pump toilet. It's not la-di-da but we liked it.' I said I didn't care about la-di-da. Perhaps your chappy can fix it up.' 'I don't have a chappy. How much?

It was £6,500. 'I'll get you the money tomorrow,' I said, and I did. I took out my savings and got a loan for the rest.

I met him by the boat. He was a grumpy old thing with a stick. 'They're all right,' he said, waving his stick towards the next boat up, 'but the rest of them, you'd be wasting your time.' He could barely get on the boat. Once inside he gave me a history of every single object plus all the trips they'd ever taken. 'I wanted to do the locks at Devizes, but Betty wasn't up to it. Before she went she said, "Ern, you do the locks at Devizes," but my leg's been worse. The engine's good. I always saw to that. I started her up last week.' There were cups and plates in the cupboards and knives and forks in the drawers. There was a gas bottle under the sink. 'Don't forget to keep the bilge pumps going.' He gave me a short lesson about navigation and where to get diesel and other provisions. I think he doubted my sanity. I was doubting it myself.

I gave him the money and he stuffed it down his shirt. He refused any help getting off the boat. He looked back only once and, when he saw me, gave a surly 'be-off-with-you' wave.

I sat in the little kitchen-sitting room and listened to the water lapping against the sides. It was late afternoon and the light was fading. I already had an urge to stoke up the stove and take away that damp, empty chill of neglect. I hadn't told my mother yet. I hadn't told anybody.

I told her on Sunday when Stephen came round. She reacted much as I thought she would, as if I were seventeen and about to run away with a strange man.

'Why do you want to leave? Haven't you got everything here? I mean has it got hot water, has it got a flushing toilet, how will you wash your clothes? Oh Mireille, what a lot of money to spend on a whim!' But I knew of course what she was really worried about was being left alone.

'I'll only be at the end of the garden,' I said. 'I can see you every day.'

'Why? Why?' She got so upset she couldn't eat her lunch.

'I'm nearly forty. Don't you understand I might want my own place?'

Stephen, who had been listening to it all, surprised me by taking Vivienne's side. 'Mum, don't you think you're being a bit mean, leaving Grandma without any warning, and as for an investment, a leaky old boat is not a good bet. You could have got a decent little flat, I know you don't earn much but you could have sorted out a mortgage package, I'm sure. I mean, can you work this thing? What do you know about narrowboats anyway? And what if Grandma has a fall and can't get to the phone?'

'Oh no!' wailed Vivienne.

It went on like this all afternoon. I was irritated by both of them. In the end I had a row with Stephen. He said, 'I mean, why do it now, Mum, buy a boat? Don't you think you're just a bit too . . .'

'Old!' I shouted. 'You think I'm too óld to have a life!'

'It wasn't going to say old,' he snapped. 'I was going to say weird, you know, odd. Well, you've always been odd, haven't you? Living in France and all that. Don't you think it's time you settled down, I mean you've got to be pretty together to live on a boat.'

Then I realised Stephen thought I was an incompetent. I realised he had written me off because I didn't have a well-paid job. Me living in France, cooking, chopping up wood, managing on nothing, singing, looking after him, meant absolutely nothing because he couldn't remember it. His memory of me was as Vivienne's unpaying guest. This was my mother's view of me and I had long ago ceased to pay attention to it, but this view had leaked into Stephen. We had all been together so long, of course it would.

'I have different values from you,' I said to him and to my mother if she was listening. 'Why is it OK for you to pursue your life and not me? Why is it OK for you to make decisions about your life but it's not OK for me to make decisions about mine?'

Stephen couldn't answer that, nor could Vivienne, blowing her nose. She sniffed loudly. Stephen sat next to her and said, 'There, there, Grandma, I'll make sure you're safe.' They deserved each other.

'Excuse me,' I said and left. I walked down the garden, over the bridge and on to the tow-path. I was going to spend the night on the boat even if it was freezing cold.

'Mum! Mum!' Stephen was running after me. We met on the tow-path. He scratched his head. 'Um ... look ... sorry ... I didn't mean to call you weird ...'

'Weird means different. We're different. We want different things.'

'I don't understand what you want,' he sighed.

'No you don't, and that's what makes us different.' He looked more like Gregor than I'd ever seen him, but Gregor would have understood.

'I wish you'd married Tony,' he said suddenly.

'I don't. I'm fine the way I am.' We were walking towards the line of boats.

'Do you think I should stay with Grandma tonight?'

'She makes a lot of fuss but she can cope you know.' I was standing by my boat. 'Do you want to see it?' I said.

Stephen shook his head. 'Next week. I'll help you move some stuff.'

I sat in my boat and listened to the water slap the sides. This is what it was to be alone.

*

This is what it *is* to be alone. Sitting at the table outside my hut writing my life history. Writing the choices I have made. Stepping away from what is considered normal.

Alone isn't lonely. Lonely is a gap, is a hole that can't be filled, is a dull pain that won't go away, is a longing for company, for anybody to distract you. Alone isn't that. Alone is the choice of quiet. Alone is the slow movement of silence. Alone is the thoughts streaming through my mind becoming these words. Is the scratch of this pen across the paper.

A moment, another moment, another moment.

CHAPTER NINETEEN

Thursday 26th May. Evening

The sun is just going down. It's warm enough to sit outdoors. Later, when it gets dark, the cold air comes up from the river. By mid-June the nights will be warm as well. Sticky nights with open windows and the cicadas singing, but now in the evenings it's cold enough to wear a jumper.

On the canal the mist settled towards nightfall. A thin layer of white and the puffs of smoke from people's stoves. The smell of woodsmoke, the smell of coal smoke, the smell of cooking.

This is what my narrowboat looked like. There was a large kitchen-sitting room, with a hinged table and red upholstered chairs. The seats were hollow and I stored my clothes in them. Steps led down into this room from above. The windows were slanting but the curtains hung down straight. Flowery blue and pink curtains, a bit like one of Jeanette's dresses. There were cushions on the seats of the same material. The stove was squat and black. It was possible to cook on it, but there was a separate cooker fuelled by the gas bottle which also heated the water above the kitchen sink. It was necessary to have the stove burning all the time, it was the only form of heating. Leading off the kitchen end was a small bathroom with a pump toilet and a shower. The water for this was collected in a tank on the roof. A cold shower. Definitely not la-di-da. Beyond the bathroom, at the engine end, was a small bedroom that I didn't use. It was the coldest room. My bedroom was at the other end, leading off the main room. I loved my bedroom. A large double bed, windows all round. Shelves for books and an oil lamp hanging from the ceiling. The boat rocked gently even when I wasn't moving. Under the bed were more cupboards. Betty and Ern had been fond of cupboards, there were far more than I needed.

At the back of the boat there was a petrol generator for the electricity and a bilge pump. It made a comforting sort of whirring sound. I didn't use the electric lights. I used candles and lamps. I woke up with the dawn and went to bed when it was too dark to read. I liked it that way.

When it rained, water leaked from the base of the tank into the shower. I tried to fix it with tar but it wasn't successful. Ern had left the boat clean, but everything was shabby. The boat was called *Arabella*.

My mother got used to the idea. After all I was just at the bottom of her garden. She let me use her bath and washing machine. I think she pretended I hadn't left home at all and I was just playing like a child in a tree house. On Sundays I did the garden for her and she cooked lunch for me and Sanclair and it was like neither of us had left. Her darling Sanclair and grumpy Mireille, and when was I going to buy some decent shoes, surely I didn't wear those boots to work?

But my boat was mine in a way that my room at The Heathers had never been. It was as much mine as this little hut, as uncomfortable and awkward and cold, but when I sat there in the evenings listening to the pump, the water and the sounds of the other people, I felt still and peaceful.

I'm not gregarious. It was at least two months before I started to get to know the other boat-dwellers. The boat behind mine was owned by the Bigbys, a couple in their sixties who used it as a weekend holiday home. Theirs was a smartly painted outfit with tubs of geraniums on the roof and much visible bargeware inside. On sunny Sundays they sat on their roof on deckchairs, like exhibits. If ever asked, they could talk for hours about canals, and locks and barge life.

They had been great friends with Ern and Betty and told me more than once that the sort of people on narrowboats these days were not the sort of people they wanted to associate with. It was a comment directly aimed at the boat in front of mine.

This was a long, scruffy hulk with old bicycles and a pushchair on the roof. Bags of rubbish and a pile of reclaimed wood. In it lived a young couple and their baby. They had long hair and dirty clothes. The baby crawled in the mud. They had frequent bonfires, invited their equally dirty friends, drank cider and banged drums until the morning. I could understand the Bigbys' irritation. I never spoke to them. I smiled at the woman, but she always looked harassed, straggle-haired, tripping over her long skirts, and the baby was always crying. Her boyfriend was not the smiling sort. Six foot plus with black dreads and a beard, torn jeans and a leather jacket.

Down from the Bigbys was a man called Jim, who was a recluse. His boat was the smallest and had a wind generator on the roof. The Bigbys said he worked for the government but I didn't believe that. He rode a bicycle, an expensive racer. I used to see him on the tow-path. He was a thin man with black hair and a beard. He didn't speak to anybody.

In the other boats was a changing community of students and bohemians, all young, all scruffy, who all landed up at the drum-banging parties.

Stephen helped me take the boat out for short trips. Devizes was the furthest we got. Canal life was a bit slow for him, but he liked the mechanics of the engine and the rigmarole of getting the boat through the locks. We learned by trial and error and a great deal of advice from the Bigbys.

We're setting out on a Friday evening. It's June and warm and the flies dance above the water. Just before we go under the wooden bridge I look up and see myself as a child standing there, waiting for the boats, when there weren't any. 'Hop on!' I say to my lost self and imagine how surprised and excited I would look. The child jumps down, 'Oh can I, oh can I?' and together we steer the boat up the canal towards Bradford-on-Avon. I start to sing. Stephen at the front of the boat looks round with a 'Mum, must you?' expression, so I stop. But I sing in my heart to my pretend child and the water and the trees dipping into it.

But by the end of the summer there weren't going to be any more trips because Vivienne was ill.

She was getting more tired and she started getting breathless as well. She hated doctors and she kept saying there was nothing wrong with her, but by Christmas she could barely get to the bottom of the garden and back. Stephen and I persuaded her to be examined. She had a degenerative heart condition. It was recommended she have a pace-maker fitted.

My mother was a coward. Being critically ill sent her hysterical, which didn't help her condition at all. We took it in turns to be with her at The Heathers. This is how I remember her, pale, but still elegant, in a cream angora jumper and beige slacks. Her hair wound up in a jewelled clip. Her feet on the sofa. Flicking through photograph albums.

'We were a happy family, weren't we, Mireille? Do you remember those parties at Bellevue and how you used to love to dress up and show off to the guests? What a funny thing you were, quite pretty really, and didn't Hugo adore you?'

My mother's version.

A Sunday evening at the end of February. Stephen has just left. In two weeks' time my mother is due to have her operation and we have managed to avoid the topic all day. She's watching 'Songs of Praise'. She can't get to church now, but the priest comes to see her once a week. She's humming along to the hymns and smoking. She never gave up smoking.

'I ought to go to the boat,' I say. I haven't been there all weekend and I'm missing it.

'Oh yes, off you go,' says my mother, 'they say it might freeze tonight.'

I can't believe she's letting me go without a struggle, but she looks contented and she's got her prayer book beside her. 'Keep warm,' I say and put a shawl around her shoulders. She squeezes my hand but doesn't look away from the screen.

'Make me a channel of your peace . . .' they're singing, '. . . Where there is darkness let there be light . . .'

I slip outside and run down the garden. The lawn is frosty and crunchy. In my torchlight the puddles on the tow-path are icing over. The row of boats have their lights on and smoke is coming from the chimneys. It looks homely and welcoming. The Bigbys are in and so are the couple on the top boat. I can hear their little girl crying and the mother saying, 'Marigold, you must go to bed!' As I get on my boat it rocks to greet me. Inside I light the lamp. The room smells moist and watery but I like that smell. I pile wood on to the stove and light it. If I can get a good fire going there's a chance the taps won't freeze. It takes some time because the wood is damp. My hands are black and I wipe them on my jeans. I make myself a cup of hot chocolate. At The Heathers I can stay awake until midnight, there's something about the arid centrally-heated atmosphere that prevents me from sleeping, but here the proximity of water and the always-gentle rocking makes me tired. I sit on my bed because it's the comfiest place to sit. I've got a patchwork quilt now, a tattered one I found in Walcot Street market, and all around the wall are cushions. I'm still wearing my coat. I put my cup down. The mother is singing to her little girl. I can just hear her. 'Twinkle, twinkle, little star, How I wonder what you are . . .' I put my head on the cushions.

The morning light wakes me up. I jump out of bed because I've left Vivienne on her own and she's probably gone hysterical again, called up Stephen, and everybody will be cross with me. I run up the slippery tow-path. The whole world is white, frosted, sparkling, beautiful and the canal has frozen. I run up the silver garden and into the house. There's a note on the table, 'Don't forget to lock the patio door.' My mother is still in bed. I look in on her. She's asleep, propped up on pillows so she can breathe. She does look old now. A little grey-haired old lady in a lacy nightdress. I go to my own room and flop on the bed. I'm unwashed and crumpled but stupidly relieved. I pull the duvet over me.

I'm woken by my mother going into the sitting room and exclaiming, 'Oh, what a beautiful day! Oh Mireille, it looks like a wedding cake . . .' I get up but she's already opened the patio door and she's in the garden in her nightie and slippers. 'Oh look, everything is so white, it's so white!' She laughs like I've never heard her laugh before, it's how Sanclair used to laugh. 'I've never seen the garden like this, have I? Mireille, surely it's never been so white before!'

But by Friday she was dead. Sanclair found her in the morning. He said he could tell she wasn't asleep because she'd fallen back on the pillows. He said she looked peaceful. At the funeral there weren't many people, but the Costellos cried. So did Sanclair. So did I.

I sometimes think I had two mothers. The woman I left behind when I went to France and the woman I came back to. I know which one I prefer. She was silly and vain, dependent and insecure, but she had been generous to me and Stephen. Yet there was always a gap, I felt we hardly knew each other. Oh, I knew how she liked a cup of tea and how she liked her potatoes cooked, but I didn't know what was inside her head, and what was inside mine only upset her. We baffled each other. When I lived at The Heathers I got to like her. I suppose that was a step.

We lived with her for sixteen years and she never complained. I had to insist on paying towards the bills and she spent so much on Stephen. She had money invested and she left most of it to me, but she left The Heathers to him.

In the months after her death I felt oddly calm. I moved the rest of my things down to the boat. I got the roof fixed. I decorated the kitchen. I watched spring come back slowly to the trees along the canal.

Stephen was in turmoil. He couldn't decide whether to sell The Heathers or sell his own house. It embarrassed him that he had The Heathers and not me. I kept saying to him I didn't want to live there anyway. He found it difficult to throw away her things, so I helped him. I got somebody to take away her clothes and somebody else the contents of her bedroom. All those beautiful clothes, silk shirts, suits, dresses, shoes (they wouldn't have fitted me) and her bedroom furniture. I barely went into Vivienne's bedroom. An elaborate chest of drawers, a bedside table, a standard lamp and a big, heavy double bed. Stephen and I watched as the last pieces were being carted off. Afterwards we sat in the sitting room and cried and cried. Vivienne had truly gone.

Without her it was easier to see what The Heathers was supposed to be like, a work of art. A white frame for the canvas of the sky. Stephen saw it too. He put his house on the market. By the end of March he had moved in and was already decorating and buying new lamps. It's his place now and it suits him. He sleeps in his old room but bared down to just a bed and a cupboard. Vivienne's room is for guests and my room is a study, which I seem to remember is what my father originally intended.

I wish I could draw a line there and say, so we lived happily ever after, because that spring I was happy. Stephen was feeling important and stylish in The Heathers and I was down on the canal feeling undisturbed. I cycled to work. I came home and cooked a meal. I loved it.

I wish I could draw a line because the next bit is tough. I'm sitting outside the hut on a warm evening soon to become cold and I'm thinking, I don't want to write the next bit. I want to feel again what I did then. Undisturbed, uncomplicated, ticking over, ticking on.

The next bit hurts.

My lamp is flickering on the table and a moth is flying around it. A large brown floppy moth. I've flicked him away several times but he keeps coming back. The flame will kill him and apart from killing him myself there's not much I can do. He's done it, he's inside the lamp now. He's flapping about madly. Do moths feel pain? He's a lunatic, he keeps flying right into the flame. He's done it . . . he went up with a fttt!

I thought he would put the light out, but he didn't.

End of May. Stephen has a girlfriend. She's called Judy. She's not my sort of girl. She has blonde hair and a made-up face. She's in marketing. She wears suits and little tappety shoes. She smiles a lot. Stephen likes her. They have dinner parties up at The Heathers. I let them get on with it.

I'm taking a group of students to the Roman baths. It's one of the first things I do with new groups. Most of them aren't the least bit interested, but when they write back to their parents it sounds good. 'Today I saw the Roman baths, the abbey and the costume museum.' I have been to the baths so many times now I can do it blindfold and this day is no exception. We come out into the open by the great bath and I stand by the water and say, 'This is a holy place. It's not just a hot tub, it's a sacred spring dedicated to the goddess Aquae Sulis Minerva,' and I make the students stand by the stream where the water gushes out and put their hands in the water. 'See, this is a hot spring. It's a natural hot spring. Our ancestors thought this was a miracle and I want you to know that it still is. The natural world is a miracle.' I, too, kneel and touch the water.

For a second I close my eyes and I think of that other spring far away in France and I hope it's as still and secluded and private as this place is public. I open my eyes and I'm looking into the eyes of a young man. Blue eyes, grey eyes, with a dark ring around the corona. My eyes look like that and it's a shock, it's like I'm looking into my own eyes.

I stand up and the others are waiting. I assume he's with my group. 'Well . . .' I say, 'now you know more about the goddess. They say this country is Christian, but we have holy places which are far older . . . Next week we will go to Glastonbury. Now, we will visit the abbey . . .'

The young faces look at me. Teenagers from Spain, France, Italy, Scandinavia, Germany. The young man is tall and has curly dark blond hair. He's wearing a brown jumper. I assume he's Italian.

We go round the abbey. I tell them about its history. We look at various tombs. Any questions? When are we going to have lunch? Why do the French students always ask that?

We eat our sandwiches in the square. We sit on benches. The French students inspect their meal distastefully. A pigeon flies over the bench and one of the girls screams as if it's a rat. Across the square somebody is juggling on a monocycle. The tall young man hasn't sat down. He's smoking a cigarette. He stamps it out and starts to walk away.

'Excuse me!' I call out. 'We're going to the costume museum . . . What is his name?' I say to the other students, but they look at me blankly. I run after him. 'Excuse me. Where are you going? We haven't finished yet.' I look down my list. 'And who are you?'

'I'm not with your group,' he says in perfect English.

'Whose group are you with then?'

He smiles. He looks like an angel, like one of the angels on the front of the abbey. 'I liked what you said about the water. I'm not with your group.'

I look at him and again at his pond-blue eyes. Of course

he's not one of my students, he's far too scruffy. He's wearing faded jeans and scuffed black boots. 'You live on the canal,' he says. 'Next to Barney and Rosebud.'

I say nothing. I'm at work, I don't want people knowing where I live.

'I liked what you said about the goddess,' he says and I still don't answer, so he walks away.

It meant nothing. The world is full of odd people. When I thought about it I decided I didn't care if somebody had recognised me. I didn't know the people on the top boat and I had no plans to include them in my future.

It was June and it was the solstice and there was a bonfire party going on outside. The Bigbys were away, which was fortunate, because the bonfire crew had started drumming. Pots and pans, bongos, lumps of wood. It was impossible to sleep. From midnight until four in the morning I lay with a pillow over my head cursing them. Daft, dirty, drunk crusties. Eventually I got dressed. I was going to tell them to shut up. I opened the hatch and stood on the roof of my boat. I had thought there must be at least fifty of them but there were only about ten. One of them was playing a didgeridoo now. They were sitting round the dying fire, the sun just coming up. They looked like a happy bunch. The man with the dreads had his arm round his girlfriend and their child was sprawled across both of them. I remembered being on the beach with Gregor, and remembered it so acutely, being young and care-free and anarchic, flouting convention and respectability, and what was I now but a dowdy old spinster with a bad temper?

But most of all I remembered singing and I missed it so much my eyes were tearful. I went back to the boat and got my accordion. I took it to the bonfire group and sat down. The man with dreads smiled at me in a drunk, sleepy way and I started to play.

A didgeridoo and an accordion. It's an odd mix. I closed my eyes and sang the old songs I hadn't sung for years because nobody wanted to hear them, only this bunch of raggle-taggle pixies up the canal.

The man on the didgeridoo has stopped and he's lying down. The only other person playing is a young man on an African drum, and I can see in the morning light that he's the same man I met at the baths. We don't make eye contact but we keep playing. He's not the first to stop. I am, because I'm tired. The sun is shining on the water and the mist is hanging over the valley obscuring the great scar of the by-pass being dug out across it.

'What were those songs?' he asks me

'They were the songs of the troubadours,' I say and pick up my accordion.

'I'm a troubadour,' says the young man and smiles. 'I'm a poet.'

CHAPTER TWENTY

Friday 27th May. Morning

Very early morning and the sun is up. I'm not sleeping too well. Is it because it's getting hotter and I'm changing to Mediterranean mode, get up early then sleep after lunch? Or is it because I'm thinking about Felix?

I was forty. I had grey hair. I had resigned myself to a quiet, solitary life up the canal, punctuated with small moments of bliss. Like when I listened to the water. Like when I made that first morning cup of coffee. Like when I sunbathed on the roof on my boat and ignored the cyclists, the hikers, the Bigbys and the other boat people.

High June and it was almost as hot as it is here. I was sitting on the roof. It was a Sunday afternoon, Stephen had invited me out for lunch with him and Judy to some smart place in town, but I didn't want to be smart. I said I had to prepare coursework. The school was at its busiest in the summer. But I didn't work. I was on the roof in my swimsuit.

Then a voice said, 'Are Barney and Rosebud in?'

It was the young man. 'They've gone to Solsbury Hill to see the protesters.' They knew some of them apparently.

'Fuck. I've just hitched from Bristol.' The sun made him look dusty. He wore faded red trousers and a patched shirt, which flapped in the breeze like a flag.

'They'll be on the boat tonight,' I said.

He didn't move. 'You're not friendly,' he said. 'You like to be alone.' He went to where the bonfire had been and lay down on the grass.

At six o'clock he was still there. I went to check up on him.

He was asleep with his head on his arm. I shook him. 'Do you want a cup of tea?'

We sat in the kitchen. It was warm in the boat even with the windows open. He put his hands around his cup of tea as if he were cold. He coughed, like an old man with a wheezy chest. 'Fuck!' he said. I was just about to start cooking. 'Are you hungry?' I asked.

He piled up his plate as if he hadn't eaten for a week. I was beginning to get worried he wasn't just a stray dog he was a nutcase. He didn't talk much and when he did it was pretty obscure.

'. . . I heard they sprayed the protesters on Solsbury with CS gas. What do you think about that? . . . there's more two-headed sheep being born . . . and the male fish are turning into female ones in Canada . . . sometimes I think I'm being followed . . . have you seen a white Cortina around here . . .?'

I wanted Barney and Rosebud to come back, quick.

'So . . .' I said, 'I don't know your name.'

'I'm Felix.'

'Felix the cat?'

He laughed. 'I can be a cat. I can be an owl. I can be a snake. I can be an eagle. I can be a fish.'

'And you're a poet?'

'Yes.' He took a bit of paper out of his pocket and read something like this, not the exact words, I can't remember them. I can't remember any of his poetry. '. . . Crazy dream bird what vision of your gorgeous moment turn the fluff of sunlight into some luscious dream forest of your pinky bed sheets, white delirious underpants, take them off . . . That was for my last girlfriend. I was dead keen on her . . .' He stood up and read the rest. When he read he was a different person, not lost but shining. I've seen that happen to people when they sing, insignificant mousy people burst open and fill the room, but he was doing it with words. My kitchen was filled with words like firework sparks.

'Phew!' says Felix and he's laughing and laughing makes him cough so he's coughing and laughing. He spins round the room in a little private dance and his bits of paper fall out of his pockets, but he's still laughing. He's as mad as a brush, but I'm not alarmed anymore. He's being passionate, being in the moment and stretching it as far as he can. I know what it's like and it's wonderful. I'm laughing too because I haven't spun any moments widdershins not since, not since, I can't think, but it must be running round the château with Julian.

He sits down and becomes serious for a few seconds. The boat is rocking like it's dancing.

'I want to learn the troubadour songs . . . they travelled from castle to forest . . . they didn't have a home . . .'

'OK,' I say, 'if that's what you want, but first I will tell you a story. Now you must be quiet and sit down . . . Once upon a time there was a troubadour called Avelard and a prince who lived in the grandest castle in the Maures . . .'

And I tell the story. He listens intently, his pondwater eyes fixed on me and one finger on his lips. He listens. It's becoming dark and I light the candles. Barney and Rosebud might be back but we can't hear them.

It's early morning. I wake up and Felix is asleep on the floor in the kitchen. He's hugging himself like a child does. I put a blanket over him and go back to bed. When I wake up again he's gone. A few days later Barney and Rosebud say they saw him at Solsbury. He was dancing.

I'm getting to know Barney and Rosebud better. He was done for nicking a car and now finds it difficult to get work. Though who would employ a surly giant with black dreads I don't know. Rosebud used to be a smack addict. She's disarmingly disorganised. Their boat is full of mouldy food and car parts. The only sane one is Marigold, who's two and a half. She helps herself to apples and clean socks. She's going to look like her mother, all big eyes and lank blonde hair. I ask them where Felix lives, Rosebud says he doesn't live

206

anywhere, he just turns up. The Bigbys are treating me like I'm a traitor.

I've got used to Felix just turning up. Sometimes he's OK but sometimes he's low. He sits with his head on the table. He doesn't change his clothes enough. He doesn't eat enough. He doesn't sleep enough. I don't want to look after him but I don't mind him being there. I say, 'Think about a place you can go to in your mind, your best place, your special place and go there.' I know this, I've been doing it for years. But he says, 'I can't. All I see is people's floors.' It was then that I told him about the Ferrou.

This is Felix's story. His mother married late, an older man who died before Felix was born. He was brought up by his mother and her twin sister. His mother's a headmistress at a girls' school in Bristol and his aunt's a probation officer. They're a formidable pair. He's a darling child, doted on and loved in a firm, stern way. Much is expected of him. But Felix is dreamy and solitary. Instead of his homework he writes stories and poems, which he hides from his increasingly baffled mother. He becomes a dreamy solitary adolescent and does badly in his exams. His mother sends him to a crammer. He finally gets to art school and leaves after two terms. His mother is furious. His auntie scolds him. He leaves home and stays with friends. His mother calls him a drop-out. He's depressed, he can't find work. He experiments with drugs, acid, speed, ecstasy. He's spun-out on self-neglect and chemicals. He starts writing again, poetry, which he reads to his equally spun-out friends. They call him a genius. They say he's remarkable and he knows he is. He knows that inside he is truly and genuinely remarkable. He has seen stranger places beyond the mind, beyond the heart. He's a traveller, a quester, he doesn't want to shut his eyes in case he misses something. The goddess has called him to be her messenger.

And that's where I met him. He was twenty-one.

*

Why don't parents understand their children? My mother, despairing of my lack of interest in clothes. Me, down on the canal bored to bits with Stephen's new coffee machines and designer toasters and Felix's mother disowning her odd son.

She should have had Stephen, with his company car and his chic girlfriend. We love our children but they are not like us, isn't that what we have to learn? People who are like us are not our children, don't we have to learn that too?

For me, Felix was a lost boy landed up in Never-Never Land because he had fallen out of his pram. I didn't think of him in any other way. I could see he was beautiful, like a Botticelli youth, but one with hollow eyes and a few days' beard growth. He had the most sensitive hands. Long, bony fingers and pointed finger tips. He used to put one finger on his cheek when he was thinking. He talked with his hands. You could tell what he was feeling by his hands.

For me he was beautiful, like an opium poppy with the thinnest of petals.

We went to Solsbury Hill to see the protesters. Barney, Rosebud, Marigold, me and Felix. I hadn't planned to go. I saw them when I came back from work, they were congregating outside Barney's boat with bags of drink and food. 'Come with us,' said Rosebud. 'Come and sing for the warriors.' So I did. I took my accordion. We walked there, across the huge scrape of land that was going to be the by-pass. It was an eerie sight, great curls of earth and flat dry mud, not a blade of grass in sight. There hadn't been any rain for weeks and it was like walking across a desert and we were those ragged people you see on the news from war-torn countries, walking to the nearest refugee camp with too much to carry and a crying baby.

'The goddess is crying!' said Felix. 'I can hear her crying!' and the seagulls above us did sound like that. 'It's monstrous,' said Rosebud and she started crying too. By the time we got to Batheaston we were all emotional.

The protesters were in a clump of trees on the side of the hill, living in benders and makeshift tents. They were trying to stop the trees being cut down, but this was the third camp they had set up. What saddened me most was the futility of it. Their earnestness and defiance were nothing when pitted against government plans and the police force. They were a mixed crew. Old men with grey beards, young girls with dreads, men with dreads, women with shaved heads and somewhere in the middle of it local grannies with Barbour jackets and tweedy skirts. Thermos flasks of tea and gigantic spliffs. Green wellies and bare feet.

Barney's friends were called Dog-ear and Paignton. Dog-ear wore a Peruvian hat. He had watery eyes and a goatee beard. He was a wasted old thing. Paignton was much younger, shaven-headed, coffee-coloured skin and the blank black eyes of somebody who had done too much, seen too much. They weren't talkative.

Rosebud handed out the food: bread, cheese and apples, and Barney passed round the cider. For a moment he looked like the Ghost of Christmas Present, all smiles and munificence. Dog-ear rolled joints and Paignton said to Felix, 'Give us some words, man.'

Felix stamped his feet, looked at the sky, then shouted out, 'The goddess is here! The goddess is here! Even in the felled trees, even in the parched earth, do not forget the goddess!' Paignton banged on Barney's drum and it went on from there.

Nightfall and a summer sky full of dusty stars. Woodsmoke and the lights of people among the trees. Drumming, but this isn't a celebration. This is a vigil because tomorrow the security men will come and move the protesters, and when they do the trees will be cut down. Big oaks, beech and hawthorn, they'll turn this little grove into a graveyard of stumps. I'm playing my accordion, slowly like a dirge. Marigold and Rosebud are asleep in Dog-ear's bender. Dog-ear and Barney are mindless on dope and Paignton is drumming like a wild thing. So is Felix. Wild, wild, they have wild eyes. Towards dawn I've had enough. I've got to go to work later. I don't want to see the eviction. I'm sad and I want to be alone.

That evening Felix taps on my window. I let him in. He's still wild, with twigs and leaves in his hair. I say, 'I know, it was awful, don't tell me.'

He shakes his hands as if there's electricity coming out of them. 'Paignton got arrested,' he says.

I say, 'I'm exhausted, I need to go to bed.'

He looks at me and says, 'Can I stay here?'

I point to the spare room. As I shut my door it occurs to me he might have been asking for something else. As I fall asleep the idea seems more bizarre and incredible, but then Gregor and I shouldn't have happened but it did.

It was early September and the beginning of my holidays. I hadn't planned to go anywhere. I thought I might take the boat out. Stephen and Judy had gone to Seattle. They were going to hire a car and get up into the mountains. The Bigbys had returned from a trip to Oxford and had already had a row with Barney about rubbish on the tow-path. Paignton had been released without charge, but he was 'shook up' and was staying with Barney. Where Felix was nobody knew.

I took the boat up to Bradford-on-Avon. The weather was still dry and the summer felt old, a wrinkled old lady still in her party frock. But the Avon valley was beautiful, just turning yellow, and silent. Beyond the fields was a wood. I moored by the bank to listen to it, the sound of the countryside. I stayed there most of the day, on the roof playing my music.

Then to my utter amazement walking down out of the woods came Felix.

'I thought it was your boat. I thought it was your music,' he said.

210

'What are you doing here?'

'I've been in the woods.'

'For three weeks?'

He didn't answer, he wasn't good at explanations, but he looked calm and radiant. He sat in the sun on the roof of my boat.

'There's a house for sale up there. It's empty. I know where these places are.'

We stayed there all afternoon. I played my accordion. Felix read poems. Other boats passed us. In the sky the swallows circled lower and lower.

I made some food and we ate it on the roof. The sun fell gradually into the most spectacular sunset and we watched until it disappeared behind the trees.

'I'm not going to make it to Bradford-on-Avon tonight,' I said.

We sat inside and sang more songs and made more food and drank cup after cup of coffee and talked and giggled and it must have been well gone midnight.

'Are you going back to your house in the woods?' I asked.

'No. People get suspicious. Was that an owl? Have you ever been to Tunisia?'

'No,' I said.

'Can I stay here?' He traced his finger round the rim of the cup and then put it on his cheek. Our eyes met. Again it disarmed me that his eyes were the same colour as mine. Like looking in a mirror. We are two sides of the same person. He was lit up by the candle and it made his hair glow like a halo. Scruffy desolation angel. Crazy dreamchild.

When I was seventeen I had been much more bold.

'Is that all you're asking for?' I asked.

He put his finger on his lips and smiled. 'I want to sleep with you,' he said.

In the dark my hair is no longer grey, it's soft and black and

211

you cannot see the fine lines around my eyes, but you can feel the bones on my face and you can feel my skin as soft as yours. You touch me lightly. Enjoy your body. Enjoy my body, but this time it's minds and hearts as well, opening like the heart of a rose that sings with its scent.

We are young and old and wise and naive at the same time and I am as alive and vital as when I was seventeen and I ran along the canal to meet my lover.

In the dark an owl hoots and I think I'm at the Ferrou, you're breathing like the wind in the pine trees and the creak of the boat like the creak of the branches.

Here I am at the Ferrou, sitting outside. The sun already creating puddles of warmth. Above me the branches creaking like my boat on the water.

CHAPTER TWENTY-ONE

I'm running out of food. I should have gone to the village today but I didn't. I don't want to see anybody. I don't want to see Jeanette or Auxille or Odette or Madame Cabasson or any of them. I want to be alone. I wonder if I'm becoming like Old Man Henri. Perhaps that's what the Ferrou does to you, it sucks you into its silence.

I have a bag of pasta, a bag of rice, some bits of cheese, olive oil and some dry bread. There are herbs everywhere and I have enough coffee. Surely I can last until Tuesday. Today a lizard ran into the hut, looked a bit surprised and then ran out again. A small brown lizard not more than six inches long. I think the heat brings them out. Today is the hottest day so far and so still. There's no breeze at all, it feels like the air is solid. I'm on the hammock in the shade and I've just been asleep. Days and nights, nights and days. I'm getting confused. Perhaps I'm becoming like Felix.

He stayed. I suppose he had nowhere else to go. We took the boat up beyond Devizes. He was a good companion. He liked to be quiet for hours on end and that suited me. He never got up until two but on a boat that doesn't matter. It's an odd life on the canal, chugging along, watching the fields, steering the boat, reading a book, listening to music, listening to nothing and then all the drama of getting through a lock. The locks at Devizes took for ever. Halfway through we just looked at each other and laughed as if we were going to spend the rest of our lives doing this. I liked that about Felix. He could tell what I was thinking. I felt transparent with him, it felt intimate and close. That was his gift. He understood people.

Felix, when you weren't spun-out on chemicals you were a delight because there was no time, there was just now. Isn't that what Gregor says the Baba is like, living in each moment and the Baba is supposed to be a spiritual being. Felix, you lived in a state of perpetual now. Imagination and feelings were more important to you than basic needs.

Barney, Rosebud, Dog-ear and Paignton, they were like that too. Totally inept at getting through the everyday, so defeated by form-filling, job-hunting, telephones, tax returns, bank accounts, the law and fast-moving, slick-talking modern life. Yet so passionate and committed to their ideal of community, so supportive of each other. I came to learn that for Felix it wasn't what drugs he took, but why. Trying to escape to a safer place of brighter colours, intenser feeling.

'Just go there in your mind,' I said to him, but he couldn't do it.

Felix, I'm thinking about you sitting on the roof of my boat. In red trousers and with your shirt off, you are turning into autumn colours. Tawny hair and golden skin. You're writing and when you write you grimace and bite your lip as if you're arguing with the paper. Then you stop and look around you, and I can see your face and it's as if everything you see is pouring into you, every tree, every cloud. Everything is pouring into you.

We came back to Bath like explorers returning from a fantastic voyage and there was Barney and Rosebud, waving when they saw us. Felix jumped on to the tow-path and hugged them. Barney looked at me and winked and proclaimed the rest of the day a celebration.

It was the equinox and there was a big party that night. The people from the other boats came along, as did Dog-ear and a huddle of protesters from Solsbury. There was music and dancing. The Bigbys kept pulling back their curtains to scowl at us. Even Jim the recluse popped out of his hatch like a nervous rabbit. Well into the night I left them to it. Felix as well. He was dancing to Paignton's drumming, mad celebrationary dancing as if he were explosively happy.

Autumn came slowly to the canal in a soft fall of leaves on the water and mists in the morning. I hadn't yet told Stephen about Felix. I had been up there several times to hear about their holiday in Seattle, and the wonderful coffee bars and how Judy might get a promotion and Stephen might get a larger car.

Judy wasn't exactly living there but she acted as if she did, fussing about coffee cups and did the cushions go with the sofas. As if I cared. They didn't ask me what I had been up to so I didn't tell them.

It was a Sunday morning in October. I was re-tarring the roof. Felix was still in bed. Stephen was walking up the towpath. 'Hi, Mum!'

'No rugby?'

'Knee strain. We wondered if you'd like to come for lunch?'

'Yes, why not?' Felix would probably still be asleep when I got back.

'Give us a coffee. It's nippy out here.'

I hesitated. 'I haven't cleaned up . . .' but he was already on the boat and down the ladder.

I followed him.

'Instant coffee? Haven't you got a percolator . . . I'll give you my old one. Fresh coffee is so much better. God, look at your cups . . .' He sat down. We chatted about cars, bathroom tiles and the garden. The important things.

Then what I feared would happen, happened. There was an intense fit of coughing from the bedroom and Felix stumbled out, stark naked. 'Fuck! Is that the time! I said I would take some skunk up to Dog-ear! Oh, who are you?'

'And who the fuck are you?' said Stephen, staring at him up and down.

'Felix, this is my son, Sanclair . . .'

'Stephen Sinclair,' corrected Stephen.

'Fuck, get me out of here!' Felix shot back into the bedroom and slammed the door.

'Who is that?' shouted Stephen.

'That's Felix, he's my . . . I suppose he's my boyfriend . . .'

'How old is he, for Christsake?'

'He's twenty-one.'

'Mum, he's younger than me! Oh Christ! Mum!' He slammed down his coffee and left.

Felix was bumping about in the bedroom swearing. 'I'll be back in a minute!' I shouted to him and ran after Stephen.

I ran all the way to the house and banged on the patio door. He didn't open it so I went in. He was in the study. 'I don't want to talk to you,' he said and turned on the computer.

'I'm sorry but I want to talk to you. I should have told you. I don't know why I didn't. I apologise.'

'Thank God Judy's not here. I keep telling her you're not that weird.'

He still wasn't looking at me. I pulled his chair and swirled it around. 'Talk to me,' I said in French. It was years since I'd spoken to him in French and he did look at me. He was angry.

'You're old enough to be his mum.'

'I'm not his mum. I'm your mum. He's my lover. Why is that a problem?'

He didn't answer. 'I don't understand you,' he said at last.

'I know you don't. Vivienne didn't and you don't. It's nothing new.'

'And can you understand me?' he snapped. 'I mean, I might sometimes like to have a mother I could introduce to my friends without embarrassment. "Here's my mum and her toy-boy lover." How does that sound?'

'You care too much what other people think.'

'And you don't care at all . . . Christ, you don't care at all, do you?'

'No,' I said and it was true. I didn't. There didn't seem to

216

be much more to say.

'Are you going to stay for lunch?' said Stephen.

'Do you want me to?'

'Not really.' So I left. I walked down the garden and back to the boat. I was crying. When I got inside Felix had gone.

He came back in the middle of the night and I only knew he was there when he slipped into bed beside me. 'I'm sorry,' he said. 'I thought you were going to throw me out.'

'I wouldn't do that,' I said.

'Yes, I know that now,' said Felix.

For Christmas it was just me and him on the boat. His mother wasn't talking to him and Stephen wasn't talking to me. The canal was quiet, even Barney and Rosebud had gone away. We got up on Christmas morning and sat there.

'Let's take the boat out,' I said and we did. Beyond Bradford we moored by a field. Then we sang and whooped and shouted poetry and banged saucepans and made as much noise as we could because there was nobody there to hear us.

I don't know how long it would have lasted, but we respected each other's territory. I learned he needed to go away for days, sometimes weeks, to be wild, and he learned that there came a point when I got tired of dope parties and Barney's half-baked conspiracy theories and the chaos and despair that accompanied their lifestyle. Sometimes I wanted to be silent.

We were a strange pair because we weren't a pair. We were two separates, but when we were together we were ecstatic and tearful and passionate and contented and calm all within the space of an hour.

Felix, this is you and we're in bed. When you're naked you move with a grace I don't see in you at any other time unless you're dancing. Sex is like a dance for us, it involves all your body and I love this, this celebration of tongues and lips and softer parts. You're silent when we make love.

But I love silence. I love this feeling of connection with

217

another person. You want me for what I am. Forget age, forget differences, forget what it looks like to other people. You want me for what I am. I want you for what you are.

In February I missed a period and I thought nothing of it. I thought, I'm forty-two, this is going to happen, but in March I missed another and I thought, Oh shit. I took a test and I went to the doctor's and took another test, but it was true. I was pregnant. I had been careful with Alan and Tony. I had been so careful, but when I thought about it I hadn't been so careful with Felix. I suppose I thought I was too old.

He was away. He had gone to a party in Oxford. I waited. It was strange because I didn't feel any different. Perhaps my belly felt a bit soft, that was all.

Felix came back. He was coming down off acid. The wall had split open and he had seen a door to a beautiful landscape, but everybody in the party started to look like his mother and he had freaked. He ran off and was picked up by a man in a suit who took him back to a hotel bedroom and tried to have sex with him, so Felix hit him. The man started to cry then gave him fifty pounds and said he was sorry, so Felix ran off before the man changed his mind, and he managed to hitch a lift to London where he went to see an old friend who had been a smack addict. They took some more trips, but somebody in the flat nicked his money, so it had taken him seven hours to hitch back.

This was a typical Felix story. I listened. He looked thin and hollow. I thought, how can I have a baby with this man? He put his head on the table.

'Why do you do it?' I asked.

'I want to go to a beautiful place . . .' He traced the grain of the wood with a finger. 'When I was little, the pattern on the table was an island in the sea and I used to go there in a boat and I could see the waves and the mountains. I used to go there . . . it was so quiet . . .' I left him there.

In the morning he woke me up with a cup of coffee and a

packet of biscuits. He sat on my bed. His hair was tangled and he was still wearing his coat. In the winter he wore an old, grey, army coat. It had no buttons. I was feeling queasy. I suppose those were the first signs.

'I have to tell you something,' I said and he swallowed. He always thought I would get fed up with him and chuck him out. Other women had done that and I could see why.

'I'm pregnant . . .'

He opened his mouth and stared at me but it wasn't a look of horror, it was of amazement and wonder. 'If it's a girl can we call her Inanna, or Isis, like the goddess . . .'

'Hang on. I'm not sure if I want this baby . . .'

'We must, oh we must . . . I'd love a baby . . . oh don't kill it,' and he held my shoulders. 'The goddess has sent us a gift, can't you see that?'

I went through all the objections. My age, low income, small boat, but he was smiling as if I hadn't realised how simple it would all be. 'Can't you see, the goddess will provide.'

You and your goddess. 'No I can't see that,' I said.

'And I will look after you.' He held my hands. I looked into his eyes and that decided it for me, because I could see that deep down, right to the bottom of his pool, yes, he would.

The winter baby conceived in the snow and born in the frost. Not like Sanclair, made out of sand and sun and the breeze on a hot day and the patterns of light through the trees, but a water baby made out of the canal kissing my boat, turning to ice in the night and hugging it tighter.

I don't want to write that we were happy in the spring and the summer, that Felix got a job three days a week in a pizza place. That Rosebud gave me a bag of baby clothes, a bit soiled but adequate, that I felt fit and well when I cycled to work and the people at work couldn't believe it when I told them, because to them I was an old bat who lived on a boat and who would want to shag me anyway?

I don't want to write that we were happy because it makes me cry.

I don't want to write that we were happy because when I wrote and told Gregor he wrote back and said he was joyful for me. I don't want to write and say we were happy because I went to see Sanclair to tell him and he couldn't believe it. He said, 'Mum, are you certain this is what you want? Are you happy?' and I said, 'I'm very happy,' and he said, 'Well, as long as you're happy,' and suddenly all the years just flipped away and I said, 'You were my first baby,' and for the first time in ages we hugged each other and for the first time it didn't matter that I sat on the roof of my boat and listened to the water and he went to the Conran shop and bought glass fruit bowls. I don't want to remember this.

It was early November and there was a hard frost. Like the song, earth stood hard as iron, water like a stone. A grey stone sky and a cold mist over the canal. I went to the hospital for my final check-up and Felix came too. I had twinges and backache and they decided to admit me because I was four centimetres dilated. At 2 p.m. my waters broke and it had begun, starting and stopping. What I remember most is walking round and round the corridors, and blue flowery curtains (it's odd what you remember) and the clock on the wall. Every time I looked at it, it seemed to be going too fast or too slow. After midnight the baby was showing signs of distress so I got wired up to a monitor and at five in the morning I was feeling those wrenching gagging pains I had completely forgotten. I shouted, 'Why the fuck am I doing this?' but Felix was sweet and held my hand.

The baby was born just after six and they put him straight on my stomach. A small baby with dark hair. Felix was saying, 'He's so beautiful, oh he is!' A still baby, he wasn't kicking and looking around like I remembered Sanclair had done. A quiet baby, he opened his eyes and looked at me and made no sound. His eyes were dark pits of silence. Then he closed them.

The midwife said, 'He's not breathing properly,' and they took him away.

We sat there in the room, which should have been filled with noise but was so quiet you could have heard a leaf drop. I could hear people walking up and down the corridor. We sat there and waited, and a nurse gave us a cup of tea and tried to smile and look reassuring and we waited.

Then the midwife came in and tried to explain what was happening, but I don't think I heard it. Felix held my hand and held it tighter. Then the doctor came in. He said, 'I'm very sorry . . .'

There's a medical name for it. The lungs don't develop properly. They tried to operate, but his heart packed up.

A winter baby. Conceived in the snow and born in the frost. He couldn't live in the air and the sun. A water baby.

It's a bit blurry next. They said did we want to see him and they brought him in wrapped up in a white blanket with a white dress on. He wasn't stiff but floppy and his feet were cold. A pale clammed-up face. Felix held him. His baby he would never have. He said, 'I think I've just grown up.' He was too sad to cry.

A dead baby is pathetic. A little floppy thing like a chick fallen out of its nest. Bluish eyelids and soft cold skin. I must have touched a fledgeling when I was little and now, here was another one. A bigger one.

What do you do when your baby dies? You avoid people because the first thing they ask is, 'How's the baby?' What do you do when your baby dies? You move from one minute to the next. One hour to the next. One day to the next. What do you do when your baby dies? You put all the clothes and toys into a bag and say to somebody just take them away. What do you do when your baby dies? You sit and wait for the pain to go away, but you're not sure that it ever will.

In the morning in the hospital. The same day? The day after? We're in a quiet room far away from happy mothers and crying babies and a nurse brings me a cup of tea. Felix has fallen asleep on a chair beside the bed and his head's thrown back and his arm's flung out as if he's just been dropped there. 'Would your young man like one too?' My young man.

On the boat. It's so quiet I can hear a sparrow chirping in the trees. Felix is sitting by the stove warming his hands. I can't work out what sound is missing and then I do. There's no sound of water. The canal is frozen.

Stephen's come to see us. He's dressed in an expensive jumper and green cords and Felix is unwashed and dishevelled. We sit round the table, not talking. Stephen flicks back his hair.

He says, 'Look, I'm really sorry, I really am,' and suddenly he jumps up and hugs Felix and Felix hugs him back. They keep on hugging and I let them. Two young men who have never spoken to each other but who have loudly voiced disapproval about what the other represents. I let them.

I love them both.

What do you do when your baby dies? You make all sorts of ridiculous plans about going away, to Spain, to France, to India, but you go nowhere. You sit and wait for the pain to go away, but it doesn't.

It was December and a week after my birthday. The frost had gone and then come back even harder. I felt cold right through to my bones. We had been together for over a month and the strain was showing. I needed to curl up and be quiet

222

and Felix needed to run around and be mad, but neither of us could separate. I could see the strain on his pace of being caring and responsible when he wanted to be neither of these things. I wanted to hear him laugh, more than anything I wanted to hear that. A wild whoop and a giggle of joy because I couldn't laugh.

I said, 'Why don't you go and see Dog-ear?' because Dog-ear wasn't at the camp anymore, he was in a van near the gasworks in Twerton and Paignton was there too, and there was a pub round the corner they all went to. Barney told me. Felix looked at me and I knew what he was thinking. I said, 'I'll be fine. I will. I'll go and see Stephen.'

Felix said, 'I won't go for long,' and I said, 'I'll be fine, I will.'

He was wearing his brown jumper and red jeans. He put on his army coat. He kissed me goodbye and I watched him walk up the tow-path, his hair bouncing, his coat flapping.

But I didn't go and see Stephen. I walked as far as the bridge. The world was white but not sparkling. The sky was white and the trees were white. There was a light fall of snow. The water hadn't frozen but it was as grey as slate. I walked back. My head was full of whiteness like the clouds and as weightless. I lay on my bed and slept.

He didn't come back that night but I wasn't worried. Or the next day but I wasn't worried. It was so still I could hear myself breathing. I could hear every creak in the boat. It got colder and started to snow and the canal froze. I thought I could hear it, the sigh of ice like a dying baby.

In the night I was so cold I curled up tight to keep warm. I thought, come home now, Felix, come home now and keep me warm.

I woke up and I heard the police radios. They were talking to Barney and Rosebud. I thought they were being busted. I put my coat over my pyjamas and opened the hatch. It was late morning. Barney was holding Rosebud and she was crying. There was a group of students from the other boats all talking together and pointing. Pointing at me.

A bundle in the water. A body in the ice. A young man found this morning. With a grey coat and red jeans and a brown jumper.

An inquest, a coroner's report and a funeral in January. The beginning of a year with no hope, and I felt nothing. When people talked to me it was like they were behind a screen. I hated the funeral. Felix's relatives, his mother and aunt at the front. Stern, smart women, and us at the back like beggars. Barney, Rosebud, Dog-ear, me and Stephen. Paignton didn't make it, he'd been on a bender ever since they'd been tripping the night Felix fell in the canal. And he did fall in. I never believed he killed himself because he was depressed, like his mother believed, or like Barney believed he was pushed in by some police-informer anti-road protester. I suppose you have to believe something. I talked to Paignton. They had been in Dog-ear's van off their faces and Felix started talking about France, saying he had to get back and tell me we had to go to France, and he ran off into the night. I know what happened. He was running on an icy tow-path, he just slipped and fell in the dark, in the tunnel, and I know what it's like when you plunge into icy water. It takes your breath away. And what you see underwater, the curling changing shapes. Underwater in the dark, he just turned round and went down following the darkness of his own imagination.

At the funeral I thought about this. He wanted to go to the Ferrou. He wanted us to go to the Ferrou and if he had made it back to the boat and woken me up, out of his brains, ranting and saying we must go to the Ferrou, I would have said yes.

There was nothing of Felix at the funeral. The hymns and reading his mother chose were not him. I couldn't stand it. I

224

walked outside in the sleet through the overgrown graveyard. Forgotten places. He knew where they were.

We're standing outside in the sleet and the mother and aunt are thanking people and I can tell which one is the mother because she does look like a headmistress. She has a fixed smile and a mock-sincere nod. The aunt is less stylish and she's plumper. Stephen's in there shaking hands also, saying, 'I'm Stephen Sinclair,' to anybody who'll listen.

Then the mother sees us. She comes over and says, 'Thank you very much for coming,' as if we are a group of fourth years which has decided to behave. Nobody replies. Rosebud is crying and Barney and Dog-ear look at the mother now barely disguising her distaste. 'I'm sorry about the baby,' she says to Rosebud, but no, she's not sorry at all, she's furious. Felix got into one mess after another and now he's dead, and it was just like him to get a dirty thing like this pregnant.

Rosebud looks up through her tears and says, 'What?' She's confused. I could leave it like this. The mother will go away in a minute and she'll never know, but suddenly I want her to know that Felix wasn't just a mess.

'It was my baby,' I say and the mother looks at me. She didn't even consider me a candidate. A grey-haired woman in black. 'Felix was my lover,' I say. 'He was coming back to my boat. He was an extraordinary person. I miss him so much.'

She's looking at me. Her version, the one she's been telling herself since it happened, now has holes in it big enough for her to see through. There's something about her eyes which reminds me of Felix, but Felix's eyes were full of wonder and mystery, not this hardness. She's not even ten years older than me but she's starting to look older.

'How do you do, I'm Stephen Sinclair,' says Stephen to her.

'This is my son,' I say and she shakes his hand automatically and looks at me, and looks at him.

She's beginning to understand now.

'Felix was an extraordinary person,' I say and across her face there's a flush of disbelief, and also envy, because I still have a child and she doesn't and the one that's dead she didn't know.

She's rescued by the aunt who says, 'Come along, Daphne, dear,' and 'Are we inviting these people back?' But before she even has time to think about it I say, 'Thank you, we've made our own arrangements.'

We sit at The Heathers. Dog-ear and Barney uncomfortably on the leather chairs. Rosebud still crying. Stephen hands us cups of coffee and tea. Dog-ear skins up and says, 'Is this cool?' but he smokes it anyway, and Barney skins up and Stephen gets out the vodka and we sit there and get more and more trashed.

I wake up on the sofa and I feel like my mother. Empty and hollow and what's the point? Only then I start to cry.

Every day until March. Stephen was patient. He let me come and stay at The Heathers because when I was on the boat I couldn't do anything. I couldn't light the fire. I couldn't cook. I lay in bed and listened to the water. Slop. Slop. At The Heathers I lay on the sofa and listened to nothing. Then I heard it, one night when I couldn't sleep, the trickle of water from the fountain. Water over rocks.

And this is why I'm here.

I'm here because I needed to find the next step and now I'm here I'm beginning to think this is the next step. This is it now, me and silence. Me on a hammock in a patch of shadow in late May. Me and the water. Me and the rock. Me and the air through the trees. Like Old Man Henri, I shall stay here now until I die.

I don't feel sad. I don't feel lonely.

It's so still now. There's no breeze at all. In the mountains I can hear the rumble of shellfire.

226

I've just finished writing my life story. It's a strange feeling. It can't be shell fire. It's a Saturday. They never practise up there at weekends. It must be thunder.

Chapter Twenty-Two

The storm broke in the night, sweeping down from the mountains. Dry thunder and flashes of lightning forking across the whole valley. It felt as if the hut was shuddering on its rock. It felt as if any moment the lightning would strike a tree and send it crashing through the roof. Then the rain came, hailstones at first like lead shot on the tiles and then a torrent of water. It was impossible to sleep. The tiny hut seemed inadequate protection against nature raging outside one wooden door. Mireille pulled her blankets over her head. There was nothing to do except wait. Water gushed off the roof, and now the thunder and lightning were coming in unison. Flash-boom, flash-boom. The storm was right above her. She wasn't scared but the experience was like a fairground ride, exhilarating but also sickening. She couldn't relax. In the silences she was waiting for the next jolt to hurl her out of the sky.

The storm roared round the valley then grumbled back into the mountains only to return with a less violent but longer burst of temper. More rain. Less thunder. And she had almost forgotten what rain was like, but here it was, two streams on either side of the hut spurting over the edge of the rock.

Early morning, in the half light and half asleep she realised the rain had stopped. She put on her coat and looked out of the door. A wet misty morning, not unlike a canal morning, the world was sodden, but it wasn't cold.

Water was still trickling past the hut, making patterns in the mud. The sun was rising over the mountains and it was the clearest she had ever seen them. In the distance above the mist of the valley they looked so near she felt she could touch them. The pink light of morning staining a bruised-looking sky. The storm had gone to the coast and she could see it, a grey volcano of cloud far away.

She walked through the gully to the Ferrou. She wanted to see if the storm had changed the water and it had. It was pouring out of the basin murky brown, iron red. The rock seemed to be bleeding into the pool. The water was more agitated than usual, turning in a spiral like a cauldron of soup. The Ferrou was a damp, dripping place. Sunless and eerie. It made her shudder. It seemed to be filled with the ghosts of a hundred dead people, all trapped there, all unable to leave.

She was dozing. Through the open door sunlight fell on to the stone floor. Somebody was calling her name. 'Mireille! Mireille!' She sat up in bed. She thought it was her mother calling her to get up for school. 'Mireille! Mireille!' But it was Jeanette. In her pyjamas she went outside and there was Jeanette by her car squawking like a magpie. When she saw Mireille waving to her she scrambled up the path. They met on the hut terrace, Jeanette puffing and blowing and Mireille in her nightwear but delighted to see her. Jeanette had a huge basket, which she hauled into the hut and put on the table. 'Oh, it's so steep! I'm not young like I used to be.' She sat on the stool and fanned her cheeks, 'What a storm! I was thinking all night, I'm sure she's going to be killed. There were two people struck down, one farmer out by Rochas and a shepherd in the hills, it's always happening. Thank the Blessed Lord you have been spared! We have not seen you for so long I said to Macon, I must go and see her myself. The Ferrou is a lonely place. You are all right, aren't you?'

'I didn't sleep much,' said Mireille.

'Who could sleep? Mama was screaming, storms remind her of the war and when they shot Papa. Two branches came off a tree in the square and the dog hid in the cellar and we couldn't find him. What a night! Now the dog's got the runs

229

and Mama's in bed and I said to Macon, I bet a tree fell on that hut. There's trees down in the forest all over the place.'

'Thank you for being concerned,' said Mireille. She stoked up the stove and put on the coffee pot.

Jeanette patted her dress and crossed her sturdy legs. 'I've brought you some things. Nobody's seen you for weeks.' She pointed to the basket.

'For me? Are you sure? Oh, how kind!' Mireille looked inside. There was a quantity of fruit and vegetables, cuts of cold meats, two quiches, a bag of olives and a cassoulet in a pot. A baguette, some local cheese and a packet of coffee. It was like Christmas. 'Oh, all for me? Jeanette, I was going to go shopping on Tuesday . . .'

'Tuesday! There's nothing to eat, I can see. What do you live off? Roots? Look at you, you're so thin. Come on, eat!' and she whipped up a hearty sandwich.

As Mireille was eating Jeanette put the food on the shelves. 'Being a botanist doesn't pay, you need another job, let me tell you, and one that puts meat in your pot. At least you keep this place tidy. Old Man Henri, he lived like a pig, but then what do you expect, he was a man . . .' The coffee pot boiled and she poured it into the cups. Then she saw the pile of paper. 'Ah, that's why you've been alone . . . and I thought it was because you've been going mad . . .' She looked through the papers thoughtfully as if she could understand what they said. 'So thorough and not too much crossing out . . . what a great deal of writing . . . I have to admit I hardly ever write . . . won't your magazine be pleased . . . they will surely pay you well for this and then you can eat like a queen . . . and dates too . . . an excellent survey . . .'

'It's a precious document,' said Mireille, smiling, and took the journal off Jeanette and put it on her bed.

'You have your father's brains and that's for sure. You have written a complete survey of all the flowers in the valley. It's sure to be published. I shall tell everybody . . .'

230

'You do that,' said Mireille, laughing now.

They sat outside on the wooden bench Mireille had made and shared the meat and cheese. Jeanette kicked off her shoes and bared her legs to the sun. Mireille changed into her dress. The rain was evaporating from the grass and the trees, rising in a steam. Jeanette didn't stop talking, the village, her mother, Old Man Henri, the price of meat in Lieux, the topics changing like the remnants of the clouds until there wasn't anything left to talk about and the sky was a clear pure blue.

Two women sitting on a makeshift bench, staring at the sky and the view of the wooden hills across a quiet valley.

'You could sit here for ever, couldn't you?' said Jeanette, yawning.

'I sit here for hours sometimes,' said Mireille.

'In the end Old Man Henri wouldn't come to the village at all. You must not be like that. Too much silence makes you mad. There's an *aioli* next Monday. If it doesn't rain it'll be the best one yet. Madame Cabasson has already sold fifty tickets. Will you come? You must come. You must come with us. Whitsun Monday at the top of the Col de St Clair.'

'Thank you,' said Mireille. Jeanette got up to go. 'And thank you for the food and thank you for everything.' Mireille hugged her.

'We musn't let you starve,' said Jeanette, a bit embarrassed, as she collected her basket.

'I nearly forgot. Here're two letters for you. They arrived ages ago, but I haven't seen you.' She retrieved them from out of her bra. She gave them, crumpled and warm, to Mireille, and for once she wasn't curious about their contents.

Sunday 29th May
A letter from Stephen and a letter from Gregor. Happy, chatty letters asking me the same thing. How are you and what are you going to do next?

I don't want to answer them just yet.

231

LA FERROU

CHAPTER TWENTY-THREE

Aioli is garlic mayonnaise. An *aioli* is a grand picnic where boiled vegetables and fish are served with garlic mayonnaise. The whole village takes part and in Provence it is as traditional and unquestioned as our church fêtes. The St Clair *aioli* was held every year at the top of the Col de St Clair, a wooded hill with a small olive grove and a little chapel on top. Perhaps once the occasion had been after a mass, but now the chapel was semi-derelict and unused. The *aioli* was always on Whit Monday.

Mireille walked, but most of the villagers went up in cars and vans and the zig-zagging road was full of them, honking to each other, bumping over the stones. It was a long walk, hot and dusty and quite uninteresting. The pine trees were so tall there wasn't even a glimpse of a view. Even at the top there was only one place that was clear of trees, behind the church, and from here the three villages could just be seen. St Clair, Rochas and Lieux, and beyond Lieux the dark ridge of the Canjurs.

It was a hot day and due to become hotter. Since the storm there was a feeling that summer had definitely begun and cicadas had started their dry song. There would not be much rain now until September.

The top of the hill was full of butterflies, yellow and blue ones. Blown up on the warm drafts of air, they danced among the olive trees. Also flitting about were the villagers, putting up trestle tables, laying table-cloths, opening chairs and emptying great boxes of food. This was a French picnic.

Cabassons were in charge and theirs was the largest table,

laid out with the *aioli* for those who had paid for the privilege to eat it. The villagers gradually took their places according to their family groups. Noticeably absent were the Villeneuves, the North Africans and Odette and her daughter, who never went to such occasions. The Blancs hadn't arrived yet but the Gregsons were there, on a table next to the Cabassons. Mrs Gregson saw Mireille and called her over.

'I don't think we've had the privilege. Richard, this is the lady botanist.' Richard didn't hear, he was explaining loudly to a group of his friends the fiscal advantages of living in France.

'Do sit with us.' Mrs Gregson was tanned a honey colour and her hair was two shades lighter than when Mireille had last seen her. She was a fit-looking woman in her late fifties. Her friends reminded Mireille of her parents' friends. This did not endear them to her. 'Do excuse Richard, we haven't seen the Bonvilles since Christmas. Sometimes I think we entertain all summer. Some wine? It's from the château. Please, call me Pat . . .'

Mireille sat down.

'Tell me about your book . . . and who's going to publish it?'

Mireille sighed. 'It's just a personal thing. It's of no interest to anybody.'

Pat Gregson looked bitterly disappointed. 'Oh, I thought you were a specialist.'

'No, I'm a nobody,' said Mireille. 'I love the countryside here but Jeanette has a wild imagination.'

'So there's no truth in this at all.' She was quite annoyed. 'You can't believe anyone around here.'

'There is a book and Jeanette has seen it,' said Mireille cryptically, protecting Jeanette. 'But I'm not a specialist. I'm an admirer of truth and beauty.'

'I see,' said Pat, but she didn't. She poured herself more wine. She looked around the tables. 'Don't you love these affairs? They're so Provence. That's what I like about living

236

here. When we first came here I said to Richard, who on earth will we get to know? But we've met people from all over. I think there's an English family in every village now and we know a few Parisians. Dutch people are nice too, so polite. If it wasn't for people like us these villages would be ruins, you know.'

The priest was blessing the food and the mayor had started a lengthy speech about modernity versus tradition, but not many people were listening, least of all Pat Gregson. '. . . I mean the Provençals are fine and all that, but you never get to know them. They're all family, and between you and me, well, they are peasants and they have no idea about their culture. Peter Mayle wasn't wrong, you know, and I know he was writing about the Lubéron. Personally I think he got his ideas from Lady Fortescue. I much prefer her books. We've got early editions, but I do believe they're in print again. Anyway, we've been here fifteen years and that's longer than the Mayles.'

Mireille decided to play Pat Gregson's game. 'My parents bought our place in 1963,' she said.

'Good gracious! Richard, did you hear that? This lady's family's been here since the sixties. Sorry, my dear, what was your name?'

'I'm Mireille. My father was Hugo Devereux.'

'What, the architect? . . . who designed the luxury flats at Juan les Pins, and that house, what's its name, that overlooks the Cap and is open to the public? Well of course we know about that. Richard used to work for Edwin Musgrove, he designed our swimming pool feature . . . Richard, Richard, this lady is Hugo Devereux's daughter.'

'Yes, Devereux and Crawford,' said Richard and for slightly more than a minute shifted his attention to Mireille and told her about all the other architects he had worked for. '. . . and of course Edwin Musgrove designed our pool. Have you got a pool?'

Mireille hesitated. She wanted to say, my pool is a natural feature of unparalleled beauty, but she didn't want the Gregsons anywhere near it. 'No,' she said.

'Well, you've got to have a pool,' said Richard and went back to his friends.

'You must live in the most superb place if your father designed it,' said Pat, looking furtively in her diary for when she might be able to invite Mireille for dinner.

'Not at all. My father died. I live in a *cabanon*. Excuse me,' for she had just seen Jeanette and Auxille arriving with two car-loads of the second best Blancs.

'What a peculiar person,' she could hear Pat saying as she left.

But Jeanette was overjoyed to see her and the mayor's speech had nearly finished so they hadn't missed a thing. Madame Cabasson started serving the *aioli*, and oh, was the fish as good as last year, and surely they had more vegetables, and Auxille could remember when they used to come up here on donkeys. Macon opened the wine. The feast had begun.

And did the château Blancs remember Mireille? Of course they did, who could forget that little boy, and Dou-dou became a great big hound and hunted boar and fathered dozens of other good hounds. And Badouin gave them a painting and it's worth thousands of francs but they won't sell it, it's over the fireplace. And Mireille's a botanist now and Sanclair has his own business, would you believe, and his father lives in the Himalayas and wears nothing but a yellow bit of cloth.

The sun was scorching hot now and table umbrellas added to the bit of shade under the olive trees. The mayor made another speech and Richard Gregson shouted out 'Bravo! Bravo!' but nobody else did. The church choir sang a few songs, all out of tune, and Auxille couldn't help remembering that her grandfather, the shepherd, used to bring his flock up here in the old days.

238

Mireille, quiet, in the bosom of somebody else's family, but enjoying it. It was a comforting place to be.

Friday10th June. Midday
Hot June and this is the Provence that people pay to see. Bright sun, blue skies and terracotta roofs. The wind blowing the earth to dust and the long afternoons trying to find a piece of shade. I'm by the Ferrou. A daily swim keeps me fresh and I've promised Jeanette I will go and see her twice a week. If I'm still here at the end of the summer I will need some work. There must be somebody who wants to learn English. Jeanette said why don't I sing for her customers, her café's starting to get busy, but I don't want to do that. I don't feel like singing.

I've been reading through my life story and one thing keeps occurring to me. I have experienced the fantastic. I did give birth to Sanclair by the pool. I did. It wasn't a dream, it was real. And living here for four years was real too, and so was meeting Felix. If I'm sad about anything it's not just the loss, it's the stretches of the mundane I seem to get stuck in. I read my life story and I thought, why didn't I go to India? I felt guilty about Vivienne and I was stubborn and proud, but there's nothing for me to be stubborn and proud about now.

There's only me. Sanclair is a grown man and wants something different.

'Children of light, why do you protest when I help you find the path that leads to your light?'

I keep thinking about this. My light. Being here. The sun on the wet crack in the rock. The still green patch of grass. The leaves turning on the surface of the water.

She walked back to the hut, heat-hazy and with a desire to sleep. It was difficult to sleep outside now, because of the ants. She lay on her bed with the window and the door open.

239

The breeze blew in, creating little dust storms on the floor. A dog barked at the farm . . .

A car came along the road and stopped. People got out and were talking, their voices came closer, one a man's and one a woman's. Mireille could hear them, not French voices, but English ones. 'It's got to be up here . . . but I can't see it . . .' the man's, and the woman's slightly whinging, 'God, these brambles!' For an awful moment she thought it was the Gregsons and she contemplated slipping out of bed and bolting the door, but the man's voice was younger, more energetic. 'Here it is . . . down here, look . . . Mum, Mum, are you there?'

Coming along the terrace was a tanned-looking Stephen and a hot-looking Judy. Mireille was so surprised to see them she couldn't move and stood there in the doorway.

'Mum, it is you! There you are, Christ, this place is difficult to find! Come on give your big boy a hug!

She did and he smelled of clean shirts and lavender soap.

'You look well,' said Stephen and she did, even though her dress was crumpled, she had bare legs and her hair was down to her shoulders.

'I wasn't expecting you . . .' She was still so stunned she couldn't think properly, but she was overjoyed to see him, she knew that.

'I thought I'd check up on you . . . you didn't answer my last letter. I thought I'd make it into a holiday. We've been here a week already. We've been to Castellane and Moustiers and the Gorge du Verdon.'

'Those roads,' said Judy.

'And we're staying in Lieux, in a reasonable sort of place. So we've come to St Clair to see you. We asked in the café and some crazy old woman went on for hours about how she remembered me as a baby, and some drunk bloke gave us directions. I never thought we'd get here.'

'Auxille and Macon. Then you didn't see Jeanette. She's

240

probably at Monoprix.' She laughed and laughed. She hadn't felt so happy for months.

They took the table outside and sat in the shade. 'Tell me your news, then,' said Stephen.

'There isn't any. Here I am. That's the news.'

'It's quite a place, isn't it? I love the view.'

Judy didn't look so impressed. The sun was bothering her. She had fair skin and her nose and cheeks had started to go pink. Her expression reminded Mireille of Vivienne. Thinly disguised distaste, which increased when Mireille showed them the hut, the bed, the sink and the loo in the woods. She gave them water to drink because the stove was unlit.

Judy sipped hers politely. 'The perfume factory at Grasse was interesting,' she said.

'Why don't you come and stay in the village? Jeanette's got a flat,' said Mireille.

'We didn't want to rough it,' said Judy quickly.

'Come on, Jude, where's your sense of adventure?' said Stephen, but Judy didn't look like she had any. She was trying to knock the ants off her legs. 'We were worried about you,' she said accusingly, 'Out here on your own. We thought you'd be back by now.'

'I'm happy here,' said Mireille.

Judy and Stephen exchanged glances. 'Come on, Jude, we don't want to bother Mum with that just yet.'

'Why don't you stay for dinner?' asked Mireille, 'I've got bread and salad, cheese and salami.'

'Brilliant!' 'We've made other plans,' said Stephen and Judy in unison. They looked at each other again.

'Another time,' said Mireille. There was an anxious pause. 'Tell me about Bath, then, and The Heathers.'

And Stephen did. A new bookcase, a new lawn-mower, a new gate to the bridge, and Mireille felt herself taken back to that part of the world that was so familiar to her, and so sad.

'And the canal,' she said, trying to smile.

241

'Those guys that bought your boat are gay, and after the shock the Bigbys got used to it. Now they're all great pals and they've formed a clean-up-the-canal campaign, which of course means the crusties, but when I last saw them Barney said they wanted to move to Ireland anyway. They send you their love.'

'Before I left they said they wanted to get together a collection of Felix's poems.'

'No. That didn't happen. They couldn't find any. Just a few bits of paper, but nothing made sense. I suppose they were in his head. Sorry, Mum.'

Nothing left of you. Not even your words.

Stephen stood up and flicked back his hair. 'Well, I think we better go.' He gave the car-keys to Judy. 'I'll be with you in a minute,' he said. They watched her pick her way back down the terraces.

'You are all right, aren't you, Mum?'

'Oh yes,' said Mireille.

'I can see why you came here. It is beautiful.'

'It was bloody cold in March.'

Stephen laughed. They watched Judy sitting in the car fanning herself with a road map.

'It's funny . . .' said Stephen. 'It's like I remember it, but I don't remember it. Inside, with the bed and the table . . .'

'Thank you for coming to see me,' said Mireille.

'And we'll see you tomorrow. Where? Here?'

'In the square for lunch. Tomorrow I do my shopping.'

When Jeanette saw Stephen she covered him in hugs and kisses, exclaiming inaccurately, 'My baby! My baby!' The café was busy and she announced to all the customers, 'My husband's aunt used to look after him when he was a little boy.' Stephen took it very well. He blushed and smiled and ordered a three-course meal, which was exactly the right thing to do.

It was a pleasant lunch. Stephen got out a map and outlined their plans for the rest of the holiday. Jeanette, rushed off her feet, still had time to remark how Stephen looked so like his papa and wasn't his girlfriend just like Princess Diana, and even Odette managed to close her shop so she could come and look.

Macon hovered by the table. 'He's a city boy, but his father was so strong he could carry twenty bricks in a hod. That German told a good joke. This one looks serious.'

Stephen bought him a bottle of wine, which was also the right thing to do. Mireille ate her lunch and smiled. Her son, although harassed, was passing the first test. Ordeal by villagers.

The only person who was failing was Judy. Auxille had plonked herself next to her and was recounting her complete memories of Stephen as a baby, plus everything else she wanted to recall. Unfortunately Judy's French wasn't up to it. She nodded and looked more and more bored.

'Is she deaf?' said Auxille to Mireille. 'I've asked her four times when is the wedding, but she doesn't answer.'

'I think she's tired,' said Mireille, trying to be kind, but Auxille interpreted this as pregnant and starting winking and nudging Judy, who responded in horror and pushed her plate away.

'Stephen, are we going to stay here all afternoon?' But Stephen and Macon had found they had one subject in common: rugby.

'Maman!' shrieked Jeanette from the café. 'Are you going to sit there or do I get my dishes washed?!'

By three o'clock the café had emptied, but they were still there.

'So . . .' said Stephen, folding up his map, 'we'd better look round this village then and look at this flat.'

'It's a shame we can't stay in Lieux. It was much quieter,' said Judy.

'We're here to see Mum,' said Stephen. Judy pursed her lips. She started rubbing sun-cream on her nose. She looked petulant now, like a little girl who hadn't been given the present she wanted.

'You don't have to stay here,' said Mireille. 'You don't have to see me every day.'

'But I want to,' said Stephen emphatically. 'All these people remember me. It's weird. I keep remembering little bits. I remember that church door and this square and . . . I know, there's something I've brought for you.' He ran off to his car.

He came back with the accordion. 'It was a pain getting it over here, but I thought you might like it.'

He gave it to Mireille and she held it gently as if it were valuable, because to her it was.

'Oh Stephen, I haven't played this for months,' and the last time was a starry evening on the roof of her boat with Felix. A tear dribbled down her cheek.

'I thought it might cheer you up,' said Stephen.

'Thank you,' said Mireille and smiled. 'It has.' She wiped her eyes.

'My father gave you that,' said Macon. 'My father gave her that, for nothing.'

A red accordion with ivory and brass decorations. She undid it and put her fingers on the keys. She played a chord, a minor one, a sad one, then another. Jeanette and Auxille sat down. She closed her eyes.

−O *Magali, se tu te fas*	'O Magali, and if cold clay
La pauro morto,	Thou make thyself, and dead,
Adounc la terro me	Earth I'll become, and there
farai,	thou'lt be,
Aqui t'aurai!	At last, for me.'

She didn't sing but she played the tune she hadn't played in that square for twenty years.

She opened her eyes. Stephen was drumming on the table. Even Judy was listening.

She stopped. 'Can you take me home?' she said to Stephen, 'I'd like to go home now.'

A week of trips, car rides and lunches out. Mireille had seen more of the area than she'd ever seen in all the time she'd lived there. Stephen was becoming more enamoured of the countryside of his birth. He wanted to see everything in the guide book. He was already planning to stay another week. But Judy wasn't happy. Hot and bored, she was behaving like Vivienne, except Vivienne had excellent French and an icy polish. The flat was poky and airless. She hated the hairpin roads. Her shoulders were burnt and wherever they went she could only sit there like a dummy while Stephen and Mireille bantered with the waiters.

At the end of the week Stephen came to see Mireille on his own.

She was sitting outside. She had been playing her accordion. Stephen looked glum and fed up.

'I thought today was Avignon and all points due west.'

'Judy's got a headache.' He sat on the bench next to Mireille and undid his shirt. 'I'm going to take her to the airport tomorrow.'

'And what about you?'

'I want to stay another week.' He sighed and stretched out his arms. 'We had a row. She said I need to be here with you. Perhaps she's right. You see, I keep remembering things. I went to the baker's and I remembered it, and inside the church. It's like a dream I've forgotten. It's difficult to explain.'

'Tell me what you remember?' said Mireille, in French.

Stephen laughed, 'Oh yes, and I can understand the accent and that pisses her off as well. She likes organising things. She likes being in control and she's not.'

He picked a snail shell up off the ground. 'Shells . . .' he said, in French. 'I remember putting them in my pocket . . . and red plastic sandals . . . outside with a bowl of water, washing shells and putting them in a line.'

'They're still there,' said Mireille and showed him. A line of shells along the far wall of the hut. Stephen knelt down and picked one up. 'I put them there . . . that is so weird . . .' He was behind the hut under the *cannise*, he could see the hammock and the woods. 'I don't remember the hammock.'

'No, that's new.'

'I remember it raining and hiding under the trees. I'm wearing wellies and I've got a little dog and I put him in my coat and I sleep with him at night and he licks my face.' He walked towards the hammock. 'I remember it being really hot and I went to play in the woods then I think . . . no I'm muddling this up with something else . . . I remember going swimming . . . and it's not a river and it's not a swimming pool . . . Is there a pool here?'

'Come with me,' said Mireille and she led him up the gully towards the Ferrou.

They stood there looking at the rock and the still pool of water shaded by the trees.

'God, I dream about this place,' he said in a whisper. 'I didn't think it was real.' He put his hands in the water and washed his face. 'Did I swim in it?'

'We used to swim in it all the time.'

'I don't remember you being there. I was swimming on my own . . . I didn't think it was real.' He looked like a man who had just discovered fairyland.

'This is the Ferrou,' said Mireille. 'This is why I'm here.'

CHAPTER TWENTY-FOUR

Tuesday 21st June. Afternoon

Stephen's here. He's in the woods making a shelter for the toilet. He hasn't learned that you don't do things when it's hot, but I know this and I'm inside resting. He came here ten days ago. He was with Judy and they were having a holiday but it turned into something else. She went home on Saturday and there were tears and bad scenes. In the end I felt sorry for her. She's too urban and English for this place. She wanted a nice sight-seeing trip and for one week we were complete tourists. I've seen so many hill-top villages I can't remember which one is which. I hate being a tourist because you are just looking, just consuming. I want to be settled. I want to be absorbed. She couldn't do that. She couldn't understand the French and that's vital here. You have to speak French. And Stephen has started to discover his roots.

For the first time in his adult life he's asking me 'Where did we sleep? What did we do? What did we eat?' when he was little. Judy's not a part of this at all and she was right, he does need to do it on his own. They were up at Jeanette's flat for a week but now he's down here. It was his choice.

It's odd having him here. He's not my little boy anymore. He's a great big man, eating man quantities of food and planning projects and walks in a man-sized way. But then I see it. Making a shelter for the loo is a game which involves banging and sawing and much puffing, and I see it, he's four years old making dens in the woods.

Now he's gone brown in the sun with a few days' stubble and his hair's losing that office-cut look, he does so look like

Gregor. I read Gregor's last letter again and I think, he's in his sixties now and in every single letter he's written, 'Come and see me.' He's never stopped saying that. I've been thinking, isn't it time I swallowed my pride and saw him? I don't mind anymore that he chose the Baba and not us. Stephen has no memories of him and that does make me feel sad. Last night I woke up and Stephen was asleep on the floor. He was making a sort of clucking noise and I swear he used to do that when he was small. Just for a second it felt like we were all together again.

Stephen came down out of the woods, dripping with sweat, and saying, 'God, it's so bloody hot. I need a swim.' He came back wet and refreshed and they sat inside. Even with the door open the hut wasn't cool, but at least inside was out of the sun. 'Is this the botanical survey Jeanette raves about?' asked Stephen, picking up Mireille's file of papers. 'I thought she was making it up.'

'It's a journal,' said Mireille and politely took it off him. She put it on her bed. It wasn't for him to read.

Stephen shook the water out of his hair. 'I meant to tell you before, but I'll tell you now. I'm afraid I read all of Dad's letters.'

'Why should that make you afraid?'

'Well, they were private, weren't they? When you were away I was sorting through stuff and I found them in a drawer. I read them all.'

'Then you will know that whatever he wrote to me he wrote to you as well.'

Stephen poured himself a glass of water and sat down. 'Yes . . . I gathered that . . . you used to read them out, didn't you?'

'You never paid much attention.'

'I know . . . I used to think . . . why doesn't he come and see us . . . why does he stay in India . . . I thought he was a sod.'

'I thought that too,' said Mireille. 'Loads of times. I don't think that now. He did what he felt he needed to do. I respect him for that.'

'When I read his letters, I thought, he's a decent bloke, I wouldn't mind having a drink with him.'

'Gregor is a decent bloke,' said Mireille. Stephen stood in the doorway, looking out across the valley, hot in the afternoon sun.

'He never stopped asking about me.' He stood there. A young man in shorts, walking boots and a pale blue shirt.

'I'm going to light the stove. Do you want some coffee?'

'I want to go to India. I want to go and see Dad.'

'I've been thinking that myself,' said Mireille.

The afternoon slipped into the evening and they were still talking, about Gregor mostly, what he was like, what he did, but Mireille knew she was only a small episode in his life and there was plenty about him she didn't know. The more they talked, the more it became obvious to her she had been putting off going to India for far too long. If Felix had lived. If the baby had lived. But that was another stream and she thought about the rainwater pouring down the hill in so many streams all to land up in the muddy Rioux.

The lamp was flickering on the table and the moths came in and flew around it.

'Yes, I want to go to India, but I want to go to Australia and New Zealand and Thailand and the States . . . I could look up Tony.' Mireille had not seen Stephen so excited about anything.

'This is more than a holiday you're talking about, isn't it?'

Stephen wrinkled his face. 'Give up the job? That's a big one . . . but you do it, don't you? You manage to survive.'

'I don't have your lifestyle.'

That made him think. 'But you don't need these things, do you? Things. You can have too many things.'

'Sell The Heathers.'

Stephen looked at her. She had suggested something outrageous. 'I'm not ready for that. I like The Heathers.'

'Let The Heathers. For six months. You would make money out of it.'

This was a new situation. Mireille giving Stephen advice about how to manage money.

'Yes, through an agency. They specialise in these things don't they. . . ? Mum, you're quite shrewd, aren't you?'

'I like to think I am.' And they both thought about their own situations.

'I reckon I could go to India for Christmas. I could have it sorted by then,' said Stephen.

'And Judy?'

He grimaced. 'She'll hate the idea. She'll think I've gone mad.'

'Sometimes you have to leave people behind,' said Mireille and they were both quiet because they both knew how it felt to be left behind.

'And you?' said Stephen. 'What are your plans?'

'There's nothing stopping me moving forwards anymore.' When she said it she could feel Felix and the baby flying over the hut, towards the mountains. Flying with love. Flying with joy.

'Mum, are you all right?' asked Stephen and squeezed her hand.

'I am now,' said Mireille and squeezed back.

Stephen's birthday and the next day he was going back to England. Browner and a year older, but he had grown up more in that week. They were sitting by the pool. It had been a quiet day. No expensive presents or parties. Mireille had given him a leather bracelet she found in the market and they had lunch in the café. There was the sadness of things ending but also anticipation. They were going to meet again for Christmas in India.

Talking seemed unnecessary because the trickling water

provided all the varying patterns of speech. Light falling through the trees was filtered as green as water and it was impossible to tell if an hour had passed or two or three.

Stephen, who had been lying on the grass, sat up. 'Has anybody ever been up that rock?' he asked, and when he said it Mireille felt an old fear in her stomach.

'Yes . . . ' she said, but before she could elaborate he had put on his boots and was planning the climb. 'Won't take me a minute,' and he was up.

He didn't call to Mireille to follow him and he didn't look down at her. For the third time in her life she watched somebody she loved climb the rock and she was as anxious as when she was ten and her father became smaller and smaller.

At the top he was a small shape with the sun behind him. His hands on his hips looking at the view. It seemed to take a long time before he was on the ground again.

He was an experienced climber but he was distressed.

'Were you frightened?' she asked and sat on the grass next to him. He undid his boots and his fingers were shaking.

'I've done that before, haven't I? At the top I remembered . . . seeing the sea and the villages like you're on top of the world . . . I didn't go up there with you, did I?'

'It's hard to get me up a ladder,' said Mireille.

'I was on top of somebody's shoulders. Then they put me down and I was holding their hand. They seemed huge but I felt absolutely safe, holding his hand on top of the world . . .'

'That was Gregor,' said Mireille.

'I remember my dad,' said Stephen.

Sunday 26th June. Afternoon

Something's happened. A son has found his father and a mother has found her son and I am going to meet Gregor in India for Christmas.

Stephen went yesterday and now I'm alone. I don't mind. I like being alone.

I'm going to India but I'm not quite sure when. It might be at the end of the summer. I am going to meet Gregor in India for Christmas and so is Sanclair.

Full circle.

Tuesday 28th June. After lunch
I went to the mini-market today and I walked all round the village. I thought, I love this place. It was a hot walk back through the woods and now I'm by the pool. I seem to spend every day by the pool.

Wednesday 29th June. Morning
I'm by the pool . . .

She put down her pen and picked up her accordion. It was music she wanted, not words. She played every song she knew, one after the other and the sound of it echoed round the grove of the Ferrou. Suddenly the sun flashed in her eye. It had just risen over the top of the rock.

She stood up and the sun was shining in the pool and the pool was a bowl of light.

The rock stood in front of her like a challenge and she knew she had to do it now, like a flash.

Like when she ran down the tow-path to Gregor, like when she looked into Felix's eyes, like when she got up off Stephen's sofa and put an ad in the paper to sell her houseboat.

This was the energy that moved her on and she needed it now.

She put her hands on the rock, and one foot, and hauled herself up. Stephen said it was an easy climb and it did look easy, over the craggy limestone towards the split, if you weren't terrified and your hands weren't shaking and sweaty.

Don't look up. And she didn't. She looked at her hands and the next handhold and the little plants growing out of the

252

rock. Succulents with pink flowers and leaves like scales. Tiny gardens on each ledge. On the grey rock.

Don't look down. She was halfway up and she looked down once but the rock started to sway. This was her old nightmare, being hurled down from a great height, and she couldn't stop the falling feeling. Her hands were sweating more and her legs were shaking. She had to go on. There was nobody to rescue her.

Don't look down. I went out in the rain and it wasn't a monster it was a pig. A fat piggy-wig-wig. I was so scared and it was all for nothing. Hugo and Gregor and little Sanclair got up here and they were no rock-climbers. It's not hard.

She turned towards the split and climbed slowly on without a pause. The rock was darker here and wetter, but the footholds were easier. The rock smelled wet. Smelled of wet earth and moss. Her face was pressed against it. She could hear the water trickling, like a lullaby. Sung by ghosts.

Don't look up.

There was a breeze now and plants, shrubs, to cling on to, broom, sage brush, the soil drier and crumbly. She was heaving and hauling herself up and up and it felt like her heart was bursting out of her body and everybody she had ever loved was singing in her ears.

You can do it. You can do it. And the ghosts were singing. You can do it.

And the last voice was Felix's, soft and calm, a stream of magical dancing words.

You've done it.

She was lying flat on her stomach, on the bristly grass in the sun.

She couldn't move. She lay there for some time. Ants crawled over her hands. Her fingers were scratched and bleeding and trembling. It felt like all of her was trembling.

She got on to her knees and looked up. She was looking at gorse and broom going up the hill.

Too high for pine trees. She turned round slowly.

Ahh . . !

The view took her breath away. In the distance the sea was a faint strip of blue and the mountains, indistinct but shimmering like fairy mountains, white castles. In front of her was the red ruined castle of Lieux on its hill and behind her to the right the church clock tower of St Clair. To her left the dark rock of Rochas and all of this above the tree tops as if it were swimming.

She stood up and for a moment everything did swim and she held her breath and looked down.

The round pool of the Ferrou holding the sun. A bowl of light in a grove of darkness. Not water but fire. The more she looked the more she could see it. The pool was the centre.

The three villages ringed around it. A beautiful natural pattern, the order exquisite, and the pool was pouring out light towards the Rioux, which roped around all of them.

The strange order of Nature. This remarkable sight unknown and forgotten except by those who had stood there. For her father it was a trick of the light, for Gregor it was the sign he needed, for Sanclair it was the link with his father and for Old Man Henri it was what kept him there for the rest of his life.

The guardian of the Ferrou. She understood the painting now. Thank you. Thank you. She was chosen. It awed her because she was a guardian too. She looked down again and the sun was passing out of the pool and the moment was soon to be lost but she had seen it.

Now she understood.

Friday 1st July. Evening

This is my last day here. Tomorrow I take the bus to Draguignan and then to the airport.

I'm going to India. I shall take my accordion. I shall never forget to play it.

I shall remember, there is always the fantastic. I climbed the rock.

Today I said goodbye to Jeanette. She cried and so did I because she is my true friend and here is my home. I shall come back here but now I need to go travelling.

This is my last night. It's warm outside and I'm sitting by the table and the moths are flying round the light. There's a smell of thyme, lavender, sage, pine resin and the smell of the river coming up from the valley.

I shall put this journal in the tin trunk but I shall keep writing. My life fits in a tin trunk but there are more stories to be written.

I shall remember, there is always the fantastic.

I climbed the rock.

Early morning on a hot day in July. A woman was waiting for a bus in a village in the south of France. She was a tall woman with grey hair but what was most striking about her was a sense of confidence and purpose that made her radiant.

It was a rare sort of happiness.

SELFISH PEOPLE   Lucy English

Leah, 28, mother of three, married for 10 years to burned-out Al, is in love with Bailey, the feckless hulk who teaches basketball at the Community Project in Bristol where she works. Their courtship is conducted over late-night drinking sessions, loved-up parties and football videos. This is love on the dole – anarchic, destructive love that forces Leah to do the unthinkable and walk out on her children.

£6.99   1 85702 763 9

All Fourth Estate books are available from your local bookshop, or can be ordered direct (FREE UK p&p) from:

Fourth Estate, Book Service By Post, PO Box 29, Douglas, I-O-M, IM99 1BQ

Credit cards accepted.

Tel: 01624 836000   Fax: 01624 670923

Or visit the Fourth Estate website at:
www.4thestate.co.uk

*Prices are correct at time of going to press, but may be subject to change. Please state when ordering if you do **not** wish to receive further information about Fourth Estate titles.*